THE DEATHLESS GIRLS

Other titles by
Kiran Millwood Hargrave:

The Girl of Ink and Stars
The Island at the End of Everything
The Way Past Winter

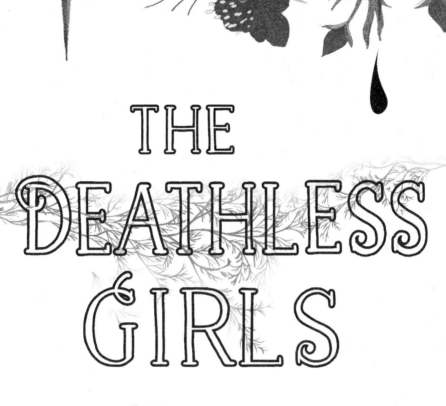

THE DEATHLESS GIRLS

Kiran Millwood Hargrave

BELL★TRIX

ORION CHILDREN'S BOOKS

First published in Great Britain in 2019 by Hodder and Stoughton

1 3 5 7 9 10 8 6 4 2

Text copyright © Kiran Millwood Hargrave, 2019
Cover illustration © Olga Baumert, 2019

A CIP catalogue record for this book is available from the British Library.

HB ISBN: 978 1 51010 674 1
TPB ISBN: 978 1 51010 691 8

Typeset by Hewer Text UK Ltd, Edinburgh
Printed and bound in Great Britain by ClaysLtd, Elcograph S.p.A.

The paper and board used in this book are from well-
managed forests and other responsible sources.

For Sarvat & Daisy,
my sisters in all but blood

That's how you get deathless, volchitsa. Walk the same tale over and over, until you wear a groove in the world, until even if you vanished, the tale would keep turning[.]

- from DEATHLESS by Catherynne M. Valente

She shall not go into that unknown and terrible land alone.

- from DRACULA by Bram Stoker

GLOSSARY

Aurar	Goldsmith
Biserică	Church
Boyar	Lord
Demoni	Demons
Dragă	Darling
Gheață	Ice
Iele	Forest spirits
Lăutari	Singer
Strigoi	Undead
Ursar	Bear dancer
Voievod	Prince

AFTERMATH

There is a time here called aftermath.

After the Settled have pulled their harvests from the ground, and long bound and placed it in dark stores, shored against rats by cats starved in narrow houses where they fight and mate and sleep until they are loosed. After the turning seasons light the trees red gold in the cold, the ground hardening underfoot, wrinkling with frost. After the snow comes like a heavy, smothering blanket, pillowing the mountains and setting off the soft fury of avalanches, finding the cracks in rocks and splitting them easy as the seeds that are deeply furrowed in the stilled earth. After the melt and pivot of another year, after all this, comes the aftermath.

The first, green moments of a new harvest, the emergence of the slow work happening beneath the thawing soil. For the Settled, it is a heralding of the work to come, always the same, sure as seasons. For us, it is a time to move on.

The aftermath had just started that year when the soldiers came through the narrow mountain pass, up through the coppery trees, and onto this land we lived upon but laid no claim to. It was a beginning into which they arrived, bringing with them the end.

CHAPTER ONE

Kizzy saw the flames first. She always was the first to everything, always half a step ahead. I was out of Mamă eight minutes before, but ever since I've been falling behind.

We were under a spreading oak, late afternoon sunlight filtering to golden needles, piercing our dark skin as we searched the ground. We were looking for white mushrooms, bright and slender limbed as sapling birches.

The next day was our seventeenth birthday, our divining day. The day Old Charani would stretch our palms over her own gnarled one, and we'd learn what the rest of our lives held.

My whole body shimmered with nerves, as if my blood were mixed with crushed glass, but Kizzy could hardly wait. I could feel her humming with excitement as she snapped the mushrooms from their stems. But then my sister had spent months, years, her whole life knowing what her future would be. We were born under a blood moon, and whilst the Settled saw it as a bad omen, for us it was thought to be lucky – who knew? It was so rare I'd never heard of another child born to it, let alone two.

Perhaps both were true: perhaps it could be a curse or a blessing. I often wondered if that meant one of us was cursed, and another blessed. Kizzy certainly thought she was the latter. She'd wake from dreams, her face alight and smooth – peaceful – and say:

'I've seen it again, Lil.'

Not 'dreamt'. *Seen.*

Kizzy was always sure that she had the gift, too, like Old Charani, though it is unusual for a camp to have more than one true Seer, if that. Divining days are most powerful on the day of your birth, but Seers can read a person for a full moon-cycle after. The Settled think all Travellers are gifted, or at worst, sorcerers, but Old Charani says it is the rarest of all fates.

'Plenty can read people,' she'd say. 'But very few can read their futures.'

Still, I wouldn't be surprised if Kizzy does have some of Old Charani's skill. The gift is, at its most simple, about knowing more, seeing more. And Kizzy has always noticed things I miss.

She was certain she would be an *ursar*, a bear trainer, like Mamă. If Charani confirmed her gift, then our next route would take us through the highest parts of the mountains, and she would go with Mamă to steal her a cub from the dark mouth of a cave. She would train it as well as Mamă has her bear, Albu, and live out her fate the way she did all things – with an ease bordering on recklessness.

And me?

I guessed my place would be as it always had been: a step behind Kizzy. Perhaps an *ursar*, if I'm lucky. All the women in our family have been, from when our stories began. I used to believe it was this blood-bred affinity that meant Albu listened to me, obeyed my commands when Mamă helped us practise; but now I think it is more out of loyalty to Mamă than to me. I love the bear – his soft white fur, a rarity that is prized and combed daily, his gentle brown eyes set in his long face, all the fierceness bred out of him by Mamă's coddling – but there is no bone-deep understanding between us. No connection that runs like a gleaming golden line, twining us together.

In my wildest, most secret moments, I dreamed of being a *lăutari*, a singer. Kizzy said my voice is sweeter than any bird's, but she is only being kind. She's the only judge I've ever had – I've never sung for anyone else. Once, Kizzy dragged me to Mamă and demanded I sing, but my voice caught in my throat like a lump of unchewed bread.

Perhaps it was just as well, for the best living for a *lăutari* is in a boyar's court, and they were brutal places, far more dangerous for a Traveller than the forests. Worse than the lords, though, are the Voievodzi, the princes that parcel up this country between them.

Power has made them beasts. There's a story of a Voievod in Northern Wallachia who had a particular liking for young Traveller girls with talent. They called him the Dragon, and it is said he made them perform until they were husks, the prettiest expected to do more than perform: he ruined them, then drank their blood, and so was immortal. It sounds like stories, but Old Charani said all stories have their roots in truth, however deeply buried.

Anyway, my becoming a *lăutari* was probably just a dream. Most likely even being a *ursar* was out of my reach and I would be a cobbler, or woodworker, like all those who have no talent and must instead learn a trade.

We should have moved on that very day, the wagons' stairs folded up, painted shutters secured, the horses saddled, and Albu and Dorsi, Erha's bear, shut in their travelling cages. But in honour of our divining day, Mamă asked Old Charani that we might stay the camp until the day after tomorrow, so she could spend it stewing the mushrooms overnight with wild garlic and sharp, green onions to make our favourite dish. If anyone else had asked, Old Charani would have refused. But no one refused Mamă. She and Kizzy had that alike.

Kizzy's apron was full, the plants torn neatly at the base so the roots were left intact and could feed us the next time we passed this way. Our lives had the cycle of slow seasons: we had been by this valley only once before, when we were swelling Mamă's belly. We try to leave no trace, take only what we need.

My apron was mucky with thick clods of mud that clung to the roots – no matter how I tried, I could not get them to break cleanly, each wrench a small destruction.

'You should have brought a knife,' sighed Kizzy, bending to snap another stem.

'You didn't.'

'I don't bite my nails to nothing,' she said, dropping the mushroom lightly into her heaving skirts and flashing her hand at me.

Her nails were curved as crescent moons, sharp bright against the smooth brown of her fingers. How were they so clean, after an afternoon scrabbling in the dirt? I clenched my own ragged claws into fists. They were more like Albu's, rough and blunt, more paw than hand.

She scanned my apron. 'Lil, that's a death cap!' She pointed to a mushroom greener than the others, flecked with what I now saw was not dirt but dark grey specks. The difference was so subtle I had not seen, but of course she had.

'Throw it away!' she said.

I took it up, but as she bent to pick another mushroom, I put the death cap into my pocket, only to show myself I

7

could do as I pleased. She looked up and saw my mutinous face.

Kizzy nudged me in the ribs. 'Don't be like that, Lil. I think we have enough to feed the camp twice over anyway.'

I looked down at my apron, the meagre assortment, roots drying sadly in their graves of mud.

'Between us, at least. Here,' said Kizzy, and tipped half of her collection into my apron. I loved my sister fiercely, but hated her most when she was kind. 'No *Iele* mushrooms,' she sighed. Kizzy was obsessed with the idea that one day she would find a patch of ground blessed by forest spirits. If you ate of them, they would give you visions. 'Let's head back.'

Our camp was halfway up the valley. Old Charani's ideal spot was somewhere where the only things higher than our wagons were the birds; but then birds did not need to struggle over scree, or transport bears, or walk to find water, so her desires for height were tempered by practicalities.

Mushrooms and other things that fed on the dark were found in the valley's deep forest, gouged through the mountain by a river that once ran fast and glinting as a knife. Now it was slow and settled, lapping at the boulders it had once torn from the ground. If Old Charani were a river, she'd stay slicing and quick all her days, never easing.

Getting down had been a straight scramble, skidding on our heels in our thin leather shoes, Kizzy laughing like a child the whole way and me gritting my teeth to keep from biting my tongue. Getting back would not be so easy, which was why we had picked it.

Had the route been simpler, Mamă would have made us bring Kem. Our brother was ten years younger and quiet, intense. We were alike in that way, as alike to each other as Kizzy was to Mamă. But I was nearly seventeen, nearly a woman, and a twin, so I was protected from the loneliness, the left-behindness we inflicted on him in our role as older sisters. Kizzy and I would put our heads together and talk or not talk, and Kem would look on like an owl, large-eyed and silent. Even the other children his age ignored him, discomforted by his watchfulness. Albu was his only friend, similarly the youngest in the den when Mamă had taken him to train.

As we turned from the flickering shadows, I plucked a couple of fiddleheads, tightly furled young ferns, and placed them into my pocket for Mamă to fry for Kem. I could never stomach them, but he loved their bitterness.

Kizzy was already disappearing into the trees, bent at a slant, eyes fixed ahead. She was bigger than me, her body already settled into soft curves that made Fen and the other boys stare, but she was deft and sure on her feet as a cat.

She waited for me at the first plateau, biting flies swirling around her head, barely sweating by the time I caught up. She matched her stride with mine after that, apron held like

9

a tray before her and yet she never stumbled. She was at ease in the forests, in a way I never was.

A grace, Old Charani called it. *That you must be born with.*

But why hadn't I, born under the same sky, been given it too? Kizzy had grace, likely had the gift. And I was uneasy with everything, the world too blunt and jagged all at once. It was a painful thing, this growing up, and growing apart. To understand that forming inside the same body did not mean we were formed the same. And after the divining day, our childhood would be over for good.

I looked sideways at Kizzy as we walked. Her profile was the same as mine, but from the front we were not identical. Her lips were fuller, her cheeks plumper. Her hips were wider, her belly gently rounded. She was wearing Mamă's braced bodice over her purple top, but I had no need. My chest was flat as Kem's beneath my cotton dress.

Her eyes flicked sideways, and a smile tugged the corners of her lips.

'What are you staring at?'

'You've got dirt on your nose,' I lied, and she brought her wrist up to rub it, smearing it with mud.

'Better?'

I nodded, the spite sour as fiddleheads.

We were about a half-mile from camp when she stopped again, so suddenly some of my borrowed mushrooms went tumbling.

'Kizzy, what—'

'Do you smell that?' She sniffed the air, like Albu when he caught the scent of a wolf near camp. I felt her fear like a coin under my own tongue.

I took a deep breath, and I did smell something, felt it hit the back of my throat.

Smoke.

'It's a fire,' I said. 'Mamă will be building one for the stew.'

'It doesn't smell right. Not just of wood . . .' She began to walk again, faster now, jolting mushrooms from her skirts. 'And the forest sounds wrong. Where are the birds?'

I ran to keep up, and a moment later there was a noise that broke the absence of sound, an inhuman bellow that struck at my chest like a stone.

Albu. Albu in pain.

Chapter Two

Kizzy dropped her skirts, mushrooms tumbling like un-puzzled bones to the ground. She held out her hand to me.

'Come on!'

I couldn't move, couldn't even let go of my apron. I had never heard Albu make that sound, not since the earliest days when Mamă took him, and he cried for his mother. But he had been a cub then, and his mewling had been pitiful. Now it was terrible, terrifying, seeming to crash through my chest to snatch at my heart.

'Come *on*!'

Kizzy yanked at me, hard, and like always I followed her, mushrooms quickly trodden into the dirt, my legs and lungs tight, Kizzy pulling me on, on, onwards toward noises I wanted to do nothing but turn and run from.

Because now, it was not just Albu screaming.

We reached the border of our camp, usually invisible even up close, disguised by fallen branches and brush. But now, you could not miss it. Kizzy cried out, and though I did not want to look, I did.

Flames, higher and wilder than any cooking pit, strangely coloured with blues and purples, were dancing at the edge of camp. At first glance I thought them *Iele*, spirits of the wind and forests that dance in fires and whip them higher. But another blink, eyeballs scratched with smoke, and I saw I was wrong.

It was much, much worse.

Old Charani's wagon was on fire. The paint was bubbling, loosing its dyes, turning the smoke poisonous shades of green.

And a man, a man I did not recognise, with a white face and a blood-red beard that trailed down his black clothes, was placing a torch to the carefully carved wheels, holding it to one until it caught, before moving to another.

I shrank back, searching for cover in the shadows cast by the trees, but Kizzy charged forwards, right at him, knocking the torch from his hand. He spun around and I saw he had no beard, but that he wore a crimson sash around his mouth and nose, like a bandit, the ends tied diagonally across his chest.

My airless mind raced. Were we being robbed? Did he not know we had nothing to take?

The world sharpened again as he kicked out at Kizzy like a dog, and my sister went down, rolling away from the hot ash, batting at her clothes as they smouldered. *Come on, Lillai*, I screamed at myself. *Move!*

I snatched up a branch from the boundary and ran before I could think better of it. As the man raised the torch to swing it at Kizzy, I parried it with the branch, and though he was far stronger it deflected the blow just enough for the torch to fly loose from his grip. He roared as I dropped the branch, my wrist aching at the impact of his strike, and pulled Kizzy to her feet.

The man's torch had lit the ground before him, and we stumbled away, briefly shielded from his advance by the rearing of flames. As we moved clear of the burning wagon, the wind gripped at the smoke and hurled it skywards, clearing our view of the camp beyond.

The circle of blazing wagons was crawling with black-clothed men in crimson sashes, wielding long, glinting sticks. They brought them down on bundles of cloth at the centre of the caravan, and Kizzy howled. I realised, a moment after she did, that they were not sticks, but swords. Now everything slowed to a nightmarish pace as one of the bundles reached up a hand—

A thin, dark hand on a delicate wrist, whorled with knotted bones and age. A hand that all my life had pressed kindness or punishment upon me. A hand that tomorrow would have taken mine and showed me my fate.

Old Charani's hand.

It fell as the sword sliced down again, and again, in an awful, ceaseless rhythm until she stirred no more. Beside her, Dika and Erha were on the ground too, and all of them wore crimson slashes like sashes.

Kizzy started forwards but I held her back. 'Kizzy, we need to find Mamă and Kem!'

We tore our gaze from the bodies, searching. In the far corner of the camp where the bears were staked, Albu was rearing, his white fur singed dark and streaked with ash. His muzzle was leaking red spots of blood to the ground, and he slashed with his front paws, swiping at the men's arms. His long claws were marred with gore, and several men lay broken before him, dragging themselves away.

But more were advancing, swords raised. Beside him was a mangled heap of brown fur. Dorsi was dead, and the remaining men were drawing closer to Albu. 'He's still tied to his stake!' shouted Kizzy. 'Where's Mamă?'

The first thing Mamă would have done if Albu were threatened would be to free him, so he could either flee, or fight freely. He was doubtless our best warrior.

And then, in step for once, we both turned our gaze along the burning circle of the wagons and saw our home at the same moment, flames eating it faster than any other.

'Mamă!' Kizzy's scream seemed to tear my own throat. 'Kem!'

Kizzy ran at the wagon, and I followed, but it was too late. I could see a thick length of wood throttling the doors, which we never locked. The awful cruelty of the sight made me stumble.

The men had shut them inside.

The shutters were ashen already, and the curtains swallowed by flames. Those curtains had been dyed purple with elderberries, stitched with blessings. Mamă's bed was beneath them, and when she rose at dawn to feed Albu I'd untangle myself from Kizzy's stifling grasp and lie down in her cooling sheets, place the fine material of the curtains across my face, breathe in the mingled smells of cooking and herbs and Mamă.

Seeing them gone was to know, even as Kizzy danced at and away from the licking flames, trying to rip open the door. Know with the same certainty I knew my sister's face, my own hands.

Mamă and Kem were dead.

Pain slammed into my stomach, and I bent double, holding myself together. They had died trapped, not even able to fight for their lives. Not even able to raise their eyes to the sky one last time. Rage flared inside me like a swallowing flame.

Mamă and Kem were dead.

But Albu was not.

I straightened and picked up Mamă's axe where it lay in its block beside our flaming wagon. The men's backs were to me, occupied with Albu's flailing paws. I raised the axe.

One of the injured men crawling away cried out a warning, and another turned to see the axe coming towards him. He stepped aside, alerting his companions. The men scattered and converged, darting clear and circling closer to me, like buzzing black flies, but in the moment they scattered, I reached Albu.

He kept them back, bellowing, as I swung at the leather connecting the stake to the chain. Two desperate hacks, and the bear was free. He stood fully, swiping behind him, the chain flying. His claws caught one of the men across the cheek, spilling blood.

As he reared, I saw what Albu had been crouched over: a small, shivering shape.

I darted between Albu's thrashing paws. My broken heart swelled.

'Kem!' I pulled at my brother's shoulder, shaking with relief, and he cowered away. 'It's me, we have to go!'

He looked up at me, his owl eyes swollen with tears, but as his soot-stained hand reached out to me, an arm came around my waist, and with the force of a hook, yanked me back.

I dropped the axe. I could see Kem's knuckles whiten into a fist. Albu bounded forward, raising his paw to strike, but he had left Kem exposed. I held out my empty hands, just as I did in training. His wet nose touched me for just a moment, flaring nostrils filling my whole palm, his breath searing.

'Kem!' I said. 'Take Kem! Go!'

Albu did not hesitate. He scooped up my brother like a salmon, throwing him onto his enormous back. Kem's hands tightened in his fur as the men rattled their swords, raised them to hack, but Albu was fast with fear and fury. He turned and ran from the smoking camp, into the thick trees beyond.

Some of the men started after him, but the one holding me stayed them.

'Leave it!' he called. 'Catch the girls.'

He stank of smoke and sweat. My hands were covered in blood from Albu's muzzle, and I threw a wish to the forest that he was not badly hurt.

The man threw me into the bears' caged cart. I landed on something soft and sobbing. Dika's son, Morsh. He squealed as I crushed his leg, and I shifted off with a murmur of apology.

He didn't respond, only curled tighter into his ball. As I looked around for Kizzy, I saw no one over sixteen was alive except Fen, whose divining day had fallen three weeks ago. He had a peculiarly shaped bruise on his cheek, and it was flaring the same blue and purple as Old Charani's wagon.

I could not bear to look, but knew our mothers and fathers, older sisters and brothers lay slain in the ring of our scorched homes, or else were caught and burned inside them. My nostrils were full of the smell: wood-smoke and something sweeter, like meat. I swallowed down bile.

'Mamă. Mamă.' Morsh's murmurs span away from his lips like prayers, face slick with snot and soot. I placed my hand gently on his shoulder.

'Have you seen Kizzy, Morsh?'

He shrank back from my touch, still muttering.

I looked around the survivors. 'Has anyone seen Kizzy?'

Terror sank me deep inside myself, a gnawing cold like an icy stake through my chest. Had the men killed her, too? We were tall for our age, and she better formed than I. And her face had been twisted with such rage – could they have mistaken her for older?

Fen crawled forward to peer through the bars of the cage. His face was heavy with worry too – he loved my sister, though I don't think he had admitted it to even himself. But when Old Charani had flattened her rough palm over his mere weeks ago, and told him he was an *aurar*, a goldsmith, and that before the year was out a woman would be placing a promise ring onto his finger, his eyes had searched for Kizzy.

'There!' His arm stretched out through the bars. 'She's alive!'

I heard her before I saw her, howling like a *demon*. She was heaped over two men's shoulders, writhing, hissing and biting. She was thrown into the cage a moment later, still kicking.

One of the men who threw her in was the same man who had caught me, only now his appearance was altered. He had scratch marks all down his face, and I saw Kizzy's hands had been bound behind her back with one of their sashes. I felt pride in her then, and my own sickening shame at being taken so easily.

He spat at her as the cage door closed and she scrambled upright, tripping over her skirts, and spat right back, banging her head against the metal slats.

'Kizzy,' I reached out to her, but even I was afraid. 'Kizzy, calm.'

She wheeled around on her knees, and her black hair was matted with blood, her dark, lovely face frenzied as a cornered wolf's.

'Kisaiya,' I said. Only Mamă used our full names, and her eyes focused on me. 'Look at me.'

I held up my hand to her, palm out, fingers splayed. It was a gesture we had always made to swear on, or calm each other, something so natural that I wondered if we had lain inside Mamă like that, our fingertips touching. Unable to bring her own hand to meet it, she leant her forehead into my palm. I leant down and kissed her head. She tasted of the sickening, sweet smoke.

She started to moan. The other children, even Fen, shrank back, but I wrapped my arms around her.

She was heavy against me, and I looked down at her bound hands. Her fingers, her beautiful, careful fingers, were burned and raw, the neat crescents of her nails now blood moons.

'Why?' she keened. 'Why?'

The camp was still behind us. Nothing stirred except the flames still licking the trees, the terrible heat of our homes making my arms slick with sweat. But I did not let go of Kizzy.

The men climbed atop our best horses, and I saw Erha's beloved old mule still twitching as he died in the dirt.

'Where are they taking us?' said Morsh, eyes bright with panic. 'Where are we going?'

'They're boyar's men,' said Fen. 'See the sashes?'

I remembered Old Charani, wearing a sash of her own blood, and closed my eyes against the sight. My throat was sore with smoke and screaming.

'Soldiers?' I asked.

'Or slave gatherers.'

'Where will they take us now?'

Fen closed his brown eyes, and a tear licked a line through his sooted face, polishing the bruise, which I realised now was in the shape of the flat of a sword. 'Wherever they want.'

The cart began to move. Within moments, the forest closed over our camp, over everything we'd ever known, like a mighty hand closing a book.

As the smoke receded into the distance, I drew the fiddleheads out of my pocket, shared them around. Uncooked they were more bitter than ever, but no one refused one except Kizzy.

The death cap was still in my pocket. I thought of slipping it into my mouth, swallowing it down. It made you sweat, then see bright colours, then it closed your throat and stopped your heart. Kizzy was still in my lap, and I pushed the thought away.

We watched the forest pass us by, as though it was the thing that moved, its great trunks of protection, its wise whorls like eyes, turning away from us. Even at this distance, I could smell the smoke that killed our mother, on the air and my skin and in my sister's hair.

I thought of Albu, and my brother caught like a seed in his fur, and prayed for the trees to cradle them safely, and carry them far, far away.

CHAPTER THREE

The way was rough and overshadowed by inscrutable canopies of oak and beech, thin boughs of larch scraping the sides of the cart and showering us with needles. I picked them from Kizzy's hair as she lay in my lap, staring up and through me, through even the thick trees. Staring, it seemed, further than any star. I wanted to follow her there, to this other place. Anywhere was better than here.

Two men rode behind the cart, their crimson sashes pulled down now, so their faces were revealed. They were pale in the growing darkness, gleaming like ghosts, but I could see the black-hearted smiles on their faces when I was stupid enough to make eye contact. I pressed my back to the bars, and their stares bore into my nape.

As soon as darkness had fully encased us, I felt for the sash that bound Kizzy's hands. When I began to untie it, I realised it was not a soldier's sash, but the purple cloth that

Old Charani used to keep her long grey curls back from her forehead. It was mottled with red blood.

I held it in my hands until Kizzy took it, and bound up her own hair with it, wincing as her burnt hands chafed. Then she lay down again in my lap, silent as dirt.

I kept myself hunched over Kizzy, letting my smoke-soaked curls hang forward over her face, hoping to shield her from view. Settled men liked her better even than our own boys did, but it was always edged with something darker. There was something glinting and hard to their desire.

Fen sensed the threat too. He kept his broad back turned beside mine, his face half slanted so he could watch them through the corner of his eye. The bruise on his cheek was deepening, purple and red as Old Charani's scarf.

We had long given up trying to speak to each other. Every time we tried to talk, the men would jab the scabbards of their swords through the bars. As they did so they called us names, names I'd heard before in the Settled villages. Gypsy, tinker, and worse.

A miserable silence weighed down on us like a shroud. Even Morsh had stopped crying. He was curled up like a snail winkled from its shell, and Erha's eldest daughter, Girtie, had her arm across him. It made me ache for Kem, though I was certain he would be safer with Albu than in this cage. Safe from whatever lay at the end of our journey.

I didn't know the path. It was not the way we had

approached the forest, nor the route we were to have taken next. We were going lower, into a different valley, not up into the mountains. Without a view of the sky I couldn't tell the direction.

Acid rose suddenly in my stomach, and I swallowed it down. The camp should have been on its way that morning. Were it not for Kizzy and me, our divining day, and mushroom stew. Because of us, our homes were ash, our family scattered to the four winds.

I wiped the heel of my hand across my eyes, and Fen touched me lightly on the inside of my wrist. His warmth was shocking on my night-chilled skin, almost unbearably tender.

'You should sleep,' he said, his lips barely moving.

'You should sleep,' I replied.

Neither of us slept, though the men behind us did, snoring as their stolen horses followed behind, and the miles unspooled. In my lap, Kizzy's eyes were two dark pits, hollow and yawning.

The forest was full of night sounds, biting flies buzzing at my earlobes, and bright eyes watched from the shadows. I prayed for bears to come and knock the men from their horses. I prayed for wolves to give chase, and for the men to abandon us. I called on the *Iele* to avenge our families' murders. It would be better to be at the mercy of beasts and spirits than these pale-eyed watchers.

Fen's head drooped onto my shoulder, and Kizzy's faraway gaze sharpened, shifted to his face. It felt wrong to see her looking at him that way, so intently. I looked up instead, but unlike Kizzy I could see no further than the branches passing overhead.

The deepest part of night was past before the trees started to thin, and as the sun began to rise, it sliced whips of light over our tear-stained faces. I rolled my shoulders and neck, wincing as they clicked. Fen jerked awake, and Kizzy looked fast away from him, finally sitting up as the daylight called to the sleeping bodies, and our friends began to stir.

Behind us, the men were still snoring, and Kizzy didn't bother to keep her voice down as she looked around.

'Where are we?'

Fen shrugged. 'We never came down the hills this far.'

'I think we've come north,' said Girtie. 'See the sun?'

To the Settled, this knowledge would mean something different: perhaps they would know a village this way, which boyar's land we had passed into. To me, to us, the land mattered only as elemental: forests, rivers, mountains, sea. Here, tin mines. There, gold. Wolves, bears, boars. North was more mountainous, more treacherous for our kind. There were slavers, and the Voievod who liked talented girls. All our stories of the north were tinged with fear, with warnings.

I knelt up, arching my back to stretch. The hand that had been beneath Kizzy's head was floppy and numb, and I shook the blood back into it, tiny, invisible needles stabbing my skin.

My bladder was sore and full, and Girtie wordlessly passed me a bucket. I braced myself against the bars. The sound of my piss hitting tin brought hot sparks of shame to my cheeks, but no one jeered or laughed or looked. At least the men were still asleep.

I dropped my skirts and Kizzy emptied the bucket through the wooden slats of the floor. Already the thin fabric of privacy that had kept us apart from each other was shot through with holes: ripped apart by the men with crimson sashes.

We were moving through another, shallower valley now, forested hills rising gently to each side. This track was well worn, packed hard by countless feet and hooves, and as the day wore on we began to pass people travelling the other way, or else smaller convoys that overtook the lumbering cart.

No one talked to us, threw us a sympathetic glance, or questioned the men. These Settled people were maybe used to the sight of Travellers in cages, or perhaps the crimson sashes gave the slavers some authority.

Our captors were newly awake and bearing almost as many bruises as we were. I was especially proud of the injuries Kizzy had inflicted: deep nail rakes that ran from the man's forehead, across his eye and to his neck. They were weeping clear liquid, and his eye was closed. He bared small, yellow teeth when he caught me looking, and I shuffled so I was again blocking my sister from sight.

Eventually the hills evened out, rolling gently down into open fields. We must be approaching a settlement: a large one. The black earth was furrowed in straight lines as far as I could see: miles and miles of land threshed and scythed and beaten into submission.

Here and there were blackened nubs of tree trunks, cut close to the ground but with roots too deep to rip out. The Settled had painted them with tar, but beneath the surface the roots were still spreading, clinging to the ground that was theirs first and would be again, long after the people who chopped them down were buried in the dirt.

The road continued to broaden until you could have driven three wagons abreast down it. As the low, square shapes of houses began to dot the roadside, labourers started to appear in the fields.

Some of them were dark skinned like us, with wavy black hair that you never saw in the Settled. But not even they looked at us. I could only guess they were slaves: surely no Traveller would choose such a life?

Kizzy pressed her cheeks to the cold metal bars, and watched them take up their tools and begin working at the earth, still frosted and glittering.

'Why do they not use their tools to attack?' she whispered. 'Why do they not hack them all to pieces?'

The longing in her voice turned my stomach.

The houses began to line the road, and as the road took a rounded curve around a small hillock, I saw our destination: a walled hill, with houses carpeting its steep sides.

On top, ridiculous and looming, was a castle. I had never seen one so large, so in opposition to the downcast houses we had passed thus far. Its turrets pierced the sky, black needles against the clouds, sharp as bared teeth set in grey gums. A flag fluttered from the highest tower, black with a crimson slash diagonally across it. So Fen was right: the slavers were boyar's men after all.

As we drew closer I could make out shapes topping the walls: crouched, enormous. I was not the only person who'd noticed.

'*Demoni!*' Morsh moaned, pointing. 'Demons!'

'They're only statues,' said Fen, but he sounded shaken too. I could see he was right, but the shapes were so intricately made, the grey light so uncertain, that at any moment they seemed ready to spring down from their places and attack. I crossed my fingers against them, barely able to breathe.

But before we reached the walls, the cart was jerked to a halt. I pulled my attention from the castle and the statues and looked around. We had drawn over to the side of the road, in front of a large, long stone structure, the size of five caravans laid end to end.

It had once been fine: the wooden door held remnants of blue paint, and the lintel was carved where it had not rotted away. But there was obviously no care left here.

We would never allow our homes to fall into such disrepair. Curtains were replaced if stained, uneven hems mended and holes darned as soon as they appeared. We were proud of the places we lived: I guessed the owner of this house had reason to be ashamed.

The men following behind approached the cage door, swords drawn.

'Be ready,' murmured Kizzy.

'For what?' I said, but she was not listening. She bared her teeth at the man who bore her nail marks, and he hit the cage bars with the flat of his sword, the way the Settled hit Albu's cage with sticks to try and rattle him, before they were chased off by Mamă.

Mamă. The memory of the burnt wagon hit me hard in the chest.

Winded, I was too slow to stop Kizzy. The moment they unlocked the bolt she leapt forward, dark legs flailing, moving as though she would run and never stop.

But the nail-marked man was revived by his rest. He was faster than me, faster even than Kizzy. He caught her about the waist and threw her to the ground, boot brought down directly onto her long hair, bound by Old Charani's scarf.

Laughing, one of his companions placed his own foot on one of Kizzy's wrists, whooping and jeering as she kicked, her skirts falling up her thighs. I made a convulsive movement as he reached down, and pinched Kizzy just above the knee, but Fen was out of the cart first.

'Leave her!'

He was rewarded with a square punch to the jaw, but the men released their hold on Kizzy enough for her to stand up and pull down her dress. Mamă's bodice was askew, and I longed to straighten it, pull it up higher. Longed to claw out the man's other eye.

'Can't sell soiled goods anyway,' he spat, and shoved her back into the cart. I pulled her towards me. I could see a thin beading of blood along her scalp where her hair had been ripped out in her efforts to writhe free. 'But any more of that, and each of your friends gets a scar to match the one you've given me.'

Fen went to follow Kizzy, but the soldier yanked him back. 'You stay there. And you, and you, and you—' he pointed to Morsh, and two of the other older boys. 'Out too.'

Morsh looked up at Girtie, who cast a terrified glance at the blade the man had gestured with. She nodded, but could not meet the boy's eye as he clambered out, the other boys following. The cart door was locked again, and the four boys lined up along outside.

One of the soldiers returned from the large stone house with a short, stout man who put me in mind of a badger with his greying hair, long face and small black eyes.

'Morning, Captain Vereski. Where're these from?'

'The western hills,' replied our captor.

The man nodded approvingly. 'They're coming closer. We'll have a steady supply soon.'

He walked slowly along the line, turning the boys' heads this way and that, peeling back their lips with his grimy hand and making them stick out their tongues. Fen stood tall when the badger man reached him, but I could see his legs shaking slightly. His hands were grasped behind his back, and Kizzy slipped her finger through the bars and stroked his palm. He stopped shaking.

The badger man nodded. 'Twenty.'

'Fifty,' said Captain Vereski.

'Twenty-five.'

'I'll get more at the castle.'

'No you won't.'

I felt nausea rock my stomach. They were bargaining over Fen and the others like they were livestock.

'Forty,' said Captain Vereski. 'Or I'm leaving.'

'Forty,' replied Badger. 'If you throw in that one.'

He jerked his head at Kizzy. Fen stiffened, but the soldier was already shaking his head.

'She's part of a set, see?' He pointed at me, and I shrank

back. My invisibility had evidentially worn off. 'Malovski's always looking for novelties.'

The man sucked in air through his gappy teeth. 'Boyar Valcar will enjoy that.'

The way they were talking was shameful. So bald, so brutal. I wanted to scream, or cry, but only hung my head. If I could not speak I wanted to make a silence of myself, a void that could feel nothing, be nothing, or else become an *Ielă*, a spirit of wind and fire that could slip through these bars and flee to the forests. But the more the men stared, the more solid I felt. Lumpen with the impossibility of escape.

'Thirty,' said the Badger. 'Final offer.'

They shook hands, like the Settled do over cattle or crops. Morsh was crying again, and I longed to have the courage to reach out to him, as Kizzy had to Fen, but my arms felt heavy and useless as felled tree trunks. The boys were herded into the dwelling, the soldiers' hands on their sword hilts. Only Fen turned, and his eyes sought one person.

Captain Vereski glanced from Fen, to Kizzy, tracing their gaze, passed between them like a grasp of the hand. A grim smile cracked his face, causing more blood and fluid to leak from his cheek.

He came up close to the bars, right into Kizzy's face. 'Any more of this—' he pointed at his injury. 'And there'll be no more that.' He pointed to Fen's retreating back. 'Understand?'

33

He didn't wait for her to reply, moving along the cart, which creaked as he swung himself up beside the driver.

I reached for my sister's hand, but though she trembled, there was no trace of tears on her plump cheeks. Anger had turned Kizzy's face smooth and dark as polished stone. She looked like a magnificent statue, finer than any carving topping the walls, far fiercer.

I let my arm brush hers, and felt something move between us, some of her heat, her fury. As the door closed on the boys, and the cart began to move again, I let it coil around my heart, and turn it a little to stone, too.

CHAPTER FOUR

I was not the only one to cross my fingers as we passed through the gate, beneath the *demoni* atop the walls. Up close they were no less terrifying: winged wolves, and gurning men with claws long as the soldiers' swords.

There were eight of us left, including Kizzy and me, all girls. I had known each of them since our birth or theirs, but fear had placed barriers between us. I could not bring myself to look any of them in the eye. Who would be next to be taken?

I kept my arm pressed close to Kizzy's, drawing on her warmth, her anger. While I had not liked the slaver's words about 'sets', I clung onto the glimmer of hope that it meant we would be together. Together, through whatever awful fate awaited.

The cart hit the incline of the hill and began to climb towards the castle. The grey sky was lightening, and I saw the pointed towers were topped with red tiles, sharp against the black stone. It was poised on a large platform of unhewn rock, so that the walls seemed to sprout from it like a terrible tree.

The road curved around the hill in a spiral, hacked flat from rough rock. The houses were better kempt as we approached, large as the Badger's but well tended, and the people were more finely dressed too. These were richer Settled, who did not have to work the fields for a living. They likely had their own slaves, to run their households – the women's cheeks were pale, made paler by their uniformly black garb, as though they never toiled in sunlight, and their hands were encased in fine gloves of different crimson shades.

This must be the dress of this place: crimson on black. The image of blood welling on dark skin rose unbidden, and I lowered my head between my knees to keep the faintness at bay.

Halfway up the road, the castle looming like a storm cloud overhead, we stopped again, outside a house with blood-red shutters. This time we drew together, shrinking as one to the back of the cart. Captain Vereski approached the cage door, keeping a sharp eye on Kizzy. But his threat about Fen seemed to have worked: she did not try to escape as the bolt slipped, though I think he was as unnerved by her furious gaze as if she had run shrieking at him.

'Out,' he said. No one moved. He bashed the flat of his sword against the bars, harder than ever before. It set the whole cage ringing, singing a chatter through my teeth. 'Now!'

Girtie whimpered, but she began to crawl to the steps. We followed, and I stumbled a little as I jumped down, legs tingling from so many hours bent in the cage. The air here was sour after the forest's sap-sweet smell, and stale without wind to clean it.

Vereski knocked on the red door. The cart was parked right up close to the house so we had to stand with our backs pressed fast against the bars to allow Vereski to pass by. He walked close anyway, brushing his leg against our skirts. I could smell bitter smoke and unwashed skin as he moved across my body.

Up close his injury was worse, and I wondered if some of the dirt from our mushroom picking had transferred from under Kizzy's fingernails. I imagined crushing the deadcap in my pocket, smearing it into the wound.

'What are you smirking at?' His words were carried on a hot tide of rotting meat and acid.

I smoothed my treacherous face, held my breath, only releasing it when he moved on. I was proud to see he did not linger on Kizzy, clearly noting her freed hands, her murderous expression. He continued, deliberately, slowly, walking up the line.

He paused in front of Reeni, the youngest of us, raised a gloved hand and ran it from her chin up to her ear lobe. A collective shudder ran through us. A muscle worked in Reeni's jaw. I was proud of her for not crying: showing weakness to this man was like blood to a wolf.

'All right,' he spoke to us all. 'Malovski will be out soon.' His eyes bore into Kizzy. 'I'll have no spitting, no scratching, no speaking.'

Shock had caught us in its numbing grasp, but now, lined up as the boys had been, I started to feel the edges of true panic, like standing on a precipice. We waited long enough for my thoughts to chase themselves to exhaustion and fall into a buzzing agitation that meant I could not settle my mind on anything. My body felt wracked with grief, sore and tender, as though I had been beaten like Kizzy.

At long last, the door opened, and a woman stepped out.

'Mistress Malovski,' purred Vereski, bowing and holding out his hand to help her down the step. She did not take it.

If the man in the fields had been a badger, Mistress Malovski was a fox. She was wearing a high collared gown of scarlet, nipped in tight at the waist with a black sash, an inverse reflection of Vereski's uniform. She was thin, like me, and short as Reeni. Around sharp, black eyes rimmed with dark lashes, her pointed face was pale except for two spots of rouge high on her cheeks, and a crimson slash across her lips, all of which conspired to give her a feverish appearance.

Her thin lips pursed as she regarded us, mouth red as a wound. 'Gypsies?'

'As requested,' said Captain Vereski, straightening.

'I see no bears.'

'They were old, Mistress. Bags of bones.'

The woman made an angry hiss. 'I could say the same of this lot. I thought I made it clear the bears were of particular interest to Boyar Valcar. You know very well the current ones are on their last legs. Literally, after last week's dog fights.'

I wished I could stop up my ears with wax. It was not only what she said, but how she said it – with as much insouciance as if she were lamenting the cost of grain. I was almost grateful they'd slain Dorsi, if that was the fate that would have awaited him. My heart lifted at the thought of Albu and Kem, free in the forests. Our mother's beautiful bear would never dance for these people, never be forced into a high walled arena and be set upon by starved dogs.

'My apologies, Mistress. I am sure we can source some elsewhere.'

'But it takes time, Captain Vereski. I wanted one ready trained, and Gypsies do that so well.' She turned her fox face upon us. 'They have a natural affinity for beasts.'

Kizzy's hands were balled into fists. The backs of them were weeping. Her once smooth, elegant fingers were red raw with burns. In the forests there would be witch hazel and willow bark, other remedies the trees could give to soothe her sore skin. If knowing the land and all it could offer was bestial, I didn't want to be human.

Captain Vereski opened his mouth but she held up her hand.

'I will manage. I always do. Let's see them.'

She opened the red door and gestured for us to follow her inside. Vereski encouraged us with a hand on his sword, but Mistress Malovski stopped him at the threshold.

'I can take it from here, Captain.'

'There are some wild ones, Mistress. I really think it best—'

She shut the door in his face with the same finality with which she had held up her hand.

With the shutters closed, inside was dark as a grave. The candles dotted about the room only served to throw the areas outside their faded circles of light into shadow. I realised much of her wealth was in appearance only: the painted shutters and fine dress hiding these drab interiors.

Mistress Malovski turned to us, the candlelight turning her skin sallow.

'There is no point trying to escape. Even if you manage to kill me, there is no way out except the way you came in. And my life will be worth every single one of yours. Line up.'

None of us moved. I wondered if Kizzy was thinking the same as I. Whatever Malovski said, she was small and slight, older than us by two decades at least. I scanned the dim room for a weapon. The candlesticks looked like iron. I imagined taking one in my hand, swinging it at the woman's sharp face, cracking it open like a vase. My knees went weak at the thought.

Coward.

She crossed the room and took up a bowl of water, a rag. She set them down on the table. 'Clean your faces.'

My whole body felt coated in grime, and the hateful smell of smoke clung to my clothes. I wanted to scratch the skin right off myself, down to my bones, to my soul, and let it fly free. But when I reached the bowl, already grey and opaque with dirt from the others' faces, I only dipped the rag into the filthy water and wiped it across my brow, and at the back of my neck. My cheek smarted, and I felt a scratch there, a clean slice. I could not remember how I got it.

'Now here.' Malovski gestured that we should stand against the wall. I butted up close to a squat wooden dresser. The candlestick was within grasp. I could not reach for it. I dug my nails into my palms until they stung.

I tried to catch Kizzy's eye, but she didn't look at me. Malovski walked slowly along the line, as close as Captain Vereski had, but her gaze was almost more disturbing. Vereski's expression I had at least understood; I had seen that mix of disgust and desire in many Settled men before. But Malovski was appraising, focused, like Old Charani studying a palm.

I thought of the other day we could have had, the day we should have had. In that other day, I was sitting full of mushroom stew under leaf-dappled sunlight, Kem on my lap and Mamă stroking my hair as Old Charani unfurled my hand like a fern and spoke my future into it.

I squeezed my eyes shut, the better to see it. The longing was a crack running from my heart along every limb. It was painful and lovely, and took me away from the room until Malovski's sharp grip on my wrist wrenched me back.

The woman spread my hands, and I wondered what future she had in store for me. She checked my fingernails, the cool softness of her skin making my own crawl. She peered into my mouth, ran her finger along my teeth, pressing as if to check for looseness. She turned my face this way and that, frowning at the cut on my cheek.

'That will need stitches, I think. Shame. But twins . . .' She looked from Kizzy to me. 'Perhaps even better than a bear. Sure she's the beauty, but the likeness is close enough. Did your mother feed you the same? Looks like she got the better breast.' It was obviously not a question for us to answer. The mention of Mamă made my body shake.

Malovski moved on to Kizzy. 'They really are striking, your looks. If you like this sort of thing.' She made a gesture to Kizzy's hips, exaggerating their curves. 'Men are simple in their tastes, even boyars.' She tapped her lip with a thin finger. 'Are you unspoilt?'

Kizzy frowned.

'Have you been bedded?'

Kizzy narrowed her eyes. 'No.'

'So you're not dumb. I thought they might have ripped your tongues out,' said Malovski dryly. 'They did that once.'

Malovski began her examination of Kizzy, starting, as she had with me, with her hands. She recoiled at the sight of the burns.

'*Bleah!* What happened here?' Kizzy winced as Malovski turned her forearms this way and that, tutting. 'This is hideous.'

She brought her head down level with Kizzy's arms, and I could feel something in Kizzy change, tense and coil like a snake. Like she was considering striking her. I felt the urge in my own hands. She could get her in a choke-hold, squeeze until the gleaming eyes dimmed. But she bore it silently as Malovski sniffed at the skin.

'Good, no rot yet. We will have to sort that too.' She threw Kizzy's arm down with a dismissive huff, looking disgustedly from my sister to me. 'Twins maybe, but damaged. Why is my job never easy?'

She crossed the room and opened the door, daylight flooding in. She gestured the Captain inside. He dithered by the threshold, seemingly unwilling to step closer. What power did this woman have over him, to make him so afraid?

'Fine. It's not such a disaster. You to . . . you.' Malovski dragged a thin finger from Girtie to Reeni. 'Dairy. You go with him.'

She jerked her head at them, and they walked uncertainly to the door.

'These two will do for the castle,' she said to Captain Vereski, nodding at Kizzy and me. 'But I need to make them presentable first.'

'Thirty,' said Captain Vereski.

'Done.'

'For them only,' he said, pointing at Kizzy and me. 'Fifty all in.'

'You have brought me damaged goods,' said Malovski, pulling Kizzy's hand up to show him. 'It will cost me to fix.'

'I—'

'I'll pay you twenty for them, fifteen for those. Thirty-five all told. If you're not happy, tell the boyar. And I will not let him forget that you failed to bring him bears.'

Captain Vereski muttered something under his breath.

'What was that?' snapped Mistress Malovski.

'Thirty-five is fine, Mistress.'

'Good. Go, then. I'll bring these up in due course.'

'I think I should leave someone with you, Mistress. That one's dangerous.' He nodded at Kizzy.

'I have handled enough girls in my time.'

'Me too,' leered Captain Vereski. 'But few have landed harm on me.' He pointed at his cheek.

Mistress Malovski sighed. 'I'll be sure to file down her nails. You may leave a guard outside, but they do not enter this house, understood? And do not worry about that scar, Captain. If anything, it's an improvement.'

CHAPTER FIVE

Malovski shut the door on Captain Vereski for a second time, a little harder than before. I heard him barking orders, heard the cage door clang shut on our friends, and wished for them to be safe. A dairy did not sound so bad: somewhere with animals and their sounds, their simple needs. The soft work of cheese and milk and butter. I wished we could have all been kept together.

I drew closer to Kizzy as Malovski strode towards us.

'Vicious claws, eh? There'll be none of that with me. I can make your life a lot worse.'

Kizzy let out a hollow laugh, and Malovski reached out, and pinched the skin between Kizzy's thumb and forefinger. Kizzy yelped, and I bit the insides of my cheeks. If it were me being hurt, she would try to protect me, and yet I could barely bring myself to watch her pain, much less stop it. What was wrong with me? Where was the strength, the courage I had felt when swinging my way towards Albu and Kem with the axe?

I pinched my own hand in the same place Kizzy was being held. It struck on a nerve, bringing bright stars of pain to my eyes.

'Stupid girl,' hissed Malovski. 'There are much worse fates than this. I could have sent you to the fields, with the labourers. Even in the dairy you'd be up to your arms in shit, chafing your hands raw on churns. See how well they'd heal then.'

She let go, throwing Kizzy's hand from her like it was a soiled rag. 'You'd do well to learn from your sister. Your beauty may protect her, but her silence will protect you both.'

Malovski wiped her hands along the crimson sides of her gown, and stepped back, giving us both another appraising look.

'Don't see many twins around here. One usually dies, or else they are drowned. Unnatural things. Did your mother use witchcraft to birth you?'

'She was no witch,' hissed Kizzy. *Was.* The word struck like a slap.

'I thought all Gypsies were.'

'We are Travellers,' said Kizzy, placing her pinched hand under her armpit. 'Not Gyptians.'

'Kisaiya,' I said warningly.

'She speaks!' Malovski threw up her hands and clapped sarcastically. 'I was beginning to think you were her shadow. Kisaiya, is it? And you are?'

I did not want to hear my name mangled on her Settled tongue, but I had given Kizzy's – it was not fair to protect my own.

'Lillai.'

'What strange names,' Malovski wrinkled her nose. 'Still, you'll have no use for them at the castle.'

'What will we be doing at the castle?' said Kizzy.

'Did I ask you to speak?' said Malovski spitefully. 'I've a mind to start you as serving girls.'

'I am not suited to holding trays,' said Kizzy, and Malovski gave a little laugh, then put her hand to her lips.

'Your hands can heal. And besides, you can serve in other ways.'

'Other ways?' I said, dredging up my voice.

'Any way the boyar chooses.'

'We are not whores,' said Kizzy hotly.

Mistress Malovski arched an eyebrow. Her skin cracked, and I realised she was wearing a lot of powder to make her so pale.

'Of course you are not. Whores get paid.'

She turned suddenly from us, reaching up to a shelf she could not quite reach. As she kicked a wooden block into place beneath it, I tried again to catch Kizzy's eye. She had not looked at me once since the cart. *Are you angry with me?* I asked inside my head. Kizzy regarded the wall.

Malovski retrieved a wooden box with a metal hinge from the shelf, and carried it to the table, setting it down beside the bowl of dirty water. She opened it and began rummaging through it. Something clinked, like metal or glass.

'Here.' She snapped her fingers at us, as you would call a dog. Neither of us moved.

'I can split you up,' she said, without looking up. 'Send one to the fields, or further. Boyars are always looking for fresh faces, and there are worse masters than the one you'll find here. No doubt even your kind will have heard of the Voievod of these parts? They call him the Dragon.'

I flinched. The Dragon. The ruler Old Charani told tales of, who treated his slaves worse than rats, who bled them dry.

'I see you have. If you want to stay together, obey me.'

Kizzy didn't move, and I felt rooted by her indecisiveness. Had my cowardice made her hate me? But then she shook back her hair, as though shaking off a cobweb, and walked to Malovski's side. I followed, as ever, just behind.

The box was full of glinting objects: long-handled, pointed blades, needles, but just as a fresh wave of fear washed through me, Malovski pulled out a comb, fine toothed and carved of bone, pale as the woman's face.

'Boyar Valcar likes long hair, so you can keep yours, but—'

'Keep it? It's ours.'

She slapped Kizzy across the face, so fast that if I had blinked I would have missed it.

'I'm getting tired of your lip now. You must learn not to speak unless expressly told to. And nothing,' she said, running her fingernails between the tines of the comb with a scraping sound that set my teeth on edge, 'is yours any more. Common practice is to shave all the slaves' heads. Stops the lice, and keeps the whores,' she put emphasis on the word, glared at Kizzy, 'in wigs.' I looked up at her head, reassessed her lustrous black tresses, caught in their intricate swirls. 'But this means I need to check it for lice.'

We didn't have any, I knew. Mamă was strict about combing our curls through with mint and vinegar, leaving it soft and shiny. She'd catch any stray lice between her fingernails and crack them with satisfying little *pops*. Kizzy and I loved having our hair brushed, but Kem despised it. His hair was even thicker than ours, even curlier and coarser.

'Take off your clothes,' said Malovski.

My stomach contracted. Of course, it was Kizzy who spoke.

'Our clothes?'

Her black eyes glittered in the darkness.

'I would rather not send you to the boyar even more bruised, girl. Do as I say.'

I clutched at my skirts. 'Mistress,' I said, keeping my voice soft, subservient, not bothering to hide the shake. 'Please don't make us.'

'Oh, but I will. I can call that soldier in from outside, and he'd be welcome to stay and watch the examination.'

'But what are you looking for?' I continued, rushing into the gap so that Kizzy would not, and say something that would earn her another slap.

'I need to check you are as you claim – not bedded. There is added value in that.'

'Please,' I said, blood rushing to my face, tears coming hot down my cheeks. 'Please do not make us.' But Malovski made for the door, and I held out my hand. 'All right, Mistress. All right.'

It was better, I decided, to undress myself.

Malovski gave a nod and returned to her box of glinting instruments. Kizzy didn't move as I stumbled from my clothes, my knees still muddy from mushroom picking. My skin pimpled despite the close air. I had never been naked in front of anyone who was not my blood before. Malovski watched me with a dispassionate air and had me lie on the table. The wood was smooth and cool, and I felt I lay on a tomb's slab.

'You cannot touch her,' said Kizzy, and I heard the crack of another slap. A second followed, and a third.

My sister made no further sound as Malovski transferred her hands to me, running them across my skin, feeling the soft parts of my chest, checking my armpits for the swellings and traces of sickness.

I felt as though I was floating above my body, and as her cold fingers moved towards my thighs I sent my mind spinning away, my body a dead thing I left behind easy as a soiled sheet. I reminded myself of the scorched trees in the fields. They seemed conquered, levelled, but it was only the illusion of defeat.

The roots, I reminded myself. *Plant yourself deep in where you came from. Keep your feet.*

'All right,' said Malovski. 'Put this on.'

I opened my eyes, and saw she was holding out a black dress, and a crimson sash. The uniform of the people who had killed my mother. I took it, remembering the trees. It didn't matter whether I wore clothes the colour of tar: inside I was still me, still living.

I sat up and put them on, back turned to Malovski so I could transfer the deathcap to my new pocket. The dress was a little big, with too much fabric on the hips, and the sash was tight with not enough give for me to move freely as I could in our loose-layered skirts.

'Now you,' said Malovski.

Kizzy was sitting on the floor, her arms wrapped around her legs. Her eye was swelling – the rings on Malovski's fingers had caught her.

I crouched beside her, my new garment straining. 'Kizzy?'

'I don't have time for this.' Malovski made for the door again.

'Mistress, please,' I said. 'She is the same as me, we are twins.'

'A fool can see you are not formed the same, and her shape invites trouble,' said Malovski. 'I must be sure she is clean. I'm fetching the guard.'

'Please,' I said, desperation scratching my throat. 'She will fight him, and you said you wanted no more bruises.'

Malovski clucked her tongue. 'If you can convince her, do. But quickly.'

'Kizzy,' I brought my head close to hers, as I had in the cart. 'Kisaiya, my love, please. I don't want you to get hurt.'

I held out my hand in our gesture, and she looked suddenly at me, her brown eyes liquid in the candlelight. There was an anger there I had never before seen directed at me. I thought she might be about to hit me, but she only stood suddenly, and began to undress. I tried to help with the laces of Mamă's bodice, but she shrugged me off, though the coarse string grating against her sore hands made her wince.

When she was naked, she let me lead her to the table, and lay down. I felt like a traitor, the worst sort of conspirator as Malovski leaned over her. I could not bear to see her stretched out like that, like a body ready for burial.

'I have never understood men's fascination with this much body,' said Malovski, prodding Kizzy's breasts. 'They should want us small as possible, easier to handle.'

Kizzy kept her eyes locked on mine, and when Malovski brought her hands to her thighs she gave a small mew and reached for me. I took her hand and cried silent tears into her hair.

It was over soon, and not nearly quickly enough.

'That's enough. Get dressed.' Malovski threw another outfit at Kizzy and went to open the shutters. 'I'll check your hair now.'

It was nothing like how Mamă did it. Mamă was so tender it was like being stroked. She carded our hair like wool, until it puffed into halos of curls that crackled like silk. Malovski yanked the comb through, checking it in the candlelight after each wrench.

'It really would be easier to cut it,' she muttered, scraping the comb so it bit into my scalp bad as a blade.

When that was done, she fetched another box. This one was open topped, and inside were things I recognised: willow bark, and witch hazel, and gut thread.

She did my cheek first, threading a needle. I held as still as I could. It did not hurt as much as I had feared. Malovski was a deft seamstress, her needle sharp and precise. She wiped the stitches with vinegar when she was done, and that is what brought tears hot to my eyes.

'Now you.'

Kizzy sat down, and Malovski began to clean her burns with witch hazel. 'Vinegar would be better, but it makes the skin tough,' she said. 'And I need your hands as soft as your belly.'

When she was done, she laid strips of willow bark along her forearms, just as Mamă would have done, and wrapped it all with what looked like clean linen.

'I will need this back,' she said, tapping the linen. 'Do not soil it.'

She left Kizzy's hands free, spreading them with a yellow salve with a sweet scent I could not place. She gave the rest in its wooden pot to Kizzy.

'Put this on every night. Twice a day is better, but I don't want the trays slipping from your hands.'

No vinegar, no salve, I thought. *Because it would make her clumsy, or tough.* There was no real care here, though Malovski's touch had been tender as a healer's. She was merely protecting her investment.

Kizzy put the pot in her pocket, and Malovski rose to inspect us both.

'Not bad,' she said. 'I'll keep you in the kitchens a month or so, to let the healing begin. And then I think you will be quite the attraction.'

CHAPTER SIX

We travelled in a fine carriage, though anything would be better than a cage. I felt already that I was making one for myself, by obeying this woman. Her touch lingered on my skin, and though the clothes we wore were clean and of a soft material that swished when we moved, I felt as though I wore a mourning shroud.

We sat facing Malovski, travelling backwards so we couldn't watch the castle approach. If I closed my eyes it was almost like travelling in our wagon with Mamă driving, taking us high into the mountains.

Kizzy's eyes were far away, and I wished we could have a moment alone, so that we could link arms and I could press my temple to hers, like we used to in our narrow bunk, feeling for a moment that we could push all the way into each other and be two hearts in one body, as we once had been. Grown together, and not apart.

I made a grave error in helping Malovski calm her, but didn't see what other decision could have been taken. The soldier would have been far rougher. I wanted to whisper all this to her, hear her forgive me, but I contented myself with pressing my leg against hers. She didn't move away.

'The castle is well run as a clock. And you are cogs,' said Malovski as the carriage began to slow. 'Well oiled and silent. Any squeaks will be ironed out, any cogs not working ripped free.' She leaned forward, her red mouth opening wide to enunciate each word. 'If you misbehave, your beauty will not save you. I will not save you.'

Save us from what, I thought, though her examinations had given me some idea. I felt exhausted, empty. The fiddleheads were the last we had eaten, and my stomach yawned, though I did not know if I could swallow with my throat so tight, with the churn of nerves wracking my body.

The road levelled. The sound of the horses' hooves changed, from the dull thud on dusty rock, to the sharp clack of cobbles, and a moment later they were pulled to a halt.

'Here we are.'

The carriage door opened and Malovski stepped lightly down the wooden steps placed beneath the door. I followed close behind, into a wide cobbled courtyard. Stables were ranged across the boundary wall, and chickens pecked at grain scattered outside a wooden door. There were more buildings, and I wondered if Girtie and the others were in one of them.

'Out,' said Malovski. Kizzy didn't move. I don't know if she even heard her.

Malovski nodded at the soldier, and he reached into the shadows and pulled my sister by her upper arm. Kizzy tripped on the wooden steps, held aloft by the soldier's iron grip.

Malovski regarded her coolly. 'You see those spikes?'

She jerked her chin at the stone wall. There were half a dozen iron spikes set atop it, rusted and about the length of a small child.

'There are more at the front of the castle. It's rare that they are empty. Carry on like this, and you'll have the pleasure of passing your sister if you ever leave the walls.'

I swallowed hard, reassessing the red stains I had taken for rust.

'And there's worse, believe me.' Malovski's eyes flicked left. I followed her gaze to the wall. What did she mean?

'This way.'

Malovski's threat had worked. Kizzy was the first behind her, though I still felt the burn of her anger towards me, like I was a weakness she longed to slough from her skin. Again I thought of Kem and Albu, their freedom a salve to my own circling panic. For them, I had to survive this. We both did.

The wooden door was unlocked. As soon as we passed through the door, heat hit our faces. It was a low passage lit with cheap tallow lamps. I could tell the fat had been poorly rendered, because it smelt of rotten meat, like Captain Vereski's breath. I scrunched my upper lip against my nose, breathing in soap and stale water.

The smells of the forest were a distant memory, and I scraped some dirt from beneath my fingernails, placed it quickly on my tongue, searching for a taste of home. All that remained was a copper tang of blood and smoke, and I resisted the urge to spit into Malovski's skirts as we moved through the oppressive corridor, lined with doors.

Ahead came sounds of clattering pans and chattering voices, and the walls were painted red with light from a flickering fire. Kizzy stopped so suddenly I walked into her. I knew she was remembering the last time we had approached flames.

'Come along,' Malovski snapped her fingers at us. 'I have other things to attend to.'

I placed my hand gently on the small of Kizzy's back. I could feel her trembling through the black fabric, but she carried on walking, the noise and smells of the kitchens growing overpowering even before we turned right through its large double doors.

The room was hot and bright, with low ceilings that pressed down and glistened with grease. A fire roared along the length of one wall, and slaughtered pigs were hung at intervals along it. Their skin was scored and bubbling, and I had to bite my tongue to keep my nausea down. One of the kitchen girls had a large metal spoon and was ladling heaps of butter to baste them as another girl turned their iron spits.

The baster was not skilled, and much of the butter dropped to the flames, sizzling and stinking. I thought of all those hours it would have taken at the churn to make such a big pot of butter, of my friends' new place in the dairy and their chapped hands, the work wasted with every gesture of the girl's spoon, and I hated her.

Along the centre of the room, more girls were chopping green onions, steel spoons in their mouths to stop their tears. There were cauldrons over smaller fires, and everything smelled rich and salted.

'Two new ones, Cook,' said Malovski. The whole room stilled at the sound of her voice, every woman and girl shrinking into themselves a little, heads determinedly cast down, apart from one woman who stopped chopping and looked up.

Cook was dark as us, and I saw a long scar closing her eyelid, which was shrunken and hollow.

'A month before they're in the hall serving,' said Malovski. 'Keep them out of trouble.'

Cook ran her remaining eye over us and gave a short nod. I chanced a weak smile as she looked me over, but got none in return.

'I'll put them on fish,' said Cook, but Malovski stayed her with a raised hand.

'I'll see them to their task.'

Malovski wove through the kitchen towards the back wall, and we followed, the girls bowing their heads and making way. One, her hands full of sage, flinched as the woman passed, dropping the herbs onto the floor.

'Idiot girl,' hissed Malovski, turning and raising her hand to strike. I couldn't see anyone else beaten that day, so I found a strength I had not summoned for Kizzy, and stepped forward.

'It was my fault, Mistress. I knocked into her.'

The Settled girl looked sharply up from the floor, her eyes grey as smoke. Her head was fresh shaven, and her neck very pale. That was why the bruises stood so clear upon it, like a necklace of purple petals, too delicate for the brutality that had caused them.

'Is that so?' said Malovski.

The grey-eyed girl said nothing to contradict me, and Malovski only cast me an irritated glance before continuing across the kitchen, stopping in front of a wooden table where two Settled girls around our age made room for us.

The table was strewn with gaping fish and translucent bones, and one of the girls was holding a pair of wooden tweezers.

'These two will show you how it's done.' Malovski nodded at them. 'No knives. I'll be back in a month, and Saints help you if I have to return sooner.'

She left, the room visibly breathing a sigh of relief as soon as her skirts swished out of sight around the corner. The taller of the girls gave us a hard stare.

'No knives, eh? What'd you do?'

Kizzy was mute as the gutted fish, so I spoke. 'Nothing.'

The other girl, whose gaze was more interested than aggressive, raised an eyebrow. 'Not sure I believe that.'

'Thought all your sort were good at knives,' said the first. 'Or is it just sharpening them?'

'Our bear's claws were sharp enough, thank you,' I snapped, my cheeks warming.

'Oh, you're bear dancers.' The first girl turned away. 'My mother said they were all witches of low magic.'

'Better not risk it, then,' I said.

The second girl laughed throatily and stepped between us. She was a head shorter than either of us and I glared over her. 'Don't mind Szilvie, she got her bloods yesterday. She's cranky.'

'Shut up, Dot,' snapped Szilvie.

'Dorottya,' corrected the girl. 'Dot makes me sound like a stain. What's your name?'

It was a good sign, I decided, that she cared enough to ask. 'Lillai.'

'Will "Lil" do?'

'If Dot will.'

'Deal. And does she speak?' She looked at Kizzy. 'Or is she like poor Mira?'

'She speaks when she wants to. Who's Mira?'

Dot lowered her voice and jerked her head to another table nearby, where a girl stood alone, sorting herbs. It was the smoke-eyed girl with the dropped sage and necklace of bruises.

'They crushed her throat. She hasn't spoken in days. It's unusual for them to shave our heads or punish us like that; usually it's only the—'

'Travellers?' I said, sharply. 'That's all right, is it?'

Dot had the grace to look ashamed. 'Of course not. I only meant it's not usual. For them to hurt someone that badly, especially a server.'

I shuddered, my own throat closing in protest. 'She is a serving girl?'

'Was. Not good for much right now, is she?'

'Is she completely mute?'

'So far,' said Szilvie. 'But should heal up all right.'

'Szilvie's a good healer,' said Dot. 'She's the one to go to for all your Malovski-inflicted needs.'

'Malovski did that?'

'She ordered it,' said Szilvie. 'Which is much the same.'

I looked at the tall, sour-faced girl with new eyes. If she was helping the grey-eyed girl then perhaps kindness was buried beneath her frosty exterior.

'What did she do?'

'Something stupid,' said Szilvie, giving Dot a warning glance. I realised I was not going to get more.

'So,' said Dot to Kizzy. 'Do you speak or not?'

Kizzy sucked in her cheeks. 'Not to you.'

Dot raised an eyebrow. 'It's like that, eh? Maybe it's good you can hold your tongue if you're to be a serving girl. The men are beasts.'

'Not that they're much interested in talking,' said Szilvie. 'But you look like you know all about that.'

Kizzy jutted out her chin and put her hands on her hips. She looked so like Mamă I wanted to weep, or punch something. 'You don't know anything about me.'

Dot stepped between them. 'That's enough. Cook's looking, and we've got this whole barrel to finish.' She looked at me. 'Have you prepared fish before?'

'Of course,' I said. 'But never without a knife.'

'They're already gutted, see?' She indicated the barrel of glistening, slit-bellied bodies. 'We're just taking out the bones.'

She clicked the wooden tweezers together. I frowned. 'Why don't you just serve them on the bone?'

'Boyar Valcar likes smooth food, easy food. Food that slips down without protest. Same as his girls,' smirked

Szilvie, and I caught hold of Kizzy's wrist, forgetting for a moment her raw skin, slick with salve. Dot looked down too.

'What happened there?'

Kizzy put her hands behind her back. 'Nothing.'

'Doesn't look like nothing,' said Szilvie, but the taunt in her voice was gone. 'Show me.'

Kizzy wrinkled her nose like the stench of the burning butter had finally got to her. 'Not a chance.'

'Show her,' said Dot. 'She's good.'

'Malovski already salved it.'

'I am better than Malovski,' said Szilvie, holding out her hand. To my surprise, Kizzy put her own out too.

The bandages were already seeping, and Dot flinched a little at the sight of the exposed skin of Kizzy's forearms, but Szilvie only examined her with an interested look on her dour face.

'Witch hazel?'

Kizzy nodded. 'And willow bark under the bandages.'

Szilvie tutted. 'That will dry it out. It'll heal faster, but it will hurt more. You need a poultice on that, to soothe it.'

'I thought we were the witches,' said Kizzy.

'Nothing witchy about knowing your herbs,' snapped Szilvie, crossing her fingers against the accusation. 'I'll beg some oats off Cook.'

Szilvie stalked off in the direction of the one-eyed woman, and Kizzy watched her go with an air of distaste. 'Doesn't it smart someone like that, taking orders from a Traveller?'

'Cook's not a Traveller any more,' said Dot, returning to her fish. 'She's Cook.'

Kizzy raised her eyebrows at me. I could hear her thoughts in my own head. *You're never not a Traveller.* Who and what we are is blood thick, bone deep. I raised mine back, grateful for the moment of connection between us.

'You're not going to be much use with those hands,' said Dot. 'But you can help me. We've already lost time talking.'

It was mainly she who was talking, but I took up Szilvie's tweezers, and Kizzy came to stand behind my shoulder to watch. Her closeness was a comfort, the sound and heat of her breath in my ear centring me.

'So you open it like this, like a butterfly, see?' said Dot. 'And then you spread it, and hold it, like this. And then you feel with your thumb, and they're sort of like ridges, the bones, if you bend the skin up you can feel more easily, and with these kind of fish, trout they are . . .'

I let her chatter wash over me. It was a simple task I could have worked out on my own, but she obviously enjoyed explaining it. I wondered if she had younger sisters or brothers at home that she liked to boss about. Her story about Mira, the girl with no voice, was fresh as a wound in my head and I cast a quick look over my shoulder at the herb table.

Mira was staring back. The bruises around her throat had new significance now I knew what had been taken from her, and I noticed for the first time some swelling about her cheeks and jaw. What monstrous hands had held her and stolen her voice? I gave her a quick smile. She went back to her herbs.

'Are you listening?' Dot nudged me with her elbow, a huffy tone in her voice. Definitely an older sister. 'Show me, go on.'

Szilvie returned with some oats and a glass jar of something that looked like tree sap.

'Cook let me have the last of the honey,' she said, flushed with success. 'Can you believe it? This stuff is like salt, or silk. I was thinking she'd palm me off with some potato water or something.'

'Oh, let me have a dab,' said Dot, reaching out for the jar with a small moan of longing. 'I've had nothing sweet for months.'

'I know full well it was you at the brandy raisins last week,' said Szilvie, tucking the jar under her armpit so it was safe from Dot, and she had her hands free to unwrap Kizzy's bandages. 'And I know Gheorghe brings you treats in exchange for kisses.'

'And more,' said Dot, waggling her eyebrows.

I knew Settled girls were more relaxed about such things, and Dot's boldness was too entertaining to be off-putting. At least she was free to kiss who she liked. Malovski's hands on my thighs, her words about serving the boyar . . . it was something I could not think about, or I would go mad. I thought on the death cap. It was something. Not for now, but maybe . . .

It was a way out.

'We need those done within the hour,' said a harsh voice close behind, making me jump. Cook was squinting at us, her sunken lid quivering. She was short as Dot, and her hands, as she wiped them on her apron, were wrinkled as Old Charani's. They were pocked with smooth burns and other marks, and I knew they'd be rough with work.

I longed to reach out and feel them on mine, to close my eyes and imagine for a moment it was divining day after all. I realised now the risk of how we had lived: that when home was a person and not a place, once they were gone you couldn't get back. Home was lost for ever.

'Sorry Cook,' said Dot, and turned back to her work, tugging at my sleeve to make me start too. But Cook held my gaze a moment longer, then looked at Kizzy.

She placed her hands, her beautiful, gnarled hands, onto my sister's exposed, raw skin, and the moment she did so, they both jolted as though the other had dealt them a blow. Cook's brow furrowed in confusion, and she went back to her place at the onions without another word, taking short, fast steps, without looking back.

'What was that about?' said Szilvie, but when Kizzy replied, it was to me.

'She has the gift,' said Kizzy, and her eyes were bright with confusion and excitement.

My breath caught in my throat. 'Are you sure?'

It was just something to say. My sister was always sure.

Kizzy nodded, her eyes feverishly bright.

'Our divining day is not lost to us.' She looked past Szilvie's frowning face to Cook, who twitched as though Kizzy's gaze was a physical weight laid upon her. I knew that feeling well.

'Lil, we need to talk to her. She can tell us what we are to be.'

CHAPTER SEVEN

With so much food being made, I was certain we were preparing for a feast that evening, but it was barely past midday when Cook clapped her hands for silence and began to bark orders. I looked at the piles of fish being skewered by Szilvie onto long pikes ready for roasting, the hogs crisp and crackling. The whole room stank of onions by then, and the warmth from the fires was almost overpowering.

'You two,' said Cook, snapping her fingers at me and Kizzy. 'Potatoes.'

She pointed to a large pot on a roiling boil, and to a slatted spoon atop a large platter. Kizzy held the platter beside the pot as I fished for potatoes, bringing them gleaming up from the steam like precious gems.

Once they were all out Kizzy could barely hold the platter, and I helped her lower it onto the nearest surface. The unskilled baster brought her vat of butter and dumped it beside us, and we began to ladle spoonfuls on.

'More,' said Cook impatiently as she passed behind us. My stomach ricocheted between nausea and a yawning emptiness I longed to fill, and the sight of potatoes freshly boiled dripping butter tipped it firmly into hunger.

I stepped back to check our handiwork and heard a soft grunt behind me.

'I'm sorry, I—'

It was Mira. She was holding a bowl of sage and tiny specks of thyme leaves, painstakingly removed from their stems. Her fingernails were flecked with them almost as copiously as mine were with scales.

'I'm sorry,' I said again, and she only shook her head and held out the bowl. Her lips looked full but were pressed tight shut and colourless. Her nostrils flared as she sucked in air.

I took the bowl. Her hands were smooth as the fire-warmed pebbles Mamă used to place beneath our sheets in winter's depths. Serving girl hands.

'Thank you.' I hesitated a moment. 'I'm Lillai. Lil.'

Kizzy gave a gesture of greeting and as Mira looked between us I wished my sister were not so lovely and standing so close to me. 'And this is Kizzy.'

'You're Mira?' said Kizzy. But the girl had already turned away, and Kizzy took the bowl from me.

'Poor girl,' she said, as she began to scatter the herbs through the potatoes, using the ladle to move them around and coat them all. I brought my hands up to my nose and breathed in the mingled scents of my work and Mira's: the lemon-tang of thyme the strongest of all.

'What are you doing?' said Kizzy. She was looking at me keenly.

'Nothing.' I bent my head so my hair shielded me from her gaze.

'Are you done with those?' Szilvie stomped over impatiently. 'We have to put everything on the central table.'

Kizzy and I carried the platter and placed it beside the piles of stuffed fish, the fried onions, the hogs butchered and hollow eyed. My mouth watered.

Another door opened at the opposite end of the kitchens from the one we came in through, and as if pulled by some soundless bell, a line of girls came streaming in.

They were our age, and they were all, without exception, beautiful. None so lovely as Kizzy, but all well formed and long-haired, their tresses wound into thick, neat knots at the base of their skulls.

'Serving girls,' murmured Kizzy. So these were the girls chosen by Malovski to please the boyar, however he wished. Kizzy eyed them sharply.

The women of the kitchens shrank to the sides of the room, keeping out of their way, though a muttering went up like a brisk breeze. I caught nasty words, cruel and damning names. The jealousy was clear, but I doubt any kitchen worker would want to take their place.

It was a well-choreographed dance, fetching the food. Each girl took up their platter, and as though they were tied by an invisible thread, turned and trailed the one in front out.

Only one looked up, a fine-boned girl with long dark hair and blue eyes, who seemed to be searching for someone. She found them in the far corner, and gave a quick jerk of her chin in greeting, her hands full of plates.

I followed her gaze to Mira, standing in the shadows. She nodded her head back, and my chest tightened with something akin to what I felt when Mamă and Albu danced. That I was outside something I wanted to be a part of.

'Quick, before it's gone,' said Kizzy, pulling me forward. I noticed there were wooden boards laid across the tables with a meagre assortment of leftovers on them: unbuttered potatoes I had not retrieved from the pot and burnt pieces of meat and fish rescued from the ashes.

There was no cutlery, but kitchen workers were falling upon the food without even washing their hands. I searched the room for a pail of water to clean the fish and herb smell from my skin.

Cook was standing a little way off from the melee, and I could see she was cleaning her hands carefully, working between the fingers with long strokes. She even had a bar of soap. I edged around the feeding women and made my way to where she stood hunched over a bucket.

'May I?' I asked, and she jumped, her faraway eye coming sharply back into focus. She handed me the soap and stood aside slightly, body angled away.

I began to lather my hands. The soap was coarse with husks of corn to scrape away dirt, and smelt of animal fat, like the lamps. I rubbed it across the backs of my hands, scraping beneath my fingernails, keeping an eye on Cook.

'What is your name, Aunty?'

'I am not your aunty.'

Her tone was terse, and I had to summon all my courage to speak again. 'My sister says you have the gift.'

'Do not speak of such things,' said Cook harshly. She rubbed her hands dry with a clean cloth, and made for the table, which was already largely empty, but with a boldness I must have borrowed from Kizzy I caught hold of her sleeve.

'Please, Aunty. Today is our divining day.'

Cook brought her face close to mine, so suddenly I stepped back.

'Forget,' she hissed. 'Your new life began today. This is your fate.'

She walked away. Her words smarted as though I'd been lashed with a whip. *Forget.*

I gritted my teeth. It had only been a day, but even if it had been a decade, I knew I would not. As I joined Kizzy at the table, I knew I would remember as long as I lived. Like the felled trees, my roots ran deeper than anyone could reach. They could never wrench them from me.

. . .

Kizzy saved me what she could – a crust of bread and a lump of flesh so charred it could have been fish or hog – but as more barrels of fish were brought in and the fires freshly stoked, the meagre offerings we were allowed to eat only served to make my stomach gurgle and writhe.

There was a frisson of giggling when two fresh sides of beef were carried in by six young men. The meat dripped blood over the rush-strewn floor, and the men looked likely to outstay their welcome until Cook waved her butcher's knife at them. They dispersed with many a wink and thrown compliment.

'Did you see Nicholai?' said Dot to Szilvie, her face flushed. 'His beard is coming in.'

'What about Gheorghe? Nicholai's still a boy,' said Szilvie dismissively. I noticed she had not joined in the giggling. I was liking her more as the hours wore on.

'Nicholai tumbled Elena last week though,' said Dot. 'And those hands are very large.'

'Tsk,' said Szilvie, the corners of her mouth twitching. 'I doubt he knows what to do with them.'

Kizzy and I were silent as stones, and Dot turned to us as she reached blindly for another fish, her hands retracing well learned pathways. 'Anything you like the look of?'

I shook my head.

'Got a boy back home?'

'All our men are murdered or now working on farms outside the walls,' said Kizzy, and Dot's grinning face fell. Kizzy's chin was trembling and I knew she was thinking especially of Fen. I squeezed her upper arm.

'Kisaiya, calm. He'll be all right.'

'Calm?' She spat the word back. 'Have you a slave's heart, Lillai? How is any of this all right? How can you bear it?'

She walked away. My hurt ached like a splinter beneath the skin. I felt sore from Kizzy's words, Cook's reprimand. From Malovski and her probing fingers, her cold eyes. And my pain was sharpest and deepest because of Mamă and Old Charani and our lost camp.

'She'll calm down,' said Dot, and I knew it was an attempt at friendship, at reassurance. But she did not know Kizzy as I did: she was never quick to forgive, her tempers leaching from her slow as charged air after a thunderstorm.

I said none of this to Dot, smiling to show my thanks for her attempt at comfort as I reached for another fish.

'How do they eat so much?' I asked. 'Does the boyar have visitors?'

'Always,' sighed Dot. 'It's a condition of the pact.'

She said these words as though they had a significance beyond their usual meaning. Travellers had pacts, of course. To never turn away a hungry traveller, to leave the places we camped as we found them. And there were older traditions around pacts: soul pacts to bind secrets or make promises.

'What sort of pact?'

'The pact that rules these lands. It's law, really.'

'Who makes the laws?'

She shot a look in Szilvie's direction. The girl had been called to the central table to knock dough into round loaves, and Dot leaned towards me conspiratorially.

'Did Malovski tell you anything of the Dragon?'

Her low tone was nervous. I felt the hair on my own arms stand up, as though her anxiety were catching.

'No.'

'Nothing of the visitors, the offerings?'

I shook my head impatiently.

'What's this about offerings?' We both jumped. Szilvie was standing behind us, hands on her hips, floury palms powdering her skirts.

Dot flushed. 'I only was telling her what you told me.'

'Then it's not much at all, hardly worth telling. You know Cook'll learn you with a slap if she hears you talking about it.' She turned her glare on me. 'Any of it. And what if Mira hears? Do you care about anyone's feelings, Dot?'

Dot shrugged off Szilvie's anger with the practised air of someone who has done so many times before. 'Fine. You'll hear of it eventually.'

'I want to know now,' I said.

'No,' said Szilvie, her glare softening a little. 'You don't.'

CHAPTER EIGHT

By the time we were done preparing dinner and the serving girls came to fetch the platters of sliced beef, stuffed fish, and the endless mountains of steaming vegetables, my neck ached and my shoulders were in spasm. I rolled them and they clicked, full of knots.

'Mira,' called Szilvie across the kitchen. 'Time to check your throat.'

I turned in time to see Mira shake her head.

'It has to stay clean,' said Szilvie sternly. 'If it gets infected, you may lose your tongue too.'

'She bit it when they throttled her,' whispered Dot. Kizzy regarded her coolly.

'I doubt she appreciates you gossiping about it.'

Dot rolled her eyes. We watched Mira reluctantly cross the kitchen as Szilvie set down the cloth and bottles. She pulled Mira onto a stool.

Mira's eyes flicked from Szilvie to Kizzy and me, and Szilvie said, 'She doesn't like people watching.'

I didn't think she had much hope of privacy with Dot around, but I went with Kizzy to busy myself with wiping down the tables.

'I'll talk to Cook,' Kizzy's voice was low and determined. 'Ask her to divine for us.'

'I already tried,' I said.

'You did?' Her voice is surprised. 'Well, I'll succeed.'

I blinked up at my sister, surprised at her arrogance and then again not at all. Though others, likely myself included, were sweaty from the fires, pores large in their flushed faces and hair stuck to their foreheads, my sister looked as fresh-faced and lovely as if she had just returned from foraging.

I shot a look at Mira and Szilvie. Mira was gargling with something that made her wince, and when she spat the liquid was dark with blood. I pulled my attention back to my sister, the back of my neck flushing hot with anger for Mira.

'We need to be careful, Kizzy.'

'Careful? Why?'

'Because I do not want to see your voice crushed from your throat,' I hissed, just managing to keep my voice down. 'I do not want to see you beaten, or taken from me, or forced into anyone's bed.'

'But you are making it easy for them,' spat Kizzy. 'You are being so obedient, they will see you as a slave, as nothing.'

'Let them,' I said, reaching out suddenly for her cheek, and cupping it in my hand. 'They cannot know what I am thinking. I want to survive this, Kizzy. I want to see Kem and Albu again.'

Kizzy's eyes burned into mine, their soft brown transformed into deep pits of dark fury.

'Surviving is not enough for me.' She jerked away from my touch, still shaking her head. 'I will not accept this fate.'

. . .

For all her confidence in learning our fate, Kizzy was refused, and we were sent to bed with no answers from Cook. We slept on straw mattresses on a cold stone floor, in a narrow room beside the kitchens. The walls streamed with water, and green mould bloomed in the cracks.

There were ten of us, Dot and Szilvie included. Mira slept along the wall closest to the kitchen, beside a grate that wept stale water. We were given the mattresses nearest the draughty door, which snagged on the uneven floor with a sound that set my teeth on edge every time someone went in or out.

'You'll be moving in with the serving girls soon,' said Szilvie. 'Their rooms are bigger.'

'Not that they spend much time in their own beds,' said a red-haired girl with high cheekbones, who Dot had introduced as Elena. She had an evenly featured face made ugly by her cruel smile.

Kizzy stared Elena down.

'Hark at you,' said Dot. 'Szilvie told me about your tumble with Nicholai.'

Elena flushed, but managed to cast another haughty glance in our direction before collapsing, fully clothed, into bed.

I knew she hated us on sight, because we were Travellers. The thing that was my pride, was something they thought should be my shame.

The reasons the Settled hated us were many and stupid: because we had brown skin, because we lived in wagons, because we called no land our own. And they were kept in fear by the stories they were told. That we had dark skin because devils live in us. We could read the weather because the *Iele* suckled us. We travelled because we steal from everyone, and moved on before we could be caught. None of it was true, of course, but people always prefer their own explanations over the reality of things.

My disdain grew from Elena's, and made me strong. But there was fascination as well as disdain in the way she and some of the others watched us. Elena's gaze reminded me of the Settled men in the villages, who coiled Kizzy's tight curls around their thumbs and asked her to show them her gums to see if they were pink as theirs.

Szilvie lay down near me, not even bothering to unlace her boots. As the sounds of sleeping filled the room, I turned on my side and whispered to her.

'Is Mira's throat all right?'

'Not really,' said Szilvie briskly. Kizzy nudged me with her foot. I knew she wanted me to let Szilvie sleep, so we could speak, but I had a further question burning inside me.

'What did she do? Why did they crush her throat?'

Szilvie's eyes were wide in the darkness. 'It's not my story to tell.'

'She can hardly tell it.'

Szilvie shuffled closer, and brought her lips close to my ear.

'Her friend. This girl. Another serving girl, she—' Szilvie shifted uncomfortably. I heard the straw grating against her skirts. 'Cristina. She was an offering.'

'An offering for the pact?' I said.

'Dot and her mouth,' hissed Szilvie. 'Yes, for the pact.'

'What is the pact?'

'Malovski really told you nothing?' I could hear the mingled fear and hope in Szilvie's voice. She did not want to be the one to tell me what it meant.

'No.'

'I should have let Dot tell you.'

'I want you to tell me,' I said. Szilvie was drawing away, about to close off completely.

'The pact the boyar has with . . . him.'

'The Dragon?' It was a hunch, and I could tell by Szilvie's frightened gasp I was right.

'Not in the dark,' said Szilvie. 'I can't dwell on it in the dark.'

'But what does it mean?'

'For Saints' sake. I'm worn out.' She pulled the covers over her head and refused to say more on it that night, or the next morning, or at all.

. . .

Our lives quickly took on a harder shape.

My sister's certainty that we should hear our divining shrank with each passing day. We had a moon-cycle to hear our fate: a month before it faded for ever. I tried to reassure Kizzy it didn't matter, that we could do without a Seer. I didn't feel there was much point in learning my fate until I could see beyond the kitchens. But Kizzy's heart was restless, and still she went every day to Cook, and every day Cook refused.

The castle beyond the kitchen remained as much of a mystery as the world outside the walls. We saw no sign of the boyar – I refused to think of him as 'ours' – and no men but the stable boys, though the stories the kitchen girls told made me glad of that.

The boys flirted with Kizzy every time they came to the kitchens with meat or gossip, but she turned mute as Mira, though nothing about her silence was meek. They started to call her *gheață*, the Settled word for ice, because she was beautiful and cold as the frost that found us even in the kitchens.

The relentless amount of food we had to prepare made me queasy, but hardly any ever came back. This was a land of more plenty than I had ever known, and I wondered how the boyar could be so prosperous with his bounds pressed upon by the properties of many others. The ground must be worked to dust.

Mira's bruises ripened to black, and I sometimes heard her whisper to Szilvie, her voice recovering slowly, but she never talked to me. I don't know why I longed for her to do so.

Out of her earshot, I attempted to learn more of the offering, the Dragon and other mysteries kept from us, but Dot and Szilvie were deaf to my questions.

'Mamă would not give up,' Kizzy said into my neck every night. *But*, I would think. *Mamă never knew what it was to be a slave.*

In her worst moments of that first week, when the scars on her hands cracked and bled, Kizzy told me she wanted to join Mamă. She said it quietly, because on her second day she shouted and raved like a fevered beast, until Captain Vereski was drawn from his sentry place down the corridor, came with a strap and made a new scar down her perfect, soft cheek. It split like an overripe peach, bled so sudden and shockingly she did not even cry. He gave me one too, re-opening my stitches so we would match.

She stopped shouting then; not for herself, but to protect me.

From that moment on, it was clear: anything done to her would be done to me. So Kizzy didn't act on her threats of joining Mamă. She only took Old Charani's cloth out from her pocket every night and pressed it to her face. I think it made her feel better, to know death would be there, as it was for everyone in the end.

'Even the boyar,' she whispered against my cheek, breath furred with stale water. 'Even he has a grave waiting.'

She didn't say so aloud for fear of being overheard, but I knew she would dearly love to be the one to put him in it. Kizzy lost none of her bravery, but it became a harder sort, honed as a blade, and though I would never have told her, it frightened me.

It also frightened the other girls we shared a room with, but they admired her too. No matter we worked the same hours, ate the same bread – despite the hardship she remained beautiful, vital, fierce. A grace, as Old Charani said. But such grace could not last long in such a place, and with the arrival of a visitor, another boyar from the north, it turned to a curse.

Chapter Nine

Elena had it from her stable boy Nicholai that the visitor was Boyar Calazan. He ruled lands larger than these, and was a man far richer and crueller than even our master, Boyar Valcar.

'He's the Dragon's man and is to be honoured. Nicholai says the yard is red with slaughtered pigs,' she said, a strange shiver of delight in her voice.

It was not the only cruelty. The cows were kept pregnant so they would give milk, their calves killed for livers. In the dairy our Traveller sisters made skeins of cheeses. The boys produced yards of soft leather for the noblemen's boots, feet chapped from treading it in the icy storehouses.

In the kitchens, we bled the carcasses for blood cakes, and went about our work quietly. As the possibility of our having a divining day drew further away, each day brought Boyar Calazan's visit closer, and our waiting fate as serving girls into sharper reality.

Two weeks into our captivity, we were at our usual stations when Cook came to check on us. She did this less and less, bored I think by Kizzy's constant requests. But this time, my sister only stared at her. Cook glared back.

'Don't even try it, girl.'

Kizzy, for once, was silent. She reached into her pocket and drew out Old Charani's purple cloth. The bloodstains had faded to black, and the colour reminded me of our elderberry curtains. I thought she had truly lost her mind, pulling it out and showing Cook like it meant something.

But, looking at Cook, I saw it did. The old woman had gone almost as pale as a Settled. She reached up, to her white curls. And then I saw it: a purple cloth, edged with yellow stitching, holding her hair off her face. An exact match for the one held in Kizzy's hand.

Cook grasped at Kizzy. 'Where did you get that?'

Dot and Szilvie were looking at us, and Cook seemed to collect herself. She snapped her fingers at them. 'Onions. Now.'

They skulked away.

'I got it from our Seer,' said Kizzy, her eyes shining.

'Charani?' The name in Cook's mouth was like a bolt of lightning through my body: I felt every hair on my arms stand on end. 'Charani is your Seer?'

'Was.'

'Is she—'

Kizzy nodded, and Cook pressed her hand hard to her mouth. I saw her throat constrict with swallowed sobs. Others were noticing our exchange, Dot and Szilvie whispering with the girls at the chopping table, and I moved to block their view.

Cook dropped her hand, took two deep breaths. 'I have turned my mind from this long enough.' She regained her usual colour, though her eyes still shone. 'Your divining day. Is it too late?'

Kizzy shook her head.

'Tonight,' said Cook, already turning from us, the old steeliness returning to her voice. 'Come to the kitchens tonight.'

. . .

Later, in our shared room, Kizzy and I lay facing each other in the darkness. The room was soon silent, the smells of the kitchen clinging to our clothes. For the first weeks I did not think I would be able to sleep in such a place. In the forest, the sound of Albu snoring outside was like a lullaby, and the woods whispered with breezes or rang out with wolfsong. But an exhausted body will take what rest it can.

I could just make out my sister's eyes, unblinking. I wanted to press myself against her, for comfort as much as warmth, but she was coiled with a taut energy. After maybe half an hour, her head twitched, and she turned her ear towards the door, which she'd propped ajar with her boot.

She gave me a nod and started to rise before I'd even made out the sounds of soft footsteps in the stone corridor. No one knocked, but a shadow crossed the thin slice of light.

I followed Kizzy through the door, and there was Cook, her face set in a frown. She gestured for us to follow her, and we kept close as she led us back to the kitchen, closing the heavy wooden doors behind. They barely squeaked, so coated were their hinges with grease spat from the fire.

'We can speak freely in here,' she said. 'The walls are thick.'

She pulled up a stool and sat at the table where we had first seen her chopping onions.

She seemed smaller now the space was empty and she didn't have her workers buzzing about her like bees attending to their queen. Her remaining eye raked over us both, settling on Kizzy.

'Charani was my younger sister. I had three, all of us Seers, but she was the most talented. Did she not see it coming?' Grief shook her voice. 'But then, I did not see the path that brought me here.'

'You parted?' I said. I somehow thought Traveller sisters would stay together, no matter what.

'I left, two days after my divining day. I knew I would never make my mark under her shadow. She was already the favourite.' An old bitterness rose in her voice, and she took a deep steadying breath. 'I was young and wanted to make my own way. My divining said my place was in the camp, and I wanted to prove it wrong.' She eyed us beadily. 'I would not place too much importance on such things. In fact, it really would be best if you did as I said that first day.'

'Forget?' said Kizzy, taking the word from my mouth. 'Impossible.'

Cook barked a laugh. 'You're a fierce one. That makes it harder to live this life.' She pointed to her eye. 'Let me assure you, I know.'

'I don't care,' said Kizzy, and there was no tremble in her voice, no doubt. 'The month is nearly done, and we cannot go on without knowing our path.'

She began unwrapping her bandages. Over time, the honey had worked some of its magic: her skin had stopped weeping, but it was still peeling.

Cook tutted. 'Did they do that?'

'No,' said Kizzy. 'I did it myself.'

She did not explain how – that she had been trying to reach Mamă in her burning wagon – and Cook did not ask.

'It's been a long time since I read a palm.'

'But you can,' said Kizzy. It was not a question. 'I felt it that first day, when you touched me.'

Cook spread her hands. Again, with their callouses and curled fingers, they reminded me so strongly of Old Charani's I wanted to weep. 'Seeing it doesn't make it true.'

'But you are reading our fate—'

'Fates can change, child.' Cook gestured around us, as if to add, *as you can see.*

'I know how it works. And I'm not a child any more,' said Kizzy. 'We're seventeen.'

'Don't be in too much of a hurry to grow up. They'll take it from you soon enough.'

'Better I do it myself than let them.'

Cook laughed again, but softer, and her eye was sadder. 'There's little choice, child.'

'My name is Kisaiya,' said Kizzy. 'What is yours, Aunty?'

'My name does not matter,' said Cook. 'In time, yours will not either.'

Kizzy held out her palm. 'Tell me what I am. Tell me what could be.'

Cook looked at her a long moment, and then took it. There was the same jolt, as though Kizzy's burnt skin still held the heat of the flames. Cook brought her eye down level with Kizzy's palm, gently running her finger along the lines, scored too deep for the fire to erase. Kizzy winced.

'You're good with bears. And birds, and cats. All animals. You would be an *ursar*, or animal healer.'

A smile split Kizzy's face as she looked at me, like sunlight piercing clouds. 'I told you.'

'Shame all that will be good for here is butchering. Now,

let's see.' Cook peered closer, turning Kizzy's raw hand this way and that. 'No husband, here. No children.'

Kizzy's smile faltered. She swallowed hard, and I knew she was thinking of Fen.

'Someone though. Someone – important. He will change you for ever.'

Kizzy snorted, regaining her composure. 'You sound like the frauds in the market, Aunty.' She put on a mystical voice. 'A tall dark stranger—'

Cook threw her hand down. 'I'll not be talked to like that. I'm not your Aunty, child. We are not kin. I could tell Mistress Malovski what's gone on here.'

'And lose your other eye?' Kizzy said smoothly. 'We're in this together now.'

Cook looked at me. 'Doesn't her boldness make you want to stuff up your ears?' She turned back to Kizzy. 'It's not just you who will suffer if you don't behave, girl. They know how to hit you where it hurts.'

Kizzy put her palm back on the table. 'I'm sorry. Please, what else can you tell me?'

Cook sucked her teeth with a smacking sound. 'It's hard to tell, but I think there's a journey ahead.'

'A journey?' I said, tensing at the word. 'You think she'll escape?'

'Maybe. Maybe a journey against your will. But this will not be where you die.'

'No,' said Kizzy with certainty. 'It will not. What about my death?'

'Death's the hardest thing of all to place.'

'I know,' said Kizzy, and I could tell she was thinking of Old Charani, who had not seen her own end.

Cook looked closer. 'It is strange though – perhaps it's only the burns, but . . .'

'What is it?'

Cook studied her hand a moment longer and shook her head. 'Can't make sense of the lifeline. There's another running beside it, but they both seem to . . . I can't tell with all this scarring.'

'But there's no time to wait until it heals,' said Kizzy. 'It has to be today, our divining days are nearly done.'

'That's all I can tell you,' said Cook. 'Your sister needs time too.'

She reached out for my hand, but I held it to my chest. I was suddenly not sure I wanted to know. Before it was because I was sure my future held nothing special, but now I had a feeling of foreboding, like a circling shadow crossing the back of my neck.

'Come on, Lil,' said Kizzy. 'You've got to do it. Mamă would want you to.'

I met my sister's eyes, feeling tears well in my own. Kizzy reached out to me with her un-bandaged hands. 'I'm going on a journey, Lil. And I know you're coming with me. We won't die here. Let her tell you.'

I could never refuse Kizzy. I gave Cook my hand. Her own was coarse as Old Charani's and I closed my eyes, imagining the sounds of the dying embers of the fire came from one burning birch and larch, that my belly was full of mushroom stew and that Mamă's hands were on my shoulders in place of Kizzy's.

'There's something in you.' Cook's voice cut through my dreaming. 'Something in you and shining – special.' I opened my eyes. Cook was staring intently at me. She brought up one of her hands to my neck and touched me very gently upon the throat.

'She sings,' said Kizzy, almost vibrating with excitement. 'That's it, isn't it? She's a *lăutari*. Lil, I *told* you!'

'There's one way of truly telling,' said Cook.

I frowned. 'What?' Cook looked hard at me. 'I can't sing. Not in front of–' I broke off.

'Then don't sing for me. Sing for her. Sing,' Cook said, leaning into me, her eye looking straight through my skin into my heart, 'for your Mamă.'

Tears came in earnest now. Cook looked away, and Kizzy wrapped her arms around me. 'Sing, Lil. It's your fate.'

So I did. I hauled my breaking heart, my hurt, into my throat, and sang something low and sweet: a mourning song. A song for Mamă, and for Old Charani, and Dika, and all the other burnt and broken bodies that had once held the souls of those we loved.

I sang their spirits free and safe and unburdened with the knowledge of what had become of us, and sent them spinning up to the stars, or into the trees, or wherever they felt happiest. I sang them love and pushed it into every note of my song until it shone.

The silence rang like a bell afterwards. When Cook, tears running down her face, smiled, it was a real smile that lit her whole face like a lamp.

'A *lăutari*, certainly. You didn't need an old woman to tell you that.'

'And the rest,' sniffed Kizzy, wiping her face. 'Read the rest.'

Cook took a deep breath, composing herself, and took up my hand again. 'No children, nor husband for you either. But a love, a great love. I can feel it strongly.'

'A love?' said Kizzy. 'Is it me?'

Cook shook her head. 'A romantic love.'

'Oh.' Kizzy sounded a little put out. 'Is she on the journey too?'

'Hush, it is not your reading,' said Cook, but gently. She seemed to have softened to Kizzy. Everyone did. 'Yes, I can see the journey. Perhaps you are together after all.'

Kizzy leaned in. 'And her death?'

Cook ran her finger across a line in my palm. She shook her hand slowly.

'What?' I said at last. The soothing effect of the song had

worn off, and anxiety was breeding in my belly again. 'What do you see?'

'I can find no death for you.'

'What?'

Cook looked up. Her jaw was tight beneath its dark, wrinkled skin. 'I cannot find your life's end.'

'That's good,' laughed Kizzy. 'Perhaps she will live for ever.'

Cook fixed her with a sharp gaze. 'That would not be a blessing, child. We die because we are meant to, as do trees and birds and all things on this earth.' She broke off abruptly, looking weary. 'It's all I can tell you. Midnight is past, and I must be up soon.'

Kizzy rose to leave, but I stayed sitting. I wanted to ask the question that had been burning inside me for days and days. 'Cook, can I ask you something else? Not about our divining.'

Cook raised her eyebrows at me.

'Who is the Dragon?'

The woman's face drained so completely of colour it was as if she wore a layer of Malovski's powder. She crossed her fingers as Szilvie had done against the mention of witchcraft. 'Who told you, child?'

'No one told me anything,' I said, my heart beating faster. 'Only the word.'

Cook ran a shaky hand through her greying hair. 'It is best if he stays as a word.'

'Please,' I said. 'I'll never ask another thing.'

Cook closed her eye. I could see her eyeball working side to side beneath the dark, papery skin.

'This place is worse than you know. This land is cursed, not only for us Travellers. For the Settled too.' Her eye opened. Her sealed lid twitched. 'We are not the only ones who have cause to be afraid.'

'Tell us,' said Kizzy, leaning into her. 'It is surely better we know.'

Cook looked at the banked-up fire, the lit heart glowing redly through its crust. 'This land is cursed, because its Voievod is a curse. They call him the Dragon, because he razes whole villages that disobey his command. He is an evil man, with a black heart. Some say he's worse than a man, has no heart at all.'

'Old Charani spoke of him,' said Kizzy.

Cook nodded, and licked her lips, as though her mouth had gone suddenly dry. 'I doubt you know the worst of it. It's barely talked of. For years, this whole land was a place of bloodshed. He'd send his . . . I'd call them men, but there are rumours they are worse.'

'What's worse than men?' said Kizzy, and Cook snorted, without humour.

'Not much, but what this Voievod makes of men . . . anyway. He used to send his servants to pillage, but then an accord was struck with all the boyars of the land. And now, he lets them alone mostly. The land is fruitful, lush. But there's a cost. A pact.'

The hairs on the back of my neck stood on end. I did not want to hear what she was going to say and yet could not bring myself to stop her.

'Once every year, on the middle dying moon, each boyar sends an offering. That is the Dragon's price. They are sent to him.'

'An offering for what?' I said, recalling Szilvie's words.

'Peace. Blood for a sacrifice. It's as if the fields are fed by the bone meal of innocents. And you'd do best to keep yourself out of notice, or else it might be you—'

She broke off suddenly. Kizzy had clamped her hand across Cook's mouth.

'Kizzy,' I said. 'Let her finish—'

'Shush!' Kizzy snapped urgently. 'Someone's coming!'

Cook dropped my hand and snatched up a nearby discarded rag.

'Quickly,' she said, motioning for Kizzy and me to get into a cupboard. 'Hide.'

But it was too late. Before I could even stand from the stool, the door opened smoothly on its greased hinges, and Malovski stepped into the kitchen.

CHAPTER TEN

Surprise flickered across Malovski's face. It was only for a moment, before her usual cold detachment took its place, but I could tell she had not known we were here. It had not been my singing that brought her.

'Mistress,' started Cook. 'I—'

'Well, well,' said Malovski softly, and it was more terrifying than if she'd shouted. 'I just went by your room, Cook. Needed to talk to you about our guest.'

'I was running them through the schedule,' said Cook. 'They slowed down service today. I did not want it to happen again tomorrow.'

'Very diligent.' Malovski's eyes took in Kizzy's unbandaged hands. 'You have never taken such care before. But I suppose rats run together, don't they?' She strode over, dark skirt swishing. 'Cover up your hands. It's disgusting.'

Kizzy snatched up the bandages.

'Get out,' said Malovski. 'Don't let me catch you three alone again. I'll have no Gyptian covens in this castle.'

'It was nothing like that, Mistress.'

'It had better not be, or I'll have your other eye. And trust me, a blind old Gypsy won't find shelter here, or anywhere on this land. Out,' she barked at Kizzy and me. 'Now.'

We hurried to the door, holding our breath until we pulled it closed behind us. I started gratefully to our room, the door still held ajar with the boot, but Kizzy yanked on my sleeve.

'What?' I whispered, but she held her finger to her lips, and with her other hand pointed along the corridor. I followed the direction of her finger. At the end of the long stretch of stone passage, lit by the stinking, smoking lamps, was the door. The door we had come in through, almost a moon-cycle ago.

My heart began to race.

Kizzy pulled on my arm again, beginning to move down the passage. I hesitated only a moment, looking back at the kitchen door. It was firmly closed and I could hear nothing from inside, just as Cook had said.

Quickly, mouthed Kizzy, already many steps ahead. I followed.

It was all we could do not to run. The corridor seemed to stretch interminably, the door growing no larger, no closer. My heartbeat pounded louder than my footsteps, and my mind raced with thoughts of all the things that could go wrong. Malovski could emerge from the kitchen any moment, and the well-lit corridor would offer no places to hide. The door could be locked, or guarded outside.

We reached it, and Kizzy eased the ring pull. I held my breath. The ring pull handle turned. It was unlocked.

Kizzy pulled it open and we spilled into the dark courtyard. There was no guard. The night air was sharp and cold at the back of my throat. Though tinged with the smell of horses and rotting vegetables, it was fresh after days indoors.

I sucked it in, almost drunk on it. The night was sprinkled with stars, and I thought of my song, spinning up to my family's spirits. Kizzy was already moving through the dark, almost invisible in her black clothes, and the gate with its fearsome spikes was closed but we would open them and soon be through, and—

'Hello, girl.'

The voice was awfully close, awfully familiar. A voice I'd hoped never to hear again. It brought back the smell of burning, the screams of dying ponies and slaughter.

Uneven teeth flashed at me in the dark and then my arm was in a vice-like grip. The smudged shape of Kizzy, sharpening as my eyes adjusted, was at the gate, and turned at the sound.

'Go!' I said. 'Run!'

I could hear the grin in Captain Vereski's voice. 'Oh yes. Go on little girl. Run. I'll take care of your sister.'

Kizzy turned.

'Go!' I cried again. 'Kizzy, please!'

But Kizzy was walking back into the channel of light cut by the open door.

'I'm sorry,' I moaned. 'I'm sorry.'

But Kizzy did not look angry. She looked broken, her moment of hope so brief and so quickly snatched, like a moth drawn to a beautiful flame and finding its wings singed to dust.

'Let her go. We'll go back,' she said. 'We'll not give you any trouble.'

Captain Vereski chuckled. 'I may find time to give you some trouble. I got landed on the night watch thanks to you and your filthy bears. I suppose I should thank you for livening it up.'

I looked up into Captain Vereski's face, and it was rapt, staring at Kizzy. Her nail marks were still red and ragged down his cheek. 'It's very dull.' He licked his lips. 'Terribly lonely, too.'

Kizzy stopped short. 'Let her go.'

'Come closer then,' he said.

'We'll go straight to bed.'

He leered. 'You and I?'

'Let her go.'

'Come closer.'

Kizzy came to us. She did not tremble, but there was a set to her jaw that betrayed her fear. I could almost hear her mind racing. I tried to wrench myself free, but it only caused Captain Vereski to pinch my arm harder.

'I'll trade,' said Captain Vereski. 'Her for you.'

I could see she was considering it.

'Kizzy, no—'

'Captain Vereski.' For the second time that night, Malovski's voice was dangerously soft. 'Let the girl go.'

The captain wheeled around, tugging me with him. I stepped on the hem of my dress and stumbled. Vereski let go and I fell to my knees on the hard cobbles.

'Mistress Malovski.' The commanding tone was gone, and Captain Vereski was again reduced to an obedient servant. 'These two were trying to escape.'

I looked up from beneath my hair, heart still pounding. Malovski was silhouetted against the light. With her dark clothes and narrow waist, she looked like a wraith, a vengeful spirit. Her nostrils were flaring.

'I apprehended them,' said Captain Vereski into the silence.

'I see that. Though I also heard some bargaining.'

'I was only – I was just trying to make that one come close enough to catch her.'

'And then what?' said Malovski. 'These are not for you, Captain. These are my girls, and my girls do not associate with the likes of you. Go to the tavern like the rest of the servants.'

'I am a soldier,' said Captain Vereski, drawing himself up to his full height, but though he was at least a foot taller than Malovski, she still seemed to tower over him.

'A servant with a sword,' she said dismissively, and jerked her head at Kizzy and me, turning back to the passage. 'Come.'

He spoke quietly, so quietly that had the wind not dropped for a moment she may not have heard him. As it was, his mutter carried on the dead air. 'Better a servant than a whore.'

I caught my breath. Malovski stopped so suddenly she might have been turned to ice. She pivoted on her heel, smoothly, her long skirts giving the impression that she floated above the floor.

'You will pay for that,' she said simply, and snapped her fingers at Kizzy and me. The sound made me jump. 'Come.'

I could almost hear the blood draining from Captain Vereski's face as we followed Malovski into the passage, her heels clicking, Kizzy's and my bare feet slapping on the cold stone. I was almost looking forward to the thin straw mattress, the warmth of other bodies, but Malovski did not stop at the bedroom door where our fellows slept.

Neither of us dared speak. I could not imagine how Kizzy was feeling: the adrenaline and relief and fear coursing through my body must be doubly strong in hers. Compared to whatever Captain Vereski had wanted with her, I was almost sure that what Malovski had planned wouldn't be as bad.

Unless . . . my mind raced. We would not be offerings?

She turned sharply left before the end of the passage, and instead of climbing, we descended slick stone steps, worn smooth at the centre with use.

The air down here was stale and dank, and the temperature dropped with every step. My soles cringed on the stone as the ground levelled out. It was unlit, and the light from the passage was lost until I felt we waded through the thick, still air like water. Malovski must have the senses of a bat, because she seized my arm with nauseating accuracy, right in the spot it was already tender from Captain Vereski's grasp.

'In here,' she said, and threw me forward.

I found myself on my knees again, on a hard floor sparingly strewn with moist straw. A smell came up from it, of unwashed bodies and other, worse things. I heard a door clang shut and wheeled around. My eyes gradually adjusting to the dim light, I saw Kizzy was not with me.

Panic coming thick in my chest, I felt for the door, and my hands met solid wood. I ran my fingers across it, and found a metal slot, an opening, and pressed my eyes to it. I could make out Malovski closing another door opposite and turning a key in the lock.

My breath caught. She had not yet locked mine – there had been no sound of a bolt. I scrambled for the handle, but Malovski closed the gap with short, fast strides, and locked my door too. She lowered her eyes to the metal slot, her crimson mouth made black by the darkness, a pit lined with neat white teeth. I reeled away.

'This will learn you, slave.'

And then she was gone.

CHAPTER ELEVEN

I waited a few moments before pressing my face to the metal slot.

'Kizzy?' I called.

I lowered my eye to the slot again. The darkness was a grimy grey, lightening by the moment. I saw the flash of my sister's teeth through the slot opposite.

'I'm here.'

'Are you all right? Did she hurt you?'

Kizzy let out a strangled laugh that sounded more like a sob. 'No more than she had already.'

I wilted in relief.

'I didn't know these places were real,' said Kizzy. 'I thought they were a story made up to frighten us.'

'What places?'

'Places without light where they keep people prisoner.'

I wanted to cry. 'Kizzy?'

'Mmm?'

'Do you – did we . . .' I could not think how to say it. The thought had swelled like a tumour in my mind over the past weeks. Now it caught on my tongue. 'The mushrooms,' I managed, finally. 'If we had not—'

'Lil,' she interrupted, her voice firm. 'You cannot think it. Mamă would not want you to think it.'

'How can I not?' My tears were hot on my chilled cheeks. 'If it hadn't been for our birthday—'

'Who's to say they wouldn't have found us anyway? Lillai, if we go down that path, there is no turning back.'

'But I cannot forget.'

'Then forgive. And if you can't forgive yourself, forgive me.'

'You?'

'I'm your twin, aren't I? We are together in all things.'

I pressed my hands to my chest, as though I could claw out my heart. 'But you tried to save Mamă. You fought. You have fought every moment.'

'And look where it's got us,' said Kizzy, so softly I had to press my ear to the slot to make out the words. 'Perhaps I should be more like you, Lil.'

I snorted. 'Definitely not.'

'You should be prouder of what you are,' said my sister. 'Your voice earlier – it was more lovely than ever. Don't give it to anyone who doesn't deserve it. Save it for that great love Cook mentioned.'

The bitterness entered her voice again, and I hurried to speak. 'And you, an *ursar* after all.'

'No love though.' I could tell she was thinking of Fen again.

'I love you,' I said, and she laughed.

'I love you too. And,' her voice grew serious, 'I forgive you.'

Her words unknotted a little of my twisted heart.

'I forgive you,' I replied, and heard her sigh.

'A *lăutari*.' The pride in her voice swelled my heart. 'Didn't I always tell you?'

I nodded, though I could not speak through a throat tight with tears. I realised now, though presumably the thought had always nestled deep inside me, that one of my greatest dreams was dead – had died with Mamă. For a lifetime, I had longed to sing while Mamă and Albu danced.

There was one dance they did, that held the most tenderness. Mamă would take Albu's paws in her own small hands, dark against his white fur, his enormous claws retracted. She would step close to him, and bring his arms around her, rest her cheek into his warm, combed chest, and they would sway. He would rest his mighty head upon her shoulder like a lover, and they would turn slow as the moon hiding its face.

'It's an apology,' Mamă told me once. 'From me to him.'

'You're saying sorry? Why?'

I remember Mamǎ's hand on my head, doubly warm from Albu's grasp.

'For taking him from his mother.'

'But you are an *ursar* – you needed a bear.'

'For me to fulfil my destiny I had to change his. There is always a cost.'

'But he loves you.'

'And I love him. But by taking him I have changed his destiny, his nature, who and what he is. I dance that dance to tell him I know the sacrifice I forced him to make. I atone in the only way I can.'

'How?'

'Kindness.'

Her words came to me now, as I sat shivering in the eternal gloom of the cell, the stench of myself so enveloping it was all I could do to keep breathing in the stale, stolid air.

'Where do you think Kem is now?' I asked, my voice tight. 'Do you think—'

'Kem's tough,' Kizzy said briskly, though our owl-eyed, watchful brother would cry at the sight of a butchered boar. 'And Albu will be caring for him. That bear was more human than beast, the way Mamǎ spoilt him.'

She laughed, so suddenly I jumped, the side of my face grazing the rough wooden door. 'He loved her, so much . . .'

She trailed off, and I felt rather than heard the restrained sob in her voice.

'Was it quick, Lil? Tell me it was.'

I thought of the swallowing heat, the smoke carried away on the wind and the flames stoked high as trees. How Mamă would have fought to the last, knowing we were out there.

'It was quick, Kisaiya.' The lie was soft and easy as a sigh.

I felt her tears on my own cheeks, and took my hand in my other, imagined they were her fingers linked through mine, drawing warmth and strength.

'We should sleep a little.'

I examined the smelly floor. 'I don't want to lie down.'

'Imagine it's a moss mattress,' said Kizzy. 'Use that imagination of yours. We'll need our strength.'

It felt like the old Kizzy was back: reassuring, taking charge. It felt good. And so I did as she said, and lay on the stinking straw, my head propped on my arm, and sank into a fitful sleep full of roaring bears and stone forests that arched like cages over my head.

CHAPTER TWELVE

Something was moving about outside the door. I eyed the gap beneath it. I knew rats were good at slipping through impossible spaces, making their bodies collapse down like their bones disconnected. But no flattened, furry body emerged through the narrow space. Instead, light blossomed through the slot, and then was blotted out as two eyes blinked through. Grey eyes, the colour of smoke, or storm clouds.

'Mira!' I stumbled to my feet, body stiff after a night on the hard floor. She stood a little back from the door, so I could see her through the slot. In her hands she held a plate, full of steaming porridge, and there was another at her feet. My stomach ached at the sight.

'Did Cook send you?'

She shook her head.

'Malovski?'

Another shake. How must it feel to have your voice snatched away so brutally, like a spirit in one of Mamă's stories? They were always vengeful and I wondered if Mira felt the same anger as the *Iele* who sometimes guided *strigoi* to their tormentors' doors.

I frowned. 'Who, then?'

She passed the plate through with a spoon and pointed at her chest.

'How did you know we were here?'

She crossed carefully to Kizzy's cell, and pushed the other plate through. I saw my sister's sore hands reach for it and take it into the shadows with a murmured word of thanks. I began shovelling the porridge into my mouth, moaning with the relief of having something warm inside me.

Mira returned to my door and knelt up so I could see her face and upper body. She tapped her ear. I realised she was humming a sort of tune, and understood.

'You heard me sing?'

She nodded, and a wide smile spread across her face. She clasped her hands over her heart. I remembered the grate beside which she slept, the swallowing dark of the gap in the wall that vented into the kitchen. She might have heard everything. We hadn't bothered to keep our voices down.

'Did you . . .' I trailed off. Had she heard me ask about the pact, the offering? Had I roused memories of her friend who had been taken?

'She's good, isn't she?' said Kizzy's voice through the narrow slot in her door.

Mira nodded hard, and looked at me even harder, her gaze unflinching and bold, her stormy eyes fierce. I could almost hear her say, *Yes*.

I ducked into the safety of the shadows, glad it was not obvious when I blushed. 'Thank you.'

Mira shook her head and reached her fingers through the slot. I brought my face close and let her brush my cheek.

All three of us sat silently, Mira kneeling before my door. Even if conversation had not been impossible, I think I would have chosen not to speak. It was almost restful, the flickering glow of her lamp reaching into the cell and the porridge salty and good in my stomach. I wondered what she ate, if she could eat at all. Thinking back, I had never seen her take more than water. She was too thin, even set against me. Perhaps Cook made her broth and let her drink glasses of milk from the dairy.

Then she gestured that she should leave. I handed her back the tray, and she collected Kizzy's too, then was gone up the stone steps, her footsteps light as falling leaves.

'Kind of her,' said Kizzy. 'Did you sleep?'

'A little.' I drew my legs up to my chest, cold biting at them like an animal.

'You should ask your Mira for a blanket.'

'She's not *my* Mira.' My voice was sharper than I'd intended.

'What is it with you two?' said Kizzy. Her voice wasn't unkind or accusing. She sounded puzzled, which I knew she would not be enjoying. She was used to knowing everything I thought or felt.

'I feel I know her,' I said. 'There's something about her . . .'

'You just feel sorry for her.'

'I don't,' I snapped. 'I think she's brave.'

'For a Settled, maybe.'

'Are you determined to hate her?'

'I don't hate her. I just don't understand why you like her so much.'

'I don't—'

'It's obvious,' said Kizzy, firmly. 'You do.'

'All right,' I said. 'I do. But not because she's pitiable.'

Kizzy did not reply.

I searched for something to move her on from the subject. 'How long do you think we'll be here?'

'Longer the better,' said Kizzy. 'Maybe Malovski will go off the idea of us being serving girls.'

I could make out the dark curve of my sister's face, her plump chin, full lips. I knew that whatever Kizzy did, short of killing someone – which I did not put past her – Malovski would not let her beauty go unnoticed by the boyar.

My teeth clattered with the fear of what awaited us, but I let Kizzy chatter hopefully into the ringing echoes of the cells, and thought instead of Mira, and how she seemed able to speak to me even without words, how I had not felt such recognition in a person apart from Kizzy, who shared the same body, had the same blood rushing through her veins.

The oats sat warm and solid in my stomach, and my cheek tingled where Mira had brushed it. I had sung to her, without even knowing it, and I didn't mind. It didn't make me cringe to think of it. Perhaps if we were ever freed, I would sing to her again.

. . .

The next day, our doors were unlocked and our buckets taken away by an unsmiling Szilvie, watched by a scowling soldier. I was glad Malovski had not sent Captain Vereski, but no doubt he had told his men about our encounter. The hatred on the man's face was clear, though it made a relieving change from the queasy look of desire that the captain had when he looked at my sister. It was worst of all when hatred and desire went together.

Szilvie was also allowed to remove my stitches, and tend to my sister's hands. I didn't hear them speaking, but shortly after Szilvie entered Kizzy's cell with bandages and willow bark, the guard banged on the metal slot, making it ring, and said, 'Not a word, Malovski said.'

117

Malovski had, at least, sent Szilvie with bowls of soup. They were evidently boiled up from peelings, thin and grey as dishwater, and served with a crust of black bread. It was just about edible, though the stale smell of rotten vegetables stayed in my nostrils as they disappeared up the steps.

'What did Szilvie say?' I hissed through the door. Kizzy's lips appeared instantly.

'Malovski's in a towering mood. The guest is coming early.'

My stomach churned on the disgusting soup. 'Are your hands any better?'

'Szilvie brought more honey, and the paste that Malovski gave me is having an effect I think.'

'I wish she'd bring a blanket.'

'Calazan is meant to be the Voievod's man,' she said, after a long pause. 'I thought the Dragon was a story.'

'A nightmare,' I shuddered. 'Do you really think he can be as bad as Cook said?'

'I'd wager the boyar here is hardly any better than the Dragon.'

'The blood though,' I said. 'Remember Charani said he kills people and drinks their blood.'

'Waste not, want not.'

'Kizzy!'

'I'm sorry. It just sounds . . . impossible. Surely no one believes he is what they whisper he is. Surely no one can be so cruel. But then . . .'

'Here we are,' I finished her thought for her. Again, the bizarre horror of the past few days returned to me like a physical weight, pinning me in place.

'I used to think to make people feel afraid was a curse, an awful thing,' said Kizzy. 'But I'd love for Malovski and that bastard Vereski to fear me like they all seem to fear the Dragon. I want them to look at me and weep.'

I could think of nothing to say to that.

Chapter Thirteen

It was nearly a week before we were let out.

Szilvie did not come again, and were it not for Mira who brought us scraps, and rags when our bloods came, we might have starved, or frozen, or gone mad in those dark cells. Instead I felt a great, swallowing anger. How could Malovski ever atone for all the cruelties she had committed? She would have to feed and clothe every beggar in the land, the world. And she was only a puppet for a larger evil. I was not ignorant of the system she worked within, that at the head of it were men.

Even as the thought crossed my mind, the woman's voice sliced through the door's slat, as though I had conjured her.

'Learned your lesson, slave?'

I saw her crimson mouth in its paper-white setting only a moment, before she took my silence as an agreement. The next second, the door was wrenched open. The air inside the cell was stirred for the first time, and though it was far from fresh it was still a relief.

A guard placed heavy chains at my wrists, linking them together, his nose wrinkling as he stepped into the space. He retreated quickly, and repeated the process with Kizzy, though I noticed his hand was hovering at his sword as he entered her cell. Her reputation must precede her.

As he nudged her out before him, I gasped: she was so altered in such a short time. She had lost weight, her plump cheeks shadowy, the angles of her face more harshly cut. Her hair was a matted tangle, and I supposed mine was no better. I had long since given up running my hands through it. She was still beautiful, of course, but her eyes were dull as the fish we spent days gutting.

I tried to catch her eye, but she kept her gaze trained at a point on the floor by Malovski's feet. The woman nodded approvingly.

'Much better,' she said, looking Kizzy up and down. 'Life will be easier now, slave, if you only keep this demeanour. Especially as our guest arrives tonight.'

I looked up to her face. Kizzy did too – she too must have noticed the quiver in Malovski's voice. Could it be that the fearsome Mistress was as afraid of the Dragon's influence as any of us?

'Lost weight too,' said Malovski, raising a handkerchief white as her skin to her nose and squinting at Kizzy. 'You'll be suitable serving girls once we get you cleaned up.'

She turned, and at last my sister caught my eye. The panic was reflected in my own face. Serving girls. So our duties had not changed. My thighs started to shake, and I gritted my teeth.

Steady. I spoke to myself in Kizzy's voice. *Calm.*

'Come.'

The guard nudged Kizzy in the back, and I walked ahead of her, behind Malovski's swishing skirts. She had lost weight, too. Her waist was narrower than ever, as though she was a toy made of two parts that could come open at the middle. I imagined wrenching her apart, the joins of her spine splitting like a wasp pierced at its hinge by a nail.

She turned to check we were following and I almost stumbled at the sight of her face. There were cracks in her white make-up, dry patches where the powder clung at the corners of her mouth. Her lipstick was not as artfully applied as usual and it bled into the lines. She had drawn dark kohl around her eyes, which served only to make them cavernous. She looked like how I imagined a *strigoi* to look, an undead soul doomed to wander the earth, feeding off living things.

She narrowed her eyes, as if she could read my mind. 'Do not look at me so impertinently, slave.'

The slap was expected, but stung no less for it.

. . .

We ascended the stairs, the guard following behind, and it felt as though we were emerging from a grave, birthed into hellish light and noise. There were people everywhere, calling orders and responding, carrying cleaning rags, swatches of cloth, thick wax candles the size of my torso, jars of milk and flagons of dark, syrupy-smelling wine. After days in the dark, it was overwhelming; my weakened legs gave way and I stumbled against the wall.

'Watch it,' said Malovski viciously, pulling me upright and wiping her glove immediately on her skirts. 'Careful of your filthy hands.'

I noticed the once-bare stone walls of the corridor were hung with blazing colours: pennants of black and red thread.

Malovski led us towards another, narrower passage we had never taken before. This was just as full of people, all women and girls around our age, their clothes more fitted and cleaner than those we had worn in the kitchens, their make-up done in the same style as Malovski's. They hoisted tight-lipped smiles onto their faces as we passed, letting them drop when Malovski was through. Then they covered their noses with their hands and sneered at Kizzy and me, drawing their skirts away from us so we would not even brush against them.

These were presumably the serving girls, the ones chosen to come into direct contact with the boyar, to wait on him in any way he wished. I tried to feel pity, but their obvious dislike of us made it hard.

'Edina, here.' Malovski stayed a girl rushing past with a click of her fingers. It was the girl who had smiled at Mira on our first day in the kitchen, and as she eyed us I glared right back. She had a haughty gaze like a cat. 'Go to the kitchens and fetch Szilvie.'

'Szilvie, Mistress?'

'Ask Cook to point her out. Bring her to the bathing room. You too – I need a serving girl to help.'

'These are the new girls, Mistress?'

'Obviously,' said Malovski dryly.

Edina looked Kizzy and me over, her lack of enthusiasm obvious, but she did not delay and continued up the narrow passage to the main, tapestry-strewn corridor.

'Hurry up,' said Malovski. Kizzy's hand settled softly on the base of my back as we walked, and I leaned briefly into it until the guard shunted us apart.

The way was lit with lamps, but they were burning a more clarified fat, perhaps even an oil, scented with some herb. I thought of Mira, her arms full of sage, her face pale through the slat in the door.

We had never used lamps in the forests, only campfires that sent woody smoke climbing into the night air. Nothing wasted, nothing much needed beyond the light the day chose to give us. I missed the sun and the stars, and knowing when to rise and sleep by their token. I would be glad never to see another lamp or candle so long as I lived.

The corridor opened out slightly like the mouth of a river, and, like a river, the pace slowed here, the movement less urgent. This was lined with doors, and through some open ones I saw bedrooms, better furnished than the kitchen workers', with low wooden bedframes set to the floor, and mattresses twice as thick. My back ached with longing after so many nights on the bare, hard stone floor.

Malovski took another sharp turn to another door, which she unlocked using a thin metal key taken from a ring at her belt. I felt a sort of sucking at the bottom of my skirts, as though there was a high wind, or a furnace inside, swallowing air.

Malovski held out her hand and the guard placed the handcuffs' keys into it. 'Wait here,' she said to him, once we were released. 'Listen at the door. Any trouble,' she shot a dark glance at Kizzy and me. 'I'll be sure to let you know.'

Chapter Fourteen

Malovski turned the brass ring in the door and stood aside so we could enter ahead of her. Kizzy gasped, and clutched at me.

I had been right about the high wind coming from beneath the door. The door opened onto – nothing. We stood on a slim platform cut into the side of a precipice. We were used to heights, but the unexpectedness made my head spin.

Far, far on the horizon, was a spiked smudge of trees. The forest from where we had been wrenched. It was so close, within sight, and yet a lifetime away. The wind snatched at our hair and dresses, and I considered briefly that Malovski may be about to pitch us down the steep side of rock below.

Instead, she parted us roughly. The platform we stood on was hewn from the same black rock of the castle and, looking up, I noticed that though the turrets towered above us, this side of the castle was not nearly so finely made as the one we had seen as we approached. It was brutish and rough, windows cut leeringly at intervals up its endless height. At the top, the flag whipped in the wind, its pole stabbing the sky.

Through my sleep- and food-starved mind, I watched Kizzy realise at the same moment I did that once again we were alone with our tormentor. This time though, it could be an accident, couldn't it, if she fell? Kizzy's hands went up at the exact moment the door opened again, and Malovski turned away as Kizzy froze.

'Ah, Szilvie. And Edi—'

Malovski narrowed her eyes as Szilvie stepped through the door. But following her was not the thin, scornful Edina. Instead, Mira raised her grey eyes to meet mine. Her arms were heaped with dresses.

'Where is Edina?' hissed Malovski.

'She would not come, Mistress,' said Szilvie. 'Sent Mira instead. Said she was trained as a serving girl and would do just as well.'

'Did she now?' Malovski's voice was as narrow and tight as her gaze. 'I don't know where you girls get the gall. Let's get this over with. Get undressed.'

I froze. Kizzy's eyes narrowed.

'You're welcome to let the guard do it. But he's like to throw you in,' said Malovski dryly, pointing below us.

I peered over the edge. Tucked beneath the overhang of our platform was a pool of water. Cupped as it was in the black rock it looked like it could be bottomless, but the bubbles rising to the surface told me it was filled by a natural spring. My skin itched at the sight of fresh water.

'Go on. Szilvie, I want you to check that one's hands.' She pointed at Kizzy. 'You know Boyar Valcar is fussy. I will hold you responsible if anything is amiss. Mira, dress them both. I presume you remember the standards I held you to. When you're done, bring them to the holding room and report back to me before you go to the kitchens.'

My whole body seemed to unknot as I realised she was leaving, that we would not have to show our bodies to her and be touched by her hateful hands. She raked her gaze over Kizzy and me. In the stark grey light her appearance was more unpleasant than ever. She looked ill.

'The guard will remain outside, and you will wear your cuffs again after you have washed. There are pumice stones and soap down there – I want you soft as peeled fruit.'

She reached out suddenly and stroked her gloved hand down Kizzy's cheek. I flinched, though my sister held herself steady.

'He will be pleased,' purred Malovski. 'And such good timing, too, with our guest coming.'

She left the platform. I caught a glimpse of the passage beyond, the guard turning to cast a curious look at the four of us assembled on the platform, before the door closed again.

Kizzy let out a long, shaky breath. I wrapped my arms around my sister for the first time in days, and we held each other a long moment. We had never gone so long without touching each other, and I felt the bones of her ribs clearly through her back. She had lost too much weight, too fast.

Kizzy let go first, massaging her wrists. I noticed for the first time they were nearly healed, the scars left by the blisters demarcated by shiny patches of light brown skin, but smooth and not nearly so bad as I had feared they would be.

'Your hands!' I exclaimed, taking them in my own.

'Szilvie worked wonders,' said Kizzy, casting a warm look at the Settled girl, whose pale cheeks coloured.

There was a bang on the door. 'Hurry up out there!'

I hesitated a moment. 'How do we get down?'

'Here.'

I turned in astonishment. The word had come not from Szilvie, but Mira.

'You can speak,' I said.

Mira's cheeks reddened too. Szilvie beamed. 'She's working on it, aren't you Mira? She has to stretch her voice, or else she won't have any.'

'You really are a wonder,' said Kizzy warmly, causing the Settled girl's blush to deepen. 'Those steps there, Mira?'

Mira nodded. 'Yes.'

Kizzy was already descending the stone steps cut into the platform's edge, more like a ladder due to their steepness. I turned from Mira and followed after.

The thrum that soon set up in my arms, the burn, was

welcome. Days of doing nothing had made me long for movement and here it was, sending blood cantering around my body, setting my heart racing with fear – but a fear I understood, fear of the steep drop, the slick steps. For these few metres, I could forget what awaited us after the pool. For these few moments, my sister and I were at home again.

Kizzy was already stripping off her filthy clothing as I reached her. Her curved stomach was smaller, her ribs showing through her back. She was transformed into a shape more akin to mine, and it did not suit her. Her scars shone on her arms, stopping at the elbow like gloves.

'Don't worry,' she grinned, seeing my expression. 'We'll be better fed soon.'

'You're still beautiful,' I said.

'Don't,' said Kizzy, sitting beside the pool. 'I would be glad to never be called that again.' She dipped her feet into the water up to her ankles. Instantly, her teeth began to chatter. 'It would've been too much to hope it was a hot spring, wouldn't it?'

I quickly pulled off my dress, the wind licking over my pimpling skin as Kizzy plunged into the pool.

She came up gasping, her curly hair heavy with water.

'Oh!' She cried. '*Căcat!*'

Szilvie and Mira snorted with laughter above as I hastened over the rocky ground and lowered myself in too. *Shit* was right. It was the kind of cold that burned, licked like flames along the lengths of my calves and ate through my meagre barrier of skin, through to my bones.

But it was also exhilarating to feel my skin sing like this, with this awful glorious icy-hot pain. Even as the numbness raced from my toes to my ankles, up my legs to grip at my waist and clasp itself about my chest, I couldn't help laughing with the relief of it. It felt like breaking the first winter ice and plunging in.

Kizzy's hand found mine through the dark water, which swirled with tiny particles and frothed with the current sent up from below us. My toes crept over pebbles and smooth passages of rock, and I noticed the wall of the pool was built up from stone too. High above, I heard a man's voice, and a moment later Szilvie called down to us. 'Not too much longer.'

The air was even harsher now my hair was wet, and I wrapped my hands across my chest as the wind bit at my shoulders.

'We need our clothes,' called Kizzy. 'We didn't bring them down.'

There was a short pause, then Szilvie said. 'Mira's coming, she's a better climber than me.'

We waited in the pool, our bodies dark beneath the dark water. I could see Kizzy's fingers trembling just below the surface like tiny fish. Mira came quickly into view, her footing sure on the steps, the clean dresses and clothes flapping where she had wrapped them about her neck. She jumped lightly down the last few rungs and held out a length of grey cloth.

'Dry,' she said simply. Kizzy pulled herself out and hurried for the cloth, wrapping it quickly about herself and dancing about on her bare feet in the sharp wind. Mira looked away, and I kept my hands crossed over my breasts, suddenly aware of my body in a way I never had been before, even under Malovski's scrutiny.

When it was my turn for the cloth, now damp from Kizzy as she struggled into her new outfit, I found I wanted Mira to look at me. She did not, keeping her eyes trained out at the fields.

I dried myself and took the dress Mira held out to me. It was navy like Edina's, and more fitted than our kitchen outfits. I placed the death cap into yet another new pocket.

There were buttons to draw it closer in at the waist, and I fastened Kizzy's with trembling fingers. Before Kizzy could return the favour, Mira's hands were at my waist, and she deftly hooked the buttons and tied the crimson sash snugly. Too soon, she was finished, and her hands moved from me.

'Hurry up,' called the guard. 'It's been too long.'

'We're coming,' said Kizzy, her feet, still bare, on the bottom rung. Mira held my gaze only a moment. I saw the glint of her teeth on her lip, her pulse fluttering like a caught butterfly beneath her ear. Then she turned and followed my sister back up to the door cut into the rock.

CHAPTER FIFTEEN

The holding room was about the same size as the kitchen and lit by a vast overhead chandelier, brass and gleaming, dripping wax caught in little dishes cupped around the bases of the candles. It was furnished better than Malovski's house, with settees of upholstered wood and a fur rug on the floor still with its bear's head. I hoped for its sake that it was the suffering bear Malovski had talked of on our first encounter, the one baited by dogs. I hoped that its pain was now at an end.

We stood in the centre of its back, and Kizzy bent and brushed her fingers through its fur. Szilvie wrinkled her nose.

'People have trodden on that pelt.'

Malovski entered a few minutes later. She looked us up and down and nodded approvingly. 'Much better. Hands?'

Kizzy held them out.

'Good. Mira, you remember how to fix their hair?'

Mira nodded.

Malovski crossed the room and pulled down cloths the same colour as the wall, so I had not noticed them. Behind were long lengths of metal, polished to a shine. Mirrors, larger than I'd ever seen before. I caught sight of my shape in its tight dress. Malovski's reflection was almost wraithlike: she glowed.

'Back to the kitchens,' she snapped at Mira. 'When you've fixed their hair.'

Malovski shoved Szilvie out of the room ahead of her.

Kizzy and I were once again alone with Mira, and I felt I could breathe again, like the laces at my waist had been loosened slightly. The dim mirrors gleamed with a golden light, and I searched the walls for windows, but there were none. We must be on the unhewn side of the castle.

Mira pulled a cloth-covered stool from a corner, set it so it stood before the mirrors, and patted it.

Kizzy sat poised as a queen at her vanity, and Mira stood behind her, raked her hands through my sister's hair, and began to twist its still slick sections into a low bun, as we had seen Edina and the other girls sporting. Kizzy didn't wince once, and Mira's face was tight with concentration. It took only a few minutes, and then it was my turn.

The feel of Mira's hands through my hair, her calloused fingers running against my scalp, warm and careful, was close to bliss. I watched her in the burnished surface of the mirror, her white teeth coming again to her lip, eyebrows creased with effort. She, too, was so pale as to seem a spirit in the mirror, but her features held none of Malovski's malice. Mira had an intensity to her, an intelligence that set her eyes alight with their silver brilliance, and her lips, which I had only seen before now pressed thin in pain, were full and pink.

Her eyes flicked to mine in the mirror, and I felt her hands hesitate on my hair.

'Do you need me to help?' said Kizzy. Her voice was light enough but when I pulled my gaze from Mira to my sister's face, I saw she was frowning. Mira cleared her throat.

'No.'

Kizzy nodded slowly, still looking at me quizzically, a faint expression of warning on her face. Mira did not catch my eye again.

All too soon, she had pushed the pin into place. I stood up and felt her handiwork. It was neat and taut, a precise mirror of Kizzy's. With her newly gaunt cheeks we looked more like twins than we had in years.

'Thank you,' said Kizzy, and I could tell she wanted Mira to leave so we could talk. But Mira hesitated. She opened her mouth, and I caught a glimpse of the dark red inside, still swollen and sore.

'Careful,' she whispered.

'What?' said Kizzy, a little unkindly.

'Careful,' I said.

Mira nodded. She looked wretched. Without thinking, I reached out and took her hand. It shook slightly.

'We will be,' I said. 'I promise.'

Mira nodded again and left. Kizzy waited until the door closed fully, then rounded on me.

'What are you doing?'

'Me?'

'You,' said Kizzy, prodding me hard in the chest. 'Making doe eyes at that Settled girl.'

'I'm doing no such thing.'

'You are, and you need to stop. It would be bad enough if it was a boy.'

'I'm not . . . I don't . . .' I stopped. There was nothing I could say. I could not deny that I had been watching Mira, hoping she was watching me too.

'Stop,' said Kizzy again, prodding me once more.

'Ouch,' I said pointedly, rubbing the spot. 'She's been kind. I want to be kind back.'

'These people aren't our friends.'

'Mira's not one of them.'

'She's a Settled.'

'They crushed her throat for Saints' sake!'

'Doesn't mean she can't betray us,' said Kizzy darkly. 'We can't trust any of them, Lillai. Just us, all right?'

She held out her hand, fingers splayed, and unable to resist the gesture that had joined us since childhood, I pressed my fingertips to hers.

'All right. Just us.'

The door opened, and despite our seconds-old promise my heart still sank when I saw it was not Mira but Edina who passed through it. She stalked up to us and circled us both, one eyebrow arched.

'So you are the gypsy twins?' She sniffed. 'Not sure what the fuss is about.'

I knew Kizzy had a sharp retort on her tongue, so I nudged her gently with my arm. As Edina walked past me, I noticed one cheek was red under its flour-white powder. So Malovski had not allowed her to get away with her disobedience after all.

'We've a busy day ahead, so don't give me any trouble,' Edina continued. 'Lunch, then the arrival of Boyar Calazan, then dinner. The whole castle will be out on parade this afternoon, to welcome our guest. Mistress wants you to serve him at dinner, so this lunch service is a practice. You'll shadow me, but after that you'll be first out until Boyar Valcar's bored of you. He likes new things, but he quickly tires.' She let out a short laugh, painted mouth tight around the sound. 'Follow me.'

Chapter Sixteen

We kept close behind Edina as instructed, and I tried to acquaint myself with the warren of the space. I felt like a rabbit caught in unfamiliar tunnels: the fox Malovski out of sight, but her reeking threat ever-present.

I recognised nothing until we entered the kitchens. The room rang with mutters, and I searched for Cook, for a friendly face. But she was bent over her work, and did not look up at us. I instead scanned the room for Szilvie, Dot and Mira, and found them all at their usual stations. Mira gave me an encouraging nod as I took up position between Edina and Kizzy. The platter before me was a pile of ribs from one of the slaughtered pigs, wafting their scent over my newly clean skin.

I gripped it in both hands, the weight straining my arms, weak from lack of movement. I felt like a woman five times my age as I hoisted it to waist height, turned, and followed Edina back out of the room.

I could hear Kizzy's nervous, shortened breaths behind me as we approached the massive doors. They were thrown open by two guards, and I tried to close my ears to their lewd comments as we walked through, my wrists aching now, and found ourselves in a vast antechamber.

Hung with the most ornate tapestries I had seen yet, and the floor strewn with sweet-smelling rushes, it was fine as any place I'd ever seen. Another set of wooden doors opened to our right, and through them came a rush of noise.

Men's voices, as they always were when there are so many together: more like beasts bellowing at one another than any attempt at real conversation. They sounded drunk already, though it was only lunchtime, and when I stepped over the threshold it was the smell of stale beer that hit me first. Next, it was the size of the place.

If the antechamber could have held our camp, this room could have sheltered a sizeable plot of forest, tallest trees and all. Five narrow slits of windows were set high in the walls, shafts of hazy sunlight piercing the interior like blades. The whole room seemed ablaze with candlelight.

The tapestries here were threaded with gold and mostly depicted hunting scenes, great spurts of cotton and silk blood turning the walls the same crimson as the soldiers' sashes. Bile rose in my mouth at the sight of the red, and the scent of the burnt meat in my hands.

My teeth began to chatter as I pushed away the memory of our burning camp, the slain bears, the bleeding people who had raised me, our wagon's curtains turned to ash . . .

Breathe. I had stopped inhaling, was growing light-headed. I gulped in a breath of beer-stinking air, steadying myself. Our long line split into three, one for each of the tables set in the room. I did my best to absorb as much of the scene as possible.

One table was set across the room before an open-mouthed fire. Men were seated facing out towards the vast room, though none had noticed our entrance, being too preoccupied with loud laughter and sloshing goblets. We were the only women in the place. Two more tables were set length-wise along the walls, with rows of men seated at long benches along each side. The men closest to the doors turned to us as we entered, and one placed his fingers between his lips and whistled once loudly, a whooping sound.

At the table to the left, I caught sight of Captain Vereski, his wound now mostly healed, showing only brown rakes. His eyelid was still puffy and sore-looking, the just-revealed eye red. His healing was slow, and I was glad of it. He bared his teeth as we passed, and I quickened my pace.

Many men wore the garb of the soldiers, but more were clothed like noblemen, with gold rings thick about their fingers, their beards neatly trimmed. Edina motioned with her elbow, her arms being full of a tureen of soup, that Kizzy and I should follow her to the top table.

This meant enduring the whistles and leering stares of the full length of the room. Some of the men seemed to have favourites, and called out to the girls by name, but none responded. I followed Edina's lead, keeping my eyes trained ahead, borrowing her imperious tilt of the chin.

The top table was raised on a platform. The fire's heat was intense even at a distance and sweat threaded down my neck beneath Mira's careful bun. It was like approaching the burning gates of Settled people's Hell.

I stepped up to the platform, the heat almost unbearable. It was worse than the kitchens somehow, though maybe it was only that my dress was made of a thicker material, more tightly fitted against my skin.

The line of serving girls fanned out along the table's length, and my arms, desperate for respite, almost dropped the platter onto the scrubbed wooden surface.

'Not yet,' hissed Edina. I heaved it back up again, looking up through lowered lashes to see if my stumble had been noticed.

It had.

'Hello there,' said the man sitting before me. He was thin and dressed in black and red, like the soldiers, but his attire was finely constructed, with neat bone buttons glinting like chips of ice along the front. His hair was slicked back, and I could see the gleam of scalp through it as he leaned forwards. 'New girl?'

I looked at Edina, but she was staring impassively ahead, the tureen still poised above the table as she waited for the other girls to get in position. I nodded, not knowing what else to do, afraid to speak. Kizzy's arms were trembling too, beside me. The man made a sort of purring sound as he noticed her, his watery eyes flicking between us.

'Ho, ho! Boyar Valcar, have you seen what Malovski has brought you?'

He spoke these words to a man a couple of places along. I followed his address, and caught sight of a broad back, swathed in fur. The boyar began to turn, and at this moment Edina nodded for us to place down our wares. I tried to control the platter's descent, but still it landed with a square *crack* on the table, sending a rack tumbling towards the watery-eyed man.

'Sorry,' I gasped, and reached out, thinking to place it back, but Edina slapped my hand. The man guffawed and reached out too. He took up the rack, and began to eat, breathing through his nose with little snuffling sounds.

'Gypsies?' said Boyar Valcar, and I looked at his face for the first time: the man who had sent his soldiers to search for slaves in the forest, who took girls to his bed against their will, who skewered heads on spikes and chose offerings for the Dragon.

He looked, like the worst monsters often do, like a normal man.

His head was covered in a silken red, twisted ornately in a fashion I had never seen before. He was layered in several furs despite the fire, and now I was so close, and unable to tear my eyes from him, I realised that though he gave the appearance of being a large man, he was not. He was thin as me, or Malovski, with a similar feverish sheen to her, though he wore no make-up that I could see.

'Twins,' said his companion, through a mouthful of meat.

Great shadows scooped beneath Boyar Valcar's eyes, making the pale blue orbs seem afloat in his narrow face. There was a swelling on his long neck when he turned his head to observe Kizzy and me, and seeing it, I realised why the fire was up so high, the furs so thickly layered upon him, and he was so thin despite the feast laid twice daily before him.

He's sick. I had seen lumps like that before, on corpses heaped by the road when we passed the Settled villages.

Boyar Valcar pulled his collar up, as though he could hear my thoughts. He, too, took up a rack of ribs, and separated one off so it sat like a finger in his palm.

'Pretty,' he said, and I could tell he was talking about us, not to us. My skin crawled. We had walked directly into the viper's nest, bearing gifts.

'Well, Sire?' Malovski swept up behind us, wrenching my chin forward as I turned to watch her come. My jaw clicked. 'Do they please you?'

The boyar swallowed, wincing. His bejewelled hands made an involuntary movement to his neck, the spread fingers encasing the concealed lump. A flash of anger shone across his pooled eyes as he noticed that he had given away his weakness, and he dropped his hand, reached for another rib.

'Of course. Your taste is always impeccable.'

He pulled the meat off the bone delicately, carefully, using just his fore teeth, but still a stab of pain grasped him when he swallowed. It would be pitiable, if I did not want to ram the whole rack down his throat until he choked. 'Any skills?'

I expected Malovski to lament our uselessness, but instead she said something that made the blood drain to my feet. 'This one's a bear dancer. That one's a singer, if you can believe anything good can come from a Gyptian tongue.'

Kizzy swayed beside me, and I knew the same wretched question was reverberating around her mind too. *How did she know?*

'Lie to me again,' hissed Malovski through her fixed smile, so only I could hear. 'I'll have your tongue.'

I understood, suddenly, Cook's reluctance to look at us in the kitchens. Remembered the press of Kizzy's fingertips to mine. *We can't trust any of them, Lillai.*

My heart hammered in my chest. Cook must have told her. I clasped my hands behind me, to keep them from shaking.

'A bear dancer is not much good without bears,' said the man opposite me, grinning at Kizzy. 'Though I'll let you give me a turn later.'

A ripple of bawdy laughter spread through the table and the floor felt suddenly unsteady beneath my feet. The boyar had not joined in – he was watching me with watery eyes.

'A singer? Go on then.'

It was as if he had clenched his hand about my throat. Malovski rustled up close behind me and gripped my arm. 'Go on, girl.'

I opened my mouth, but my voice would not come. I could not even speak. A mewing sound emerged, and Boyar Valcar snorted.

'Sure you're not mistaken, Malovski?'

'I am never mistaken.' Her hand tightened on my arm. I felt branded by it, the skin burning beneath her touch. 'She will sing for you later this evening, Boyar Valcar. And your guest, when he arrives.'

'And her,' said the boyar, nodding at Kizzy. 'We want her to dance.'

'There are no bears left, Sire.'

'Alone, then,' said the boyar, wincing again as he swallowed.

Malovski bowed her head. 'It will be arranged.'

'After the parade,' he said. 'See to it.'

She left, and we were ordered to remain. Edina was taken by the boyar to his room, and we stayed in the dining hall with its red walls and black-clothed men and still, silent women like a scene from a damned daydream, until the serving girls finally took up the emptied platters, the piles of bones, and left.

CHAPTER SEVENTEEN

We arrived into our new quarters to find the girls abuzz with
excitement. From what I could gather, though no one talked
to us directly, usually the afternoons were spent readying the
hall for dinner. But today, the whole castle was to line the
road into the town, to welcome our guest.

We were ordered to brush out our hair and leave it down
and tighten our sashes another inch. Kizzy looked more
herself with her curls loose and shining, and it set the girls
muttering – I think they would have liked to pinch her, even
as they pinched colour into their own cheeks.

We lined along the road he'd take from the north. Slaves
and serfs, stable boys and labourers were usually kept apart,
and there was a lot of sizing up between the men and women,
who rarely saw each other in the daytime. I caught a welcome
sight of Girtie and Reeni, both thinner but seemingly
unharmed. I wanted to run to them, but all I managed was

a quick wave before we were ushered further along the line. Of Fen and the boys I saw nothing.

Whistles and lewd suggestions followed Kizzy all the way along the line, rippling out from the point where we slotted into place beside the other serving girls, who moved their skirts away as though we might cock our legs on them.

I held my hand out to her in our gesture. Her fingers were warm and it seemed to spread through my whole body, stopping my teeth from chattering.

As soon as dust was spotted on the flattened horizon, Boyar Valcar came riding out to meet his approaching guest on a dappled mare, hung with his red and black pennant. I recognised the mare at once: Dika's horse, Orsha. It made me hot with rage to see him on her, and I ducked my head as he passed.

Captain Vereski followed close behind him, riding slower. 'When Boyar Valcar and his guest return, cheer! Everyone, voices up, or no supper!'

A few minutes after, cries started to rise from the distant end of the line. A phalanx of horses came into sight, trotting at a leisurely pace. At their head were the two boyars: Boyar Valcar made massive by his furs, and Boyar Calazan riding beside him. I could see even at a distance he was a larger man than Boyar Valcar, and tall, his horse a full three hands higher than Orsha.

As Boyar Calazan got closer, it was a shock to realise he was handsome. His face was fine and his hair dark beneath his fur hat, his beard neatly shaped about his jaw. There was a crest at his breast: a dragon curled about a heart.

The serving girls blushed and giggled, cheering girlishly as he looked down at them, but it was Kizzy he stared at. And she, my beautiful, foolhardy sister, stared back. Boyar Calazan leaned into Boyar Valcar and murmured something.

I held my breath, feeling as though I were on a precipice. Was she about to be struck down for impudence? But then they were moving on towards the castle, and the servants were folding in after them, and beside me Kizzy looked calm, as though nothing had happened.

'Come on,' she said, tugging at her sash. 'I need to get out of this.'

. . .

I later realised the serving girls must have known or guessed what was coming, must have heard from one of the castle guards, because they were edgy all afternoon. Like a flock of birds, they moved through their tasks in formation, a practised murmuration of dancing, redoing their hair, making pessaries of herbs that would ensure they would keep no baby, tittering and shooting flighty glances our way. There was a deeper malice in their eyes that I felt knot beneath my collarbone. They were waiting for something to happen, and it felt as though it would happen to us.

The girls only fell silent as the dark began to settle. Dinner was nearing, and Malovski swept in.

'You two. Come.'

Her expression was almost solemn, her grip rigid as her back as she led us through the massive doors, along the corridor, and finally to the kitchen. The kitchen girls fell silent when we were shoved inside. Shoulders straightened, glances flicked between us, and Malovski's face.

I searched for Mira, found her in her usual corner. She frowned at me, grey eyes questioning. A shrug was all I felt I could risk. Cook didn't look at us, even when Malovski addressed her directly.

'Boyar Calazan has requested bite wine,' said Malovski, dropping our arms at last. I rubbed my hand over the sore skin. There was a collective shiver, and Mira's questioning eyes turned afraid. 'Two flagons.'

The set of Cook's jaw was tight and tense as she nodded to two kitchen workers and handed one of them a key. They left instantly, without looking at us, for the wine store that was a little further along the passage in the cool dark of a cellar.

Cook looked miserable, her face deeply lined, its rich brown overlaid by a grey tinge. I noticed a fresh bruise laid across her cheek like a dusting of ash. Despite my anger at

her betrayal, I felt sorry for her. She was afraid, and her fear
had made her weak.

I didn't know what bite wine was, but the reaction of
the room had made me afraid. Not as afraid as I was
of singing, certainly – I wasn't sure I could physically do it:
open my mouth to sing for them. It was like opening my
heart.

Two flagons of wine were set on the table, and the key
returned to Cook.

Malovski unlocked a small door set low in the kitchen
wall with a key from her belt, and the atmosphere in the
room changed completely, everyone watching. The narrow
door opened, and Kizzy made to follow Malovski inside, but
the woman shoved her roughly in the stomach.

'Stay.'

Obedient, we did. Kizzy kept her eyes fixed on the middle
distance, well aware of the whispers that rose like the buzzing
of flies from a carcass and were fixed upon us. My eyes found
Mira again, and she was chewing her lip. She tried to mouth
something at me, but I couldn't make it out.

Malovski emerged with two clay pots cradled in the
crooks of her elbows. I could hear something inside them,
rustling. Hissing.

The room shrank back.

'Wine,' she said to Kizzy and me, and Dot and Szilvie
helped us lift the flagons into our arms. I wrapped my arms

tightly around it, rested it on the sharp jut of my hipbones, feeling the liquid sloshing about inside like blood.

'Follow,' said Malovski, and it was only then, at the last possible moment, that Cook looked up. Her eye was wet with tears, her expression tortured.

'You should be honoured,' said Malovski. 'Bite wine is a speciality of these parts, not normally entrusted to the new girls. There's a performance to it but as it's your first time I'd just get it over with.'

Kizzy and I exchanged confused looks.

'There is time for me to demonstrate.'

She veered right, into a small antechamber opposite the stone steps that had taken us down, down into the locked dark of the dungeon. My skin crawled at the proximity. Through a high hatch I could hear the sounds of the dining hall. It was connected like the kitchen was to our old sleeping room.

Malovski set the hissing clay pots down and pulled out a thick pair of gloves from her pocket.

'A couple of weeks ago you would not have needed these.' She smiled unkindly at Kizzy's hands.

'Mistress?' Kizzy's voice was curious rather than afraid.

'Stand back.' She flipped one of the pots upside down. The hissing intensified.

'Mistress, is that—'

'Silence while I work. Watch carefully.'

Malovski pulled the cork from the wine bottle, and a look of intense concentration came over her fearsome face. It made her look older, deepened the powdered lines etched at her forehead. But my attention was wrenched from her a moment later, when she slid the lid from the pot, and lifted it.

Glistening coils unravelled, tongue tasting the stale air. Thick as a child's arm, and thrice as long. My fear of it was uncontrollable, primal, instinctive. I knew this kind of snake, had caught it slithering away as we'd tramped through the forests. A meadow viper, diamonds printed along its length. It would usually leave, as scared of us as we were of it. But here, it knew there was no way out. Except to attack.

It sprung forward, but Malovski's hands were about it faster than I could blink. I stumbled back, but Kizzy didn't even flinch. She seemed not to care if she was bitten.

The snake's tail whipped about, lashing onto Malovski's arm, but by the tensing of her jaw I knew her grip was tightening as she brought the cork up to the snake's mouth. She loosened her grasp a moment and the snake bit down, releasing its poison, enough, I knew, to kill a dog, or maim a man, turn the bitten limb black and rotten.

The snake tried to let loose the cork, but Malovski's other hand was upon its jaws, clamping them shut. It struggled, and I felt a useless stab of pity for the beast, caught threshing in the paws of something larger and more powerful than itself. I felt I knew a little of its pain, its bewilderment.

Malovski began to slide the snake's length into the glass neck of the wine bottle. At this, Kizzy finally broke her silence.

'What are you doing?'

'Showing you what you must do tonight.'

The snake was struggling more than ever, its black eyes dulling, a film coming across them like rolling fog. There was a crinkling sound, like smashing glass, as Malovski's grip on its jaws began to break them. Nausea rose, hot and bitter in my throat.

'You're hurting it.' Kizzy didn't bother to disguise the anger in her voice.

'So?'

The snake's tail was now fully submerged in the inky wine. I could see its paleness flicking at the smooth glass, like a nightmare rearing through the dark. My hands twitched.

Again, it was Kizzy who spoke, but again, I felt her words bitter on my own tongue.

'I will not do this.'

Malovski squeezed the snake's head harder, and rammed the cork into the narrow mouth of the bottle. The tail thrashed, once, twice, and stilled. Kizzy reached out as if to knock the flagon to the floor, but Malovski, still in her gloves, gripped her wrist and twisted up, so that it was Kizzy who was dashed to the ground.

I was pressed against the wall so tightly, I felt I might cleave to it if I wished hard enough. I couldn't take my eyes from the snake.

Kizzy knelt up, her chest heaving. The only sound in the room was Malovski pulling the gloves from her hands and letting them drop to the dusty floor.

'I'll call you in when it's time.' Malovski's voice was steady, almost bored.

Kizzy murmured something.

'What's that?' snapped Malovski.

'I can't,' she whispered.

Malovski sneered. 'You will.'

The snake's crushed head leaked liquid the same colour as the wine down the side of the dark bottle. I swallowed.

'I'll do it,' I said.

'Lil—'

The woman's dark eyes narrowed. 'You are to sing. You are not who was requested.'

'She can't do it, Mistress,' I said, willing my voice to be respectful as I searched for a believable reason, one beyond the fact my sister was too kind for such cruelty. 'Her hands are still sore—'

'They are no more an impediment than thick gloves.' Malovski shoved me roughly aside, seized Kizzy again by her

155

upper arm. I noticed she slid her hand above the line of her sleeve, perhaps to hide bruises from sight.

'I'll leave a guard outside the door. You can practise with that one,' she gestured at the other clay pot, 'and I will have another sent for the dinner performance. And you,' she jerked her head at me. 'Better find your voice, or I may well have your tongue.'

Chapter Eighteen

Malovski left. I heard a key scrape in the lock, and the sharp order of Malovski to a guard.

I wanted to take Kizzy's hand and run, run until my feet bled and we were in the cool shadows of the forest, where things were killed quickly and kindly, and the world had an order without slaves and masters. But instead I helped my shaking sister to her feet, and, traitorously, wiped her wet cheeks dry.

'I have to get out of here, Lil.' Kizzy's voice was a whisper, so small it could have been inside my own head. 'I can't do this, can't live like this.'

'You don't have to do it like her,' I said, searching for something comforting to say. 'You could wring its neck first, or drown it outright.'

Kizzy's eyes were sunk deep with sadness. 'Better it takes me now.'

Her gaze drifted past the dead snake to the hissing pot, where its poor, doomed companion nestled inside.

I shook her, harder than I'd meant to. 'Don't think on it. You can't, Kizzy. It wouldn't kill you anyway. It would just hurt you.'

'It would if I let it bite me here.'

She raised her hand to the base of her ear, the soft part beneath her lobe that twitched with her heartbeat. I imagined the snake's fangs sinking into the dark skin, wondered if it would have enough venom for us both. Then I pushed the thought far away.

'We have to survive this, Kizzy. Together.'

'And you?' Her eyes were suddenly blazing. 'You can't even sing for them.'

'Then I won't sing for them,' I said, my anger rising to meet hers. 'I'll sing for you, and for Mamă, and for Kem. I'll sing one of our songs, a Traveller song, and they will not be able to take anything from it. As for your snake—'

I pulled out the death cap, shrivelled now, and more potent for it. 'We can kill it now. It will be quick.'

'Where did you get that?'

'The day we were taken,' I said.

'I told you to put it back.'

'I didn't listen.'

'You didn't give it to me,' said Kizzy, her voice reproachful. 'All those nights I said I wanted to die.'

'You can't die, Kizzy,' I reached out to her. 'I need you.'

'We could poison the boyar,' she said, eyes fixed on the death cap.

'The boyar will die anyway,' I said. 'Did you see his neck? He has the disease. And we are not like them, Kizzy. We are not murderers.'

'I could be.'

'We could give this snake a clean death. A merciful one. It's better than they deserve.'

Kizzy's face softened slightly then, her newly thinned cheeks twitching in a sad smile. 'You're braver than you know, *dragă*.'

Dragă; darling. Like Mamă used to call us. She took the death cap and slipped it quickly inside the pot.

At that moment, the key scraped in the lock, and the door opened with a screech that set my teeth on edge. I stood straight, expecting Malovski - but instead a boy entered, carrying a clay pot.

His dark hair dipped into his eyes, obscuring his features, but his languid gait was unmistakable.

Kizzy cried out. 'Fen!'

He was darker than I'd ever seen him, burnished brown by his work without shade in the fields. His tunic was the same he had been wearing the night we were taken. I could see stains upon it, dried blood: mine, and Kizzy's, and his.

His face was thinner too, like Kizzy's was. The apple cheeks were gone, replaced by someone less familiar and older, his expression serious and shadowed as storm clouds.

But his smile broke at the sound of her voice, warming as high summer, and made him look more himself. He hurriedly closed the door behind him, shutting us off from the gaze of the guard. When we threw our arms about him, he smelled of fresh sweat and the clean air of the fields.

'Careful!' he said, half warningly, half laughing. 'There's a meadow viper in here.'

He placed the clay pot down and embraced me. Then he held Kizzy, and it was for far longer. I looked at my feet. When they finally broke apart, both looking dazed, he glanced from her face to mine.

'I should have known you two would be at the root of such a strange request. What's all this about?'

Kizzy's smile vanished. 'Evil.'

She gestured at the poor dead snake, still in its liquid grave.

Fen grimaced. 'What's that?'

'My evening plans,' said Kizzy dryly, without mirth. 'Bite wine. The boyar requested it.'

'Bite wine?' Fen rubbed his calloused palm across his stubbled cheeks. It made a sound like cloth brushing through brambles. 'I've heard of that. The venom is meant to—'

He hesitated.

'Meant to?' I prompted.

'Be good for men,' he mumbled, determinedly not looking at Kizzy.

'Ah.' I had heard of such things before – men powdering wolf's teeth to snort to beget sons, flavouring their honey with bee venom to make them better at bedding. I had no idea if they worked, but the cruelty made me queasy.

'Pathetic,' sneered Kizzy. 'Is this the only way they can make themselves feel powerful? Have a woman murder a snake?'

'I didn't know it was made this way,' said Fen, almost defensively.

'Had some, have you?' said Kizzy, coolly. 'Who for?'

'No, it's a speciality, only for the boyar's dining hall,' said Fen, determinedly ignoring her second question. He looked at the snake again, swallowing queasily. 'I can see why.'

'Are you well, Fen?' I said, hurrying to smooth the prickly air. 'Are they treating you all right?'

'Better than I expected them to. We're in a hut all together, Morsh and me and the rest of the boys. We're at the edge of the fields. The thatch is leaking and it's the poorest of them all, but no Settled come in. At night we're free to talk amongst ourselves. We see Girtie. Reeni too sometimes, when they bring the cows to the fields.'

'That's nice for you,' said Kizzy sharply. 'We've seen no one.'

'I know,' said Fen, trying to soothe her. 'We were all worried. The girls thought you were in the kitchens or the dining hall.'

'We've done both,' I said. 'But tonight Kizzy's meant to entertain.'

Fen looked at her searchingly. 'No one's . . . have you been hurt?'

'Not in the way you care about,' said Kizzy meanly.

'Kizzy!' I snapped, but Fen held up a calming hand.

'I know you can take care of yourself, Kizzy. But it doesn't mean I don't worry, that I don't think about you.'

Kizzy set her newly pointed chin. 'I wish you hadn't brought the snake. Take it back.'

'He can't do that, Kizzy,' I said exasperated. 'He'll get in trouble.'

'Please,' she said, and I was shocked to see her lip was trembling. 'Take it away, Fen. Set it free.'

'Kizzy—' I started, but Fen squeezed my hand.

'It's alright, Lil. I'll think of something.'

'Won't you be punished?'

He shrugged. 'It's not such a bad life, in the fields. Our master doesn't watch us much, and there are other Travellers.'

'Other slaves, you mean,' sneered Kizzy. 'Are you like my sister then, accepting your fate meek as a child?'

Fen stilled, so suddenly he may have been stone aside from the hurt flickering across his face. 'Is that what you think of us, Kizzy? That we are weak for trying to survive?'

'Survive for what?' Though she did not raise her voice above a hiss, my sister seemed to grow taller, magnificent and terrible in her rage. 'To be an errand boy? You are an *aurar*, a Traveller. Have you forgotten that?'

Fen's heart was breaking. I could see it in the pallor of his cheeks, the slump in his broad shoulders. I too felt pinned in place by her anger, the room airless as our prison cells.

Finally, he picked up the pot, and spoke.

'I have not forgotten what matters. All I have done, all I have borne, I have done it in the hope of seeing you again.'

'I'm sorry to have disappointed you.' Kizzy's voice was ice. 'Don't trouble yourself further.'

Fen nodded. He had heard all he could take. He turned to me. 'Be careful, Lil. Stay alive. To see you again—' He cast a last look at Kizzy, his pain clear and shining in his eyes. 'It is enough.'

Chapter Nineteen

Malovski arrived to a sour silence. She seemed distracted, her usually piercing gaze skimming off us like black pebbles over ice. She did not even comment on the silence of the snake in the remaining pot, the lack of another.

'Bring the pot and the wine. They're waiting.'

The potted snake was silent. I thought of the breath we had taken from it, how it should be alive and vibrating between my palms like a cupped cricket. I had the bottle of wine under my armpit, and wished I had the courage to drop the whole lot, to take the punishment that would mean, perhaps, my sister could be saved.

But then, likely nothing would save her from what the boyars, feasting above, desired. Spectacle. My sister was one, the would-be torture of the snake another. And I was the shadow behind, serving only to show up their light. Even my song would be a mere backdrop to Kizzy's performance.

I fixed my eyes on the back of Kizzy's neck, willed loving words into her, words of strength, of comfort. Perhaps she heard them, because her back straightened as she passed from the narrow passages that bellied along the castle into the lighter, broader corridors.

There was a strange, heady scent coming from somewhere, out of place and cloying. I realised the animal fat lamps had been mixed with beeswax, and that was how all of this felt: a lick of sweetness over barbarity. Like poison in wine.

'We will enter through the front doors,' said Malovski. 'As serving girls do. Performers usually come through the side.' She said it like it was an honour.

The boyars wanted a good look at her, I supposed. The noises of feasting grew louder. The floor was strewn with rushes that flashed like forest through the bars of a cage, and the candlelight made everything feel slower. My head throbbed as though I had supped on the wine sloshing under my arm. Fen and Kizzy's argument chased around my mind. *Stay alive. It is enough.*

We came to a stop outside the pair of massive wooden doors, braced with iron. Now they looked more like the gates of a fortress than the entrance to a feast hall. My skin prickled as Malovski gestured for Kizzy to take the pot and the wine. She cradled the pot in the crook of one arm, gripped the bottle in the newly smooth skin of her palm. She looked young in the soft light of the candles.

'You, follow behind,' said Malovski. 'Your sister will dance first, so sing something. Then, you leave while she serves the bite wine.'

She nodded at the guard to open the door. He heaved on the metal ring, and the noise and heat smashed into my face, along with the stink of unwashed bodies and stale wine.

I saw the already too-familiar high ceiling, the room with walls of glittering silk and plunging red, and more men than there had been even that afternoon – more men than I had seen in one place my whole life. Faces turned towards the open door, a momentary lull in the ruckus.

'You would do well to please him,' Malovski said to Kizzy. 'For your, and your sister's sake.'

Then she pushed Kizzy inside.

I went to follow, but Malovski threw out an arm.

'Let her go ahead.'

This was as easy to me as breathing. As I tripped in behind, I saw Kizzy apart from myself. I saw her as a stranger might, a woman with thick hips and curling hair, her body brown and shining in the light from Boyar Valcar's massive fire.

I pinched my own narrow waist, hugged myself tight as she walked the long length of the room. No one touched her, but I knew it was only because they didn't dare. She was not theirs to touch, and not because she was her own. She was here at the whim of Boyar Calazan, and that at once protected and damned her.

'Here she is!' Boyar Valcar boomed. His voice was high, sloppy with drink. 'Your girl as requested, Calazan.'

Valcar was seated at his usual place at the top of the room, at the long table with people sitting along only one side, an audience to Kizzy's entrance. Boyar Calazan was on his left, his heart side, as Old Charani would have said. The position of highest honour.

As I drew parallel with Kizzy, I could see their table was strewn with goblets and bowls. There were heaps of untouched salad leaves on platters, yellow-white bones of chickens. The main course of pig would be brought up soon, dripping fat. But first they would have their entertainment.

I moved along the shadows of the room, using the thin channels between the outermost table and the wall. Other serving girls slipped through them too, not acknowledging my presence, as intent upon their tasks as mice slinking past cats.

Kizzy reached the table placed for her, an arm's length from the high table, set with a smooth cloth of white, light as her dress was dark. She looked holy, like a settled priest at an altar. She placed her load down, shaking back her dark curls. They shone in the candlelight, fine as the silk in the tapestries.

Boyar Calazan took in a breath, his handsome, brutal face alight behind his thick beard. He leaned forward, so that the candle on the table threw his face into shadow. The room fell silent.

'Welcome, girl. What is your name?'

'Whatever you want it to be,' said Boyar Valcar, eyelid drooping. He was very drunk, far drunker than his guest. The room rippled with snickers, but Boyar Calazan didn't laugh.

'What is your name?' he repeated.

Kizzy lifted her face to him. She showed no fear. 'Mala.'

My breath caught in my chest. Mamă's name.

'Well then, Mala,' he said, mangling it. 'Boyar Valcar tells me you can dance.'

He gestured for her to begin. She turned her head and looked straight at me. I locked my eyes on hers as she lifted her hands, so recently healed with their new skin. She placed them to one side of her head, like Mamă before she began a dance. With the defiant jut of her chin, the focused glare of her eyes, it was almost as if it were Mamă up there. She began to clap. *One, two three. One, two three.* One beat followed by two quicker. It was a rhythm I instantly recognised.

Mamă's serenade for Albu.

I felt a tidal cry rising in my throat, tears in my eyes, but I swallowed it down, blinked them away. As my sister's hips began to sway, her feet lifting and falling on the rushes with a *hush hush* like light rain, I opened my mouth, and I sang.

I barely noticed the heads snapping to me, before they were swiftly drawn back to my sister. I barely cared about the way the men began to whoop and cheer as she span. I only saw her, in her black dress, Kizzy with one turn, Mamă with the next, the space where Albu was conjured into being with each note, each twist, each beat. The song galloped and slowed, swooped and soared, until it was not coming from me at all, but became me. My whole body fizzed with it, and despite our surroundings, I felt this moment was a gift, and all would be well.

The song ended, and Kizzy became only Kizzy again, her chest heaving, sweat lightly beading her forehead. For a beat, the room was silent as the eye of a storm, and then Boyar Valcar was on his feet and clapping drunkenly, the men about us rising to their feet and hooting their approval.

A serving girl brushed past me, and it roused me fully from my daze.

'Sorry,' I murmured, stepping aside, and Mira raised her head to me. I gasped. 'What are you—'

She pressed her finger to my lips, placed her hand to her heart.

'Edina got me in. I wanted to hear you sing.' Her grey eyes shone with pride, and I clutched her wrist briefly. Even as she hurried away, vanishing before Malovski could catch her, I wanted to snatch her up in my arms and hold her, thank her for witnessing this – the one person in the room besides my sister I did not mind singing for.

The applause died away, and a new, expectant hush took its place. I knew they were waiting for what they had been promised would come next: bite wine. But my sister made no move towards the pot. Her breathing had returned to normal, and she stood straight backed.

'Go on,' slurred Boyar Valcar at last. 'Where's the snake?'

'I'll show her one!' shouted a voice from along the table, and a man stood up beside the visiting boyar. I recognised him as the one I had served at lunch. He was drunker than even Boyar Valcar, and he stumbled to his feet to gales of laughter, fiddling with his belt. I covered my mouth, unable to look away as the room dissolved into whistles and catcalls, but then there was a flash of metal, and suddenly the man's grey wool trousers were dark.

At first I thought he had wet himself, but then I registered the blade in Boyar Calazan's hand. The rest of him had not moved, only his hand darting out, and then retracting, like a snake striking. He did not even turn his head, but the drunk man was howling on the floor, blood spreading from a wound in his thigh.

It took the beer-soaked men even longer to realise, but when they did, they rose to their feet, the collective hiss of swords being unsheathed rising all about us. I hurried to Kizzy's side, tugging on her arm. She picked up the snake's pot, and we moved swiftly through the bristling air. Malovski was standing at the door, and she blocked us from leaving, motioning for us to wait.

'Boyar Calazan . . . what . . .'

Boyar Valcar was blinking stupidly, looking between the moaning, bleeding man and his calm visitor.

'I—' Valcar seemed lost for words. He put his hand to the lump at his neck and looked out at the grit-teethed men. 'I think you should leave, Calazan.'

'So do I. I did not know your court had dissolved into such lewdness, Valcar,' said Boyar Calazan languidly, wiping his blade before sheathing it. 'I'll be sure to tell the Voievod.'

The threat hung in the air like a hovering blade.

'No, that won't be necessary,' stuttered Valcar, holding out his hand. 'You are welcome to stay, of course. I forgot myself.' He turned to his men. 'Swords away.'

Muttering spread through the room.

'Away, I say,' he said, his voice too shaky to be commanding. 'Please, let's forget this nastiness.'

Boyar Calazan rose anyway. 'I'll be on my way, Valcar.'

'Please, Calazan. I'll do anything—'

'I'll take the girl,' said Boyar Calazan. 'The Voievod is in need of a bear dancer.'

Time froze, and I looked at Kizzy. He could not do this. She was clasping the pot to her chest, her eyes still faraway. I felt Malovski draw closer to us, hemming us in.

'We have already made our offering—' said Boyar Valcar. Calazan's glare cut him short. 'Of course,' said Valcar, pawing at Calazan's cloak as he stood. 'Please, take her, and we can forget this.'

'We shall see,' said Boyar Calazan, and strode around the table, and down the room. I felt rooted in place as he drew closer, his massive bulk seeming to blot out the whole world.

He reached us and stopped. The dragon crest on his chest seemed to ripple. Kizzy was trembling now, the spilt wine dripping from her sleeves, the snake pot still clasped to her heart.

'Come, girl,' he said in a voice that was almost kind and all the more sickening for it. 'We have bears enough in Ardeal. A white one brought from the forests only recently.'

My heart started to beat again, very fast.

'A white bear?' murmured Kizzy. Her eyes slid to mine. I knew her thoughts were the same as my own. White bears were rare as blood moons. *Albu.* 'Did he have someone with him?'

Calazan brushed off her question. 'Come to the Voievod, and I can promise you none shall force themselves on you. Girls there are free to take who they wish.'

'My sister must come too,' said Kizzy, and my chest swelled with pride at her daring, bargaining with this man.

Boyar Calazan's eyes flicked over me, and he shook his head. 'We have no need of her.'

'Then I will not go.' But I knew she was stalling. The white bear, Albu, stuck in the Dragon's lair. Of course she had to go.

Boyar Calazan was done being reasonable. He twisted his hand through Kizzy's curls, as swift as he had embedded his knife in the man's thigh. Kizzy gasped and dropped the pot as she was wrenched away. The snake fell, heavy and motionless, to the floor. The death cap had dealt its mercy.

I threw myself after her, but Malovski ordered a guard to hold me back. I felt arms crushing my chest, my heart a bird flying at the cage of my ribs.

'Still, or I'll stick you,' crooned Captain Vereski's voice in my ear.

He felled me with a knee to the back of the legs, the remains of the pot cutting my knees, his elbow pressed hard into my back. I strained to watch Kizzy being pulled away, my hands grasping for her, scrambling amongst the shards of pottery, but Boyar Calazan's men closed like a cloak of night over her.

My head was pushed down, the doors of the dining hall closed on the uproar left in Boyar Calazan's wake, and Vereski's grip pushed me into blackness.

CHAPTER TWENTY

Captain Vereski pulled me away from the noise.

I assumed we were following behind Malovski, and I braced myself for the dungeon again. But when I looked up, I saw that we were in the main servants' corridor, moving past the steps leading down to the cells, past the route to the serving girls' quarters, beyond the open door and roar of the kitchens, and towards the door at the end. Malovski was nowhere in sight.

Vereski stank of beer. He was pulling me too fast, my feet skidding on dirty rushes. I was dimly aware through the numb grip of shock that I was bleeding. I could feel my palm stinging, feel something sharp gripped there, and as we stumbled out into the dark courtyard, cobbled beneath my soles, I clenched it harder, pulling a fresh gasp of pain from my throat.

'Quiet,' hissed Vereski and he pulled me left, through a creaking wooden door. I smelt manure, and hay, heard a horse snicker softly. I blinked into the gloom. 'At least in the dark I can imagine, eh?'

I could see him coming towards me, his shadow a presence already weighty over me, and I realised suddenly what he meant by taking me from Malovski's sight, by bringing me here. My hand gripped the sharp object in my hand. I felt the jagged edges, a slightly grainy texture. It was a shard from Kizzy's smashed snake pot.

I heard Vereski's belt buckle, scrape of metal on metal bringing copper to my tongue as though it were between my teeth. I felt my mind wanting to take me away. There would be no shame in it – as Fen said, it would be enough to survive. But then I knew I could not freeze, not now. Not while Kizzy was being borne away to the Dragon, to our bear and perhaps our brother. This man may not stop at forcing himself on me – I would not let him take my life.

My mouth filled with the taste of metal and fear, but I forged it into something hard and shining. As his hands came down either side of my head, trapping my hair, I brought the shard to his bare groin, and as his beery tongue rasped against my cheek, I stabbed.

'Căcat!' He screamed and, slackened by pain, he fell upon me.

I pushed him off, reaching for his sword in his discarded belt. The clay piece was slick with blood, and I dropped it, finding the hard hilt of his blade. It was like the day of the burnings, the day I seized Mamă's axe with a strength I had not known I possessed.

I hacked blindly at the dark, until he stopped trying to rise. The horses whinnied, and soon they were louder than his wet whines. I felt my body as a thing apart, my mind splitting off until I hovered over the scene in the dark as I continued to raise the sword and let it fall, again and again.

Suddenly, there was light spilling inside. I wheeled around, still raising the sword–

But it was not a guard, nor Malovski, but Mira and Cook who stood in the doorway. I let the sword drop to the floor, clattering dully on the straw-strewn cobbles. A great, swaying nausea ripped through my stomach. Mira's large eyes moved from me, to the mess beneath me, and as I went to follow her gaze, she took my face between her hands, forcing me to look at her.

'No,' she said. 'No.'

'Is he dead?' I whispered. But I could still hear wet sounds, breathing laboured by blood. I could not leave him to die slowly. I moved to pick up the sword again, thinking to stab the blade between his ribs, but Mira stilled my hand. She knelt and wrapped her hands about his throat. I kept my eyes upon her face. Her eyes were narrowed, but her face was placid, almost calm. Her fingers were strong, and quick.

The breathing stopped. The silence boomed in my ears.

'What happened?' Cook's voice was low and tight. 'We saw him dragging you past the kitchens.'

'I–' I gasped, and began trembling, so hard I thought I would fall. 'I–'

Cook pulled the stable door shut behind her and we were plunged into a dark heavy with the copper tang of blood. 'Did he touch you? Did he hurt you?'

'No,' my voice was thick with tears. 'He tried – I stabbed him.'

The horror of it was a struck drum that reverberated through my entire being. The nausea rose up my throat, and I retched, held upright only by Cook, who stroked my hair and spoke low and hard into my ear.

'He deserved it.' The venom in Cook's voice chilled my blood. 'But this will not go unpunished. You must go now. I will hide the body. We all saw him taking you.' Her voice was steadying, the plan forming in her mind. 'I will say I saw him saddle a horse, take you to the fields.'

'Me too,' said Mira. 'I'm going too.'

'Mira, you don't have to–'

'I'm not staying.' She laced her hand into mine. 'Let me come.'

I spat on the floor to rid my mouth of sourness and nodded. Cook did too, her eye gleaming in the dark. 'I'll say that he took you, and Mira went after you on foot. Malovski will have no trouble believing it. Vereski was a brute, and we all knew it.'

'But where will we go?'

'Not south. That's all Boyar Valcar's land, for miles and miles. Not north, that's where the Dragon is. Go west, to the forests, or east, to the sea. There are Travellers there. Free Travellers. But you will have to ride hard, get as far as you can under night's cover.'

She cracked the door ajar to allow some moonlight in. The horses reared, and I saw one was Dika's horse, Orsha. I placed a hand on her velvety nose, and she stilled.

Cook helped us saddle her. Our soft leather saddles were gone, and to me the Settler rig seemed inhuman, all hardboiled leather and biting metal. We placed an old horse blanket over her back, to soften the contraption. I left the whip: the sight of it made me shiver.

'I wish there was time to fetch you something to eat,' fretted Cook. 'But Malovski may be out any moment.'

'We'll manage,' I placed my hand on her shoulder, and she placed her hand on mine, in the Traveller pose of thanks.

'It is the least I can do.' Her voice broke. 'I am sorry for betraying you.'

'Aunty,' I hushed her. 'I forgive you and I thank you. You could come with us.'

Cook shook her head sadly. 'I wouldn't know how to live, now.'

Mira swung herself up onto the horse, and I climbed up behind, still not looking at Vereski's body. Cook removed the keys from his belt and, checking the yard was clear, led us outside, beneath the spikes, unlocking the gate.

There was no time for a proper farewell. She left the keys in the gate, and the whole thing ajar, to make it look like Vereski had left in haste. As we rode away through the dark town, down the steep spiral of the hill, past Malovski's house and out through the border gate, I wondered how she would dispose of the body.

I hoped she would burn it, and set his soul wandering for eternity, just as he had sent my Mamă's. Only here, in this treeless place, there would be no *Iele* to catch him. He would be alone and rootless, for ever.

Chapter Twenty-One

As soon as we hit the vast flat stretches of the fields, mounds of earth tilled and churned up in raked lines, I finally took my first full breath since my sister had been dragged from the hall.

My mind raced: I could barely process any of what had happened. I had sung and Kizzy had danced, and now we had been swirled apart, as if fulfilling our fates had undone a lifetime's bond.

And I had written myself a new fate. I was a murderer. The word grew large in my head, whispered by wet, struggling breath. I pressed my ear hard into Mira's back, turning the other to the wind.

My arms were about her, her sharp ribs biting my wrists. She rode confidently, steering the horse along the very same road we had been caged along a month previous. When we reached the edge of the forest, the crossroads would come in more ways than one.

I knew I would have to say goodbye to her. She should go to the sea, or the endless forests Cook spoke of, but me? Only one road lay ahead, and that was the very same my sister was being hauled along, towards Albu and Kem. Towards the Dragon.

I looked up to the moon, veiled by fast, skudding clouds. A day shy of seventeen years a free Traveller. A month a slave. And now?

Murderer.

Here and there, tree stumps reared in the dark, and between them huts and houses that I knew from Fen were where the labourers slept. He had told us life was easier here, and I could already see it for myself. Fresh air, and the cover of night to have a little freedom. Shadowy figures talked softly, paying us little mind: lovers and friends finding moments of comfort in the dark.

We passed the Badger's house, unlit and silent, and the dwellings grew less and less solid, less well made, slumping like shamed dogs, propped on rickety beams. There was a light on in the outermost building, shining through holes in its thatch and walls.

I sat up straighter, my arm knocking breath from Mira. She gasped.

'Sorry,' I said, loosening my grip. 'Can we stop? Just for a moment.'

She twisted her head as far as it would go, so I saw her frown in profile.

'Please? It won't take long.'

She pulled Orsha to a walk, checking around us, and finally drew the mare to a stop. I slid off the horse's back, landing hard on the packed road. It sent up the scent of earth, and I wanted to drop to my knees and bury my face in the dirt, however cultivated. It was still earth; sun dried, rain fed. But instead I moved quickly to the slumped house that leaked light.

Mira made a noise of caution, but I ignored her. 'If anyone questions me, or you, ride and don't look back.'

Mira rolled her eyes, as if to say *as if I'd go*, and it gladdened my heart.

Voices came from inside, voices I knew, had listened to many times beside an open fire. If I closed my eyes, I could almost imagine myself back there in the forest, grow the tree stumps into full oaks, the tilled fields into wildflowers. But there was no time for longing.

I knocked twice on the splintered door. The wood was patched with many different offcuts, overlaid like hands of different hues. The voices came to an abrupt stop. Fearful whispers sprang up like steam, and I called through the door.

'Fen? It's Lil.'

It was pulled open so suddenly I stumbled inside, and before I could find my footing, many pairs of arms came tight about me, laughter ringing in my ears.

'Lil!'

Morsh was at my waist, holding fast to my left side. Through the tangle of bodies and smell of sweat and dirt, I saw a square room filled wall to wall with straw mattresses, with a perilously narrow space left clear at the centre for a fire pit that was overhung with skinned game, bodies pink, eyes white.

My head started to spin. The glint of Vereski's eyes in the dark of stable—

'Let her breathe,' Fen's laughing voice drew me back to the room, and I extricated myself from my Traveller brothers. They stood back as far as the enclosed space would allow, and almost instantly their cries of joy quelled into worried mutters. Fen came forward, his smile dropping, thick brows knotting.

'Lil, you're bleeding.' His fingers came up to my face, and I brushed them lightly away.

'It's not mine,' I said, more casually than I felt. I could not think on Vereski now, could not think of the blood, the moans, the feel of the sword as I hacked - *no*.

'Fen, I need to speak with you.'

He came with me unhesitatingly, closing the door on the curious faces of our companions. The poor state of the door meant the attempt at privacy was almost useless, and so I gestured for him to move further off, into the night.

183

'Is it Kizzy?' he asked, voice tight with fear. He looked suddenly towards Orsha and Mira, noticing her for the first time. His body tensed, and I laid a hand on his arm.

'It's all right, she's a friend.'

'She's a Settler.'

'A friend,' I repeated, and the two of them eyed each other a moment before Fen turned fully to me.

'Where is Kisaiya?'

I didn't know what was racing through his head, but though my news was not the worst he could fear, it would not be welcome. I couldn't think of a way to soften it.

'She's been taken. By the boyar's guest, Boyar Calazan.'

A muscle in his jaw twitched. 'Where?'

I took a shaky breath. 'North.' He frowned, and I knew he was trying to re-orientate himself. 'To the Voievod.'

'The Dragon?' His voice was hoarse, and he began to shake his head, his eyes squeezed shut. 'It's not possible.'

I set my hand on his arm again. I could feel his body coiled as the poor snake's before it struck the cork. 'Albu and Kem are there too. She's been taken to be an *ursar*.'

'Not a slave?' I knew what he was thinking, what sort of slave he feared she'd be.

'It was still against her will,' I said. 'But I'm going after her.'

'With her?' He looked up at Mira, who was scanning the road as the horse cropped the grassy banks of the fields.

'No, I'll go alone.'

'It will be dangerous.'

'No more than what I'm leaving behind.' I looked towards the castle, hunched on its hill. I wanted to be away and moving, to leave it far behind for ever.

'Then it will arouse suspicion, a woman alone,' said Fen. 'I'm coming too.'

I knew he would say this and had my riposte ready.

'If you go, it makes our story less believable.'

'What story?'

I told him briefly about Vereski and Cook's intervention. I left out the worst of it, but I'm sure he guessed because he glanced again at the blood on my face and placed a warm palm over mine in a gesture of comfort.

'I'm coming, Lil. If you say no, I'll do it anyway. There are mules in the paddock, and they're strong, if not fast. I have a favourite. I've called her Dorsi.' We exchanged a sad smile at his tribute to the slain bear before Fen's face grew serious again. 'I have to come. You would do the same.'

I can't deny it. For Kizzy, we would both do anything.

'All right,' I said, grateful to my bones. 'What will you tell the others?'

'Nothing,' he said. 'It is best they don't know. It will make it easier for them to lie.'

We broke apart, and I returned to Mira while he went to fetch the mule. She had drawn the mare alongside a mounting post but didn't help as I hoisted myself up. Her face was oddly icy, and she stiffened as I slid my arms around her again.

'Who's that?'

'Fen,' I said. 'He's coming with me.'

She grunted, but held the mare steady until Fen clopped up on a stout mule, at least two hands too small for him, forcing his legs out at a ridiculous angle. Mira snorted and dug in her heels, taking off at a canter.

'Slow down,' I called into her ear, but she flinched away from my voice, leaning forward and only slowing when we reached the welcome cover of the trees.

'Stop,' I said, reaching for the reins, but she pulled her hands angrily away, wriggling free of my arms and sliding off the horse. She walked fast away into the trees, and in the shadows I could see her white fists clenching and unclenching.

'Mira?'

My voice pulled her up short, but she did not turn around. I frowned after her, dismounting and keeping tight hold of the horse's reins as I waited for Fen.

I heard his labouring mule huffing before I saw him coming through the gloom. He stepped angrily off, glaring after Mira, who had her back to us and was looking into the gathered dark of the trees.

'What was that about?'

I shrugged. 'We should go further in, at least to the first fork, in case anyone follows.'

He nodded, and we walked the horses along the road to give Dorsi time to regain her breathing, Mira walking some distance behind. I kept turning to her, but her eyes were fixed resolutely on the ground, her shaved head shining in the slices of moonlight.

I was used to Kizzy's sulks, but usually I could fathom the reason for them. I couldn't understand what had caused Mira to react to Fen this way, but there was no time to discover it now. I wanted to get deeper into the forest before slowing.

We remounted as soon as Dorsi stopped snorting and began to cover ground faster. Every step calmed my pounding heart a little more. The forest here was sparse and sickly, fungus knotted about the trunks and between the fingers of the branches, but still: there were leaves above me for the first time in weeks, and roots rucking the ground beneath my feet. It was like a blessing by Old Charani's hand, soothing and familiar.

The trees thickened as we walked on, and at last we reached a fork in the road. One plunged sharply right, and the other continued straight.

North.

At Fen's suggestion we dismounted and led Orsha and Dorsi off the track and some way into the trees, pausing in a

187

clearing wide enough to draw the horses alongside each other, and Mira caught up.

'Are you all right?' I asked her, reaching out.

She nodded, staying beyond my reach. I pulled my hand back and gestured between them.

'Fen, this is Mira. We worked together in the kitchens. Mira, Fen is part of my Traveller family.'

'Brother?' she croaked. Fen frowned. Though her speech was clear to me, he was unused to her whispered words.

'She asked if you were my brother.'

'Of a sort,' he said. 'We grew up together.'

'He hopes to be.' I grinned at him in the shadows. I felt his embarrassment, though he surely knew his love for Kizzy was clear as a summer's day.

'Kizzy?' She patted her chest, over her heart.

'Yes,' said Fen, understanding. 'Kizzy.'

Mira's expression lightened. 'Good.'

I didn't look at her, but warmth flooded my cheeks. My heart was heavy at the thought of saying goodbye. 'We have to go north, Mira. Fen and I, we have to help Kizzy.'

'I know,' said Mira, almost casually. I felt a stab of hurt that she didn't seem more upset at our parting.

'So,' I said, swallowing. 'Do you mind if we take the horse? It is better able to bear two of us.'

She fixed me in her stormy gaze. 'We can ride the horse.'

I blinked stupidly. 'We?'

'Yes.'

'You and me?' I could not let myself hope just yet. 'You're coming?'

She rolled her eyes. 'Yes.' She smiled at Fen. 'Slow, isn't she?'

Fen grinned. 'I'll take the mule. I don't mind.'

'You should go to the sea,' I said, unable to pull my gaze from Mira. 'It will be dangerous.'

'I can't swim,' said Mira, stepping close.

'Or to the mountains.'

'My parents are dead,' she said it briskly, in a way that did not invite pity. 'And you'll need all the help you can get.'

'You don't have to—'

'I know,' she said, lifting her chin. In the dark, her throat shone white as the inside of a shell, and though she winced with the effort of her words, she spoke her next sentence clearly. 'I swear this, Lillai. I will never do anything I do not want to, ever again.'

CHAPTER TWENTY-TWO

We plunged deeper into the dark. With every step, the horror of the night sloughed off me, replaced with the giddy joy of being back in the forest, with friends beside me and a journey before us. The fear of what lay ahead could wait: this first night I would revel in my freedom, and not allow myself to think on what I had left behind in the stables.

It would be a long ride to Ardeal, but not a hard one. It was always a source of fear and discomfort to Old Charani that the Voievod's lands melted so seamlessly into the free country, that we could cross into his borders without knowing it.

'It feels wrong, it feels devious,' she'd say. 'There should be mountains lining his world like teeth, warning us before we enter the mouth of the beast.'

But he had not been the beast who had snatched her life with its ravenous jaws. That man was dead by my hand, and his master was dying of disease. That was some slender comfort. But I had noticed – and I knew that Fen had too – that our route would take us past the place we had last seen our families alive, past the place of the burnings.

Looking back, Old Charani could not have known Boyar Valcar was taking a leaf out of the Dragon's book, stealing Travellers to work his lands. These forests had always been safe, owned by none but the birds and boars and bears who stalked into hilly climes. But the world had changed, was changing, even in her lifetime. In the months before our enslavement, I'd noticed fewer Travellers on the roads, more settling in villages, working as labourers or maids. To a Traveller, perhaps the whole world was a beast waiting to strike anything different from itself, anything that roamed outside the pack. Perhaps eventually we would be squeezed out, forced to live as the Settlers do.

But not us, I thought, *not now*. I could not know what lay beyond the Dragon's walls, but until I passed through them, I was mistress of my own path. I would be brave, like Kizzy, and would not care if it led me to a trap so long as I could willingly walk it.

It was made easier by having Mira and Fen by my side. They were talking more easily now. Whatever had upset Mira seemed to have left her and they made simple, easy chatter, soft as our horses took the road north. Within a few hours, the birds began their calls though sunlight would remain elusive for a while yet: I heard skylarks, starlings, and even a nightingale. It was sweet as honey poured onto my tongue.

Just as the birds began, Fen quietened.

'We're getting close,' he said to me, and I nodded. I could feel it too, prickling up my arms.

'Close to what?' asked Mira. I listened to the question rumble her back as I pressed my ear against it, suddenly weary with sadness.

'Where we were taken,' said Fen, his voice clouded with the same grief I felt welling inside my own throat. 'Where they—'

He broke off, looking past us into the forest. I turned my head slowly, slowly, thinking he may have caught sight of a wild bear going back to its den, or a scout sent after us. But all I saw was more trees, perhaps a little thinner here than usual, the bracken about their trunks less full.

'Is that where we came through?' I asked, remembering there was a point where we had joined the main road, but not much besides.

'Yes,' murmured Fen.

Mira pulled our horse right, towards the almost imperceptible break in the trees.

'What are you doing?' I asked.

'You don't want to go?'

I glanced at Fen, uncertain. 'We should get to Kizzy.'

Fen looked from Mira to the route north. 'We could cut through the valley. It might even be better, if someone's following. It will throw them off the scent if we follow the river.'

I nodded, but as I did so I realised that I had hoped this would not be his answer. Mira noticed my reluctance. 'Do you not want to?'

The truth was I did, and I did not. I wanted to see the place we had last been happy, truly happy, but it was also the place where that feeling had died, alongside Mamă. Whatever lay ahead of us now, good or bad, there would always be a hole in my heart, a place raw and tender and aching, made by what we had seen, what we had lost.

Fen must have seen my uncertainty, because he urged his mule forwards, and reached up to me.

'I know,' he said, simply. 'But we must. Kizzy would.'

Of course she would. I nodded again, more certainly this time, and the horses began to move along the path. The forest had not fully claimed it, not fully smoothed the signs of the caged cart's crossing. Perhaps animals had adopted the break, and this was why it was so free of weeds to catch at the horses' legs.

I was glad of the ease and sickened by it. I did not want to think that we had made this mark on the forest, however unwillingly. We prided ourselves on moving on before our presence could imprint any sort of permanence on the world. *Take only what you need,* Old Charani would say. *Leave enough for the next.*

I thought of the mushrooms collected in my apron the day of the burnings, the dying, drying roots. Kizzy's bright, precise fingernails ensuring she wasted nothing. Mamă's face as she waved us off before turning back to the fire. Fire, swallowing our caravans.

My palms stung, and my mind swung back into my body. I realised my nails were digging into them. With a great effort, I unclenched my hands, and placed them back around Mira's waist, leaning once more against her back, listening to the buzz of her voice comforting the horse.

Fen led the way, knowing the woods from his time hunting, and it was his voice that called us to a halt. 'We're here.'

I closed my eyes so tightly sparks burst before them. It looked akin to embers spitting from a fire, and I began to shake.

I can't do this I can't I can't do this.

Mira eased my arms gently from around her waist and turned around in the saddle so her legs were across mine, their weight solid and good, her hands on my already wet cheeks.

'You can,' she said, as though she could hear the mantra in my head repeating. I opened my eyes. Her face was very close, her voice very quiet. 'You get to say goodbye, Lil. It is a blessing. One I did not have.'

'Your parents were killed?'

'Not my parents,' she said. 'Cristina. They took her in the night. When I woke, she was long gone.'

My heart seemed to twist. Had Cristina lain with her? I looked away so she would not see my confusion.

The ground was mossy, throwing up green, clean scent. But overlaying it was scorch and burn, even after all these weeks. I pulled up a square of yielding moss and rubbed it beneath my nose, then took Fen's outstretched hand.

We walked to the edge of the clearing. The daylight was gathering now, trees releasing their caught dark and starting to shine with a soft, chilled light. I held out my hand to a shaft of sun, letting it dance across my palm, allowing myself these last few moments before I saw the remnants of our former lives. I would never be able to unsee them.

'Ready?' said Fen. And we stepped out from the shade.

The scorched shells of the caravans were slumped about the clearing like the skeletons of felled beasts, or beached whales. Any ash left behind had long since washed away, and the pieces of wood that remained were the largest: beams that had held our roofs steady, floorboards we had washed and walked and danced on. Open to the elements, their black was striped through with bleached strips where the paint had reacted to the heat of the fire.

The spokes of Old Charani's wagon's wheels were gone, the circles of the metal runs glinting in the growing light. I took a deep breath, and looked towards where I had last seen her, her gnarled hand reaching up, pleading mercy—

Nothing remained. There was nothing of her, or Dika, or Erha, or any of the slain. All that remained of the bloodshed was the pelt of Erha's bear Dorsi, picked clean by the wolves.

I released a long breath. The creatures had spared us the sight of our families, their bones shining through rotting flesh like so much melted metal. It was as close to a sky burial as we could have hoped for.

I think Fen felt the same relief: he grasped at my hand, and I saw tears work their silent way down his cheeks, just as they had in the cart.

I squeezed his hand back, then dropped it and began to circle the scene, taking the longest possible route to where I knew I must ultimately go: the place Mamă was murdered.

I passed the churned ground of struggles, the shattered caravans, Albu's chain sliced and left in the dirt. Mamă's axe lay beside it where I had dropped it upon seeing Kem. I reached out and took hold of its leather grip.

The moment rushed back upon me as if I were slipping through the cracks of time like a Seer. I fought the rising panic as I remembered the sound of Albu howling, Kem's silent, fearful face, the sound of our elders dying, our caravans burning and Kizzy wrenching at the wood barring the door, melting her palms—

'Easy,' said Mira, her touch on my shoulder making me flinch. I was on the ground, cradling the axe, knuckles showing white through my dark skin. 'Put that down, Lil.'

'No,' I said, a little more forcefully than I meant to. Mira drew away.

'No,' I tried again. 'It's all right. I'll keep this. We'll need a weapon.' And I liked the feel of the axe in my hand. It made me remember the strength I had as I fought to free Kem and Albu. I would need to find that strength again, and more besides.

But all of it, all my resolve, all my fight, was knocked from me clean as breath by the sight of our wagon. Or what had once been our wagon. Our home, built by my grandmother's grandmother, repaired so many times only the original door had remained. But it had remained the same in spirit, because our family lived there. If it were a body, with ageing parts replaced with new, we were its constant, its beating heart.

And now? Cinder and crumbling black, the ground scorched inches deep beneath it. I walked towards it, barely feeling my feet press on the ground. I felt I floated to it, and as I drew closer, I saw the scorched earth was patched through with reds and two flashes of unnatural purple.

I bent close, closer than I wanted to, so I could be sure. Here and there grew delicate, whisker thin mushrooms with tiny fingernail caps.

'Fen,' I said. 'Look.'

He came quickly. When he saw the ground, shot through with mushrooms, he gasped. '*Iele?*'

'What do you mean?' Mira's voice was cautious. 'Spirits?'

I nodded. '*Ielele* have been here. They've left mushrooms, see?'

'Could they not have grown anyway?' Mira sounded unconvinced. I knew the Settled had different stories, but the mushrooms, the red ground – it was evidence.

The forest spirits had saved my mother's soul.

Chapter Twenty-Three

I dropped the axe and reached carefully out to the mushrooms as though they were tiny licking flames. The pain in my chest was so mighty I felt my heart might beat clean through my ribs as I pressed my palms to the ruins, gasping as grief tightened its grip on my breath. My knees hit the floor as I pushed my face into the mushrooms, the last remnants of my Mamă, our home.

I plucked one of the purple ones, my nail going into its stalk so soft I barely felt it break.

'Lil?' Fen's voice was a warning, but some power beyond my understanding was compelling me.

I brought the mushroom up to my lips and swallowed it down. It was nutty and melting, tainted with smoke. For a moment, nothing happened. Then, it felt as though my vision filled with blood.

'Lil?' Mira was beside me, but I was already drawing away from her. I felt something ice-cold enter my body, something not of this world or of the next but between: I understood this entirely, and not at all.

'Lil?'

Mira's voice was growing more distant, and there was another voice, stronger, overlapping hers and calling me as though from inside my own head.

'Lillai?'

It was Mamă's voice.

The world dropped away. I felt caught as though another body was lying the length of mine, weighing me down. I felt old as the trees and young as Kem, I felt I was me and Kizzy and Mamă and all the bodies ever killed or hurt or healed. I felt rage and sorrow and an infinite, infinite love, swarming through me like illness, prickling like heat.

I could not open my eyes, but it did not matter: I could see the roots of the trees below me, seeking water, and the leaves above me, seeking sun. I saw the red mushrooms glow and understood they were for food. I saw the purple throb and knew they were sight. I felt a hand in mine and it was Mamă's, and though I could not turn my head to see her she was beside and inside me, lifting me high over the forests and showing me the way ahead.

White trees glowed beneath us, and Mamă swooped low, brought me up a branch of one. It was yew, sharp at its broken end, and when I held it, I felt a great strength and a terrible violence wend its way through my mind.

We were flying faster now, over the path that cut through the forest like a vine stretching through bark, curling around a dark heart.

And, when it arrived, over a hill ringed with unspeakable monsters, this was how I saw the Voievod's castle: a great, cancerous heart, bubbling rather than beating, its blood salt as tears. At the outskirts of the seething morass was the white square of a building, small as a dove flung against a bloody sky. A place of safety, of use like the white yew trees, so near to danger.

We flew closer to the dark heart of the castle, scuttling as beetles into the rock, soaring as hawks above it. We flooded the corridors, and I saw people dark skinned as me, all weeping. And inside the thrumming, lumpen swill of pain and fear was anger, anger inside the man who lived there.

Not a man, said my mother inside my head. *Nothing beating, nothing warm.*

And we were behind him in a great hall, darker and larger than the boyar's, and his eyes were trained on a white bear and a girl, dancing, dancing. And a red thread was unspooling from his mouth to hers, as though their tongues were thin and monstrous and entwined, and before I could scream, he turned his head and he smiled at me – at least, I thought it was a smile. It was more a baring of teeth: sharp and pointed, like a cat's, and white as his skin.

201

I turned to Kizzy and she smiled too, and when she spoke it was with his voice.

Deathless, they said, and their mouths spilled blood. *Lay death to rest.*

Mamă's hand was whipped away, and I was falling through black and white and purples, greens and blues until finally, finally I snapped back into my body, and felt hands – real hands – upon my shoulders, another in my mouth, gripping at my tongue.

I reared up, hands searching for the axe, thinking Malovski had arrived to rip out my tongue – but it was Fen's cheek my hands connected with, Mira's grasp I wrenched free from.

'Lil!' gasped Mira, and I saw she was panting, crumpled beside the scorched earth of our burnt wagon. 'Calm, Lil.'

'What are you doing?' I hissed, my hands to my mouth. I could taste blood. 'Why were you holding my tongue?'

'You were having a fit,' said Fen. 'You were shaking so much we thought you might choke on it.'

'I saw – I went . . .' I was trembling all over. My palm was bleeding, smearing my lips with my own blood. The taste of it was unbearable, and I longed for a cool drink of water, scooped straight from a stream. I reached around for the right words. 'I flew.'

Mira and Fen exchanged a worried glance.

'No,' I said, kneeling up, trying to sound less breathless, less fevered. 'Listen. The mushrooms, the *Iele* left them for us. They were grown from Mamă's ashes. And she took me to the Voievod, and I saw the way in, and I saw Kizzy and Albu dancing.'

'Kizzy?' said Fen sharply. 'Is she all right?'

Mira frowned at us both. 'You had a fit, Lil. That mushroom must have been poisonous, made your mind play tricks. I've seen it before, girls following lights and speaking to animals—'

'No,' I said, firmly. 'I know it sounds like madness, but it was real, Mira. Old Charani told us of such things, didn't she, Fen?' I turned to him, seeking support. 'The food of the dead entering the living, showing them prophecies.'

'Dark tellings,' said Fen. 'She'd never seen one, only heard—'

'Yes,' I said, determined not to lose him as well. 'But I did see. I saw the path we must take through the forest. The forest pass is the best way, edging the mountains.'

Fen snorted. 'How? We have one horse and a mule, and no furs.'

'We have Dorsi's fur. Dika would want us to have warmth. And we should gather some of the *Iele* mushrooms, the red kind – we can eat those. They will sustain us better than the usual sort. I am sure we can take whatever we need. We must take branches from the yew trees, make stakes for protection. Kizzy is there, Fen,' I hurried on. 'Or will be soon. She will be dancing for him. We must reach her before . . .'

203

A nameless horror gripped my throat, the same sensation I had felt when I saw their tongues, or veins, or whatever they were stretching between them. Like she was already linked to him.

'Before what?' Fen's voice was harsh and taut. 'Before what, Lil?'

'Before she is lost to us,' I said simply, though something inside my heart, something left there by Mamă, told me it may already be too late.

But still, I thought. *Lay death to rest.* Was it a threat? A plea?

I stood suddenly and took up Mamă's axe again.

'Come on,' I said. 'We don't have much time.'

Chapter Twenty-Four

We rode hard from the place my mother died.

My mind buzzed, raw and open as a wound after my vision. I felt I knew what was around each corner before we took it, saw new places with old eyes. And always, beneath it all, was the mottled breath of Vereski, keeping pace with my heartbeat though I tried to bury it.

After a half-day's gallop, I began to grow more confident that we were not being followed. Would the boyar care enough about two slaves and a kitchen girl to send men after them, especially so soon after the disgracing of his court by the Voievod's man? And had Vereski's murder been discovered?

Every time I thought of his touch on my skin, his beery breath on my cheek, my mind's eye flashed to the bloody pulp I had made of him, the murderer he had made of me, and I had to press myself harder against Mira's back to keep from falling.

My skin crawled to think of the punishment Malovski would inflict on Cook were the true events of the night uncovered. Even at a distance of miles, beneath the cover of trees, I thought I felt her gaze upon me, the vulpine baring of her teeth, pale make up cracking about scarlet lips, red as the thread connecting my sister to the Dragon. I wondered if Mira did too. She cast glances over her shoulder as often as me, sharp and searching.

I could not be sure how long our journey would take, and this uncertainty set my nerves on edge, but Fen seemed to have no such fears. The further we travelled, his joy at being back in the forest seemed to overwhelm even his worry for Kizzy. His guidance meant we found yew to make stakes like the vision showed me, and flint to strike fires, and a welling spring nestled in the crook of mossy larch roots. We ate berries and the nutty *Iele* mushrooms, and on the second night we formed a rabbit trap of moss-strewn twigs and got up a fire hot enough to roast the creature on. We slept beneath Dorsi's pelt, huddled in a pile, and prayed for dry nights.

Mira slept poorly: I could see it in the hollowing circles beneath her eyes, the irritable way she accepted her morning handful of foraged food. The Settled were unused to the outdoors, to being amongst it in such a constant, unending way. Even I found the lack of a wagon roof over my head disconcerting. But her hand often sought mine in the night, and that comforted me. I wondered how I had ever slept without it there before, and felt its absence as soon as I woke.

Fen slept like a child, curled into my side. It made me ache for Kem in a way I had mostly been able to bury till now. I wondered where my brother was, if Kizzy had reached the castle yet and found him. There had been no sign of him in my dark telling.

I listened to the trees, hoped to hear Mamǎ on the wind. The *Iele* could be playful or cruel as they were wise, but all the whispers I heard were tree murmurs, comforting and cradling. The horse and mule slept close to us, and I knew they would be the first to scent trouble.

But when trouble came, it was on the fourth day, and in no form I could have anticipated.

. . .

It was our last dusk before passing into the Voievod's territory, and we were readying to stop for the night. Our lives had settled into a sort of routine, rising early with the sun, riding past midday before eating a little, and then again until sunset. The Accursed Mountains towered to the east, and I was glad our path meant we could keep to the forests.

We were not foolish enough to try to navigate in the dark: that was the dominion of wolves, and we would be best not to intrude. We heard them hunting sometimes, their moon cry tingling across my skin, but never close enough to make the horses do more than start. Perhaps the *Iele* were offering us some protection since we ate their food.

We had paused to eat a handful of lingonberries, and to chew on dandelion roots for energy before we began the task of finding a clearing big enough to lie in for the night, when a noise came from around a bend in the road.

In this part of the country, tracks were little wider than our horses, snaking the same paths bears took to rivers. We always took care to make as much noise as possible, so the animals would know we were coming. But we had fallen silent over our meal, and when the horses started to side step, shaking their heads and whinnying, my first thought was that a bear must be close.

'Do you hear that?' said Fen.

I could hear branches snapping. I rose, taking up my axe, and saw Mira pull her yew stake from her waist. The best approach was to make ourselves big as possible, to look like foe, not food, and I took a wide stance.

The noise of breaking grew louder, like the bear was lumbering off the path, drunk on honey. I spread my feet, anchoring myself, readying a roar in my chest. But when a figure came hurrying round the corner, it was not a bear.

A man, running raggedly. His eyes were wide and wild, and in the growing dark I could see the glint of bared teeth. He looked deranged. I instinctively stepped back, out of his path, but Fen held up his hands in a gesture of peace.

'Are you—'

'Out of my way!'

The man barrelled straight into him, knocking him from his feet. Mira snarled and grasped at the man's cloak. He smelt of animal sweat and blood and the snow cold of the high mountains.

'What did you do that for?' Mira hissed.

The man's cloak tore in his urgency to escape, but his feet tangled and he fell into the dust beside Fen. Mira helped Fen to his feet as the man cast a hunted glance behind him, and continued dragging himself forward, attempting to rise to his feet. Mira went to grasp hold of him again, but I stayed her hand.

'Let him go.'

I realised then that the breaking sounds had not ceased. This man was being pursued. As I opened my mouth to voice this to Mira and Fen, a shape, small as a child, rounded the bend. It was cloaked in a thick pelt of some kind, and scurried rather than ran, like a rat. I could see no part of its skin.

'Oh Saints!' cried the man, and the fear in his voice stilled my heart.

The pursuing shape drew closer and as it did, I saw that it was indeed just a child. I thought it looked wounded and held my axe up to the man, still dragging himself away. Fen caught him and pushed him back. 'What is happening here?'

'Let me past, let me through!'

The child was closing in, and I caught sight of long, dark, matted hair. It was a girl. As she approached the man kicked out. His boot connected with the poor thing, and she stumbled back. I caught sight of a small hand, reaching out, blood dripping through its fingers. Fen caught hold of the man again and forced him down, a knee in his back to subdue him.

'It's all right,' I called to the child, but she scuttled off the path into the undergrowth, and I wheeled on the man. 'What are you doing? What did you do to that child?'

'Let me go!' He tried to throw Fen off, but Mira joined him in weighting him down, her stake balanced in her hand. I slowly approached the place where I had seen the girl enter the trees.

I glanced back at the man, assessing. Had he hurt her? His hands were bloodied too. I knew some Settled abandoned their children in the woods in times of starvation, and Cook had spoken of hard times near the mountains. Perhaps this was what we had encountered. Perhaps he had even gone so far as to wound her, to slow her down while he ran away.

I squinted through the undergrowth. There was no sign of the child.

'Let go!' The man sounded terrified. 'We need to get away from it!'

'From what?' asked Fen, grunting as the man's flailing arm hit him across the chest.

'My daughter. Or at least, it *was* my daughter, but now . . . oh Saints, let me go!'

I looked back into the undergrowth. I thought I could see a shadow, very still in the shade, watching me back. I reached out to it, but then there was a cry behind me. I turned, and saw that Fen was on his back, Mira clinging to one of the man's empty boots. The man was up and running, rounding another bend, and was gone.

Almost immediately, there was a rustle in the shadows, and the child was moving faster than I would have thought possible, breaking through the branches like paper, following after the man. Her speed was impossible, dark lightning flashing through the trees.

I ran too, with Fen and Mira, turning the corner just as the child broke through the undergrowth. It was like watching a hound catching scent, chasing down a hare. We could only watch, uncomprehending of what exactly it was that we were seeing, as the child launched herself at her father, jumping too high, much too high, and wrapped her small legs about his chest.

The man let out a yell and tried to push the girl off him. Her black hide made it hard to see what was happening, but he sounded in pain. Fen reached them first, and seized hold of the girl, trying to pull her from him, but though he managed to wrench her arms from about his neck, she still stayed attached to him, her head beside her father's throat.

Mira had stopped, still as stone with her stake hanging useless by her side, frozen by the man's desperate, gurgling cries, but I ran forward to help Fen. When I reached him, I saw the girl was still connected to her father. Her teeth were buried beneath his ear, and he was screaming and moaning, the wet sound of his throat filling with blood so awful, so like Vereski, that I wanted to be sick.

'Let go!' I screamed, wrenching at the child's cloak. 'Leave him!'

The cloak came free in my hand, and the girl's face was revealed for the first time. She was pale as moonlight, shining like new snow, her hair not dark at all, but blonde and matted with blood. Her mouth was large as a maw and unyielding, locked to her father's throat.

But as soon as the cloak fell away, and her face was exposed to the gloaming light of the early evening, the skin began to – I could think of no way to describe it – *bubble*. Just as the castle in my vision had blistered like a burning heart, her skin was scorching, weeping, and her eyes shot open.

They were red as blood, irises large and black as a fish's, or an owl hunting in the dead hours of night. Her hand scrabbled for the cloak, trying to pull it back over herself, but she was already crumbling.

'*Căcat*,' hissed Fen, and took her hair in his fist, wrapping it about his knuckles, pulling her back. She released her father and fell to the floor, keening like a wounded wolf. Her hands, where they reached for the cloak, were blistering too.

She writhed and snapped her teeth and clawed at her skin. I tried to cover her, my heart aching at the sight of her pain, but it was too late. With a great, heart-sore moan, she stilled.

CHAPTER TWENTY-FIVE

In death, her stained mouth parted, she looked like a child again. She was younger than I'd realised.

I reached out and touched her cheek.

'Careful!' said Fen, but any fool could see she was gone.

She was cold as if she had frozen to death, though her skin looked burned. My fingers came away powdery, her skin clinging like ash to my fingertips. It reminded me of our burnt caravans, the vision the *Iele* mushrooms had gifted me there.

I wiped my hand carefully on the mossy ground. I wanted no part of her on me.

Mira was crouching over the father, pressing her skirts to his neck. They were dirty after days travelling, but it was pointless to worry about infection. She manoeuvred him onto her lap, to try to elevate the wound, but I could see even at a distance he was not going to survive much longer.

There was still enough light to see the ground around them was sopping, dark as a night lake.

I left the girl and dropped to my knees beside him. His hands were clenching and unclenching on his chest, and I slipped my own into them. He flinched, his gaze snapping closer to, turning on me.

His eyes were brown, and I wondered if his daughter's had once been, too. His hands were warm, but they were cooling with every shimmering, shuddering heave of his chest. I swallowed. Was whatever sickness that had entered her now working its way through him?

As if seeing the question in my eyes, his lips began to move.

I brought my head closer to him, so close I could hear the gurgling words.

'Kill me,' he said. 'Kill me.'

'What is he saying?' said Mira.

I shook my head, as much to the man as to her. But he gripped at my wrist, and I lowered my head again.

'Before it makes a monster of me too.'

His hand was cooling fast, his skin losing pallor as I watched.

'What happened?' I asked softly.

'The Dragon,' he murmured, and I tensed. 'He would not let her die, and I would not let him drink of me.'

'Your daughter?'

215

'I tried to save her, but she would not die. I would not go with her, and I could not kill her.' His eyes flickered to mine. Their light was weak as a noon moon. 'I abandoned her to the dusk.'

I swallowed. 'What was she?'

He spoke the word into my ear. I drew back, understanding. His eyes pleaded, and before I could think further on it, I reached for Mira's stake.

'What are you doing?' she began, but before anyone could stop me, I lifted the sharpened stick and slid it between the man's ribs. Mira let out a cry and shoved me back, but I knew by the jerk of the man's body, the long slow hiss of his breath, his eyes growing glassy and sightless, that my stake had found its mark.

I had skewered the life from his heart.

Mira scrambled away from him, from me, eyes filling with angry tears. 'What are you doing? You killed him!'

'He was dying anyway,' said Fen. 'It was a mercy.'

'A greater mercy than you realise,' I said, holding up a placatory hand to her. 'He would not have died.'

'Not have died?' She grasped at the stain on her skirt, tears running down her cheeks. I longed to brush them away.

'Never,' I said. 'Not if we let the curse run its course.'

I pointed at the girl's body. She was naught but a mound of dust heaped on tiny bones. Fen sucked air through his teeth.

'Was he – were they . . .'

I nodded grimly, watching the dust lift and settle, like a flung breath. A wind would gather her up soon, but no *Iele* would let her walk with them. I hugged my arms to my chest as Mira looked from Fen to me, impatience mingling with her horror.

'What?' she said finally. 'What does this mean?'

'They were undead,' I said at last, the word bitter on my tongue. '*Strigoi.*'

Chapter Twenty-Six

Mira laughed, and the sound was harsh and unlovely as a howl. 'A *strigoi*?'

'Look,' said Fen. 'See with your own eyes. Settler or no, you cannot ignore what is before you.'

Mira grimaced down at the corpses. 'But *strigoi* are stories, made up to frighten children.'

'*Look*,' Fen repeated. 'That was no ordinary child.'

'She had a fever,' said Mira. 'Or had been bitten by a rabid dog. It happens.'

'She's ash, Mira,' I said calmly. I felt like I was floating above the scene, blood roaring in my ears. 'The sun made her ash. And she tried to drink the blood of her father.'

'What did he say,' snapped Mira, holding up her hand to quiet me. 'What did he say before you murdered him?'

Fen hissed, but I ignored the aggression, the accusation in her voice. She was afraid, just as I was. Just as the man had been. And – who knows? – perhaps as his daughter had been, too.

'He asked me to kill him.'

'That's convenient,' she said.

'And told me the Dragon had made his daughter a monster. He told me she was *strigoi*. They say the thirst for blood is like a madness – they must sate it. Even with their own kin.'

'You killed him,' said Mira. 'He was alive, he was beneath my hands. He was warm, he was breathing, he—'

'He would have been *strigoi* by morning,' I interrupted, fear making my patience snap like a thread. 'Can't you see it was kinder this way?'

Her breath hitched, and I caught her up in my arms. She pushed against me, but soon her struggles turned to weeping, and she pressed her face into my shoulder.

No one spoke, and the night drew in close, whispering in our ears. Eventually Mira quietened, her breath smoothing. She drew back, her face red and puffy.

'We should burn them, then?' she said, voice thick, and I knew that at last she believed me. These *strigoi* were dead, released from the between place at last, but it would be best to burn them. It was the only way to be sure they could not rise again.

There was not much left of the child to burn beyond the cloak. The man had not been full *strigoi* when he died and I could feel his flesh-and-blood body too solid around the stake I had pushed between his ribs.

My hands quaked as I helped drag him to the patch of ground Fen had cleared and stacked with tinder. It was worse than Vereski, this slaying, so much worse, because the man was an innocent, no matter that – what had he said?

I abandoned her to the dusk.

I felt his guilt like it was my own. Though his plea was for me to do as I had done, I was a murderer twice over. *I had no choice*, I told myself, again and again, but it made it no better.

Even the child, vicious as it was, was an innocent. I knew *strigoi* were damned by their desire for blood, the closest thing to a life force they could possess. They were fed and weakened by it. Despite my frustration at Mira's initial lack of belief, had I not felt the girl's skin powder beneath my fingertip I would have had a hard time trusting it too. Everything I knew about *strigoi* was from stories, but that didn't make the girl any less real.

As they burned, I swear they screamed.

. . .

There was no point feigning sleep. Even Fen couldn't settle, and we spent the first part of the night building another fire, our backs turned to the smouldering remains of the man and his daughter.

'He said the Dragon made his daughter that way?' said Fen, rubbing his jaw with a rasping sound. His stubble was nearly a beard. It made him look like a man. He would not look at me. I knew he was thinking of Kizzy, surely at the castle a couple of days now. 'So does that mean . . .'

He seemed unwilling to say it, so I did.

'The Dragon is a *strigoi*?' I swallowed. There was a sweet taste in the back of my throat that I did not want to think too hard upon. 'I think it must.'

'It would make sense,' said Mira, the tremor in her voice not yet faded. 'The stories we were told at the boyar's castle – I'm guessing they were not stories after all.'

'What did you hear?' said Fen, sitting and pulling his knees up to his chest: a child's pose with a man's beard. I felt a pull of love for him, this boy we had grown up with, who loved my sister enough to cross countries, to face monsters.

'He drinks blood,' Mira said in a near whisper. 'He has the fury and power of a dragon.'

I nodded. I had heard all this before, but Fen was rapt. I supposed they did not hear as much in the fields.

'The offerings have been happening for decades,' she continued. 'They always sent the best of us. They sent Cristina—' her breath hitched. I felt a wave of pity, and something else burning in my belly. 'She must be dead now.'

'Perhaps not,' I said, for lack of another response. 'Perhaps she is simply a servant.'

'Why did he become that way?' Fen asked. 'Was he once a man?'

Mira shrugged. 'Some say yes; others that he is a demon come to earth. But if he is a man, he must have made a soul pact, to become so powerful, don't you think?'

I blinked at her. I didn't realise Settled knew of soul pacts, the exchanges humans made with spirits. To do it was to be damned, one way or another.

She saw my expression and laughed. My heart gladdened at the sound. 'I'm not turning mystic on you,' she said. 'But that's something I heard. And now, after what we've seen . . .' She shivered, but did not look at the bodies, burning behind us. 'Perhaps I must believe it.'

'We need a plan,' said Fen, standing so suddenly it made me jump.

'Yes,' I said. 'If he really is a *strigoi*, and as powerful as we've heard, we need a way to fight him.'

Fen frowned at me. 'We can't fight him, Lil. The best we can hope for is to find Kizzy and escape.'

'You're happy to leave the others? She said they've taken people for decades.' I gestured at Mira. 'Her friend, and that child. You're happy for it to continue, so long as you have Kizzy back?'

'Where has this come from, Lil? You were content enough to live a life in your sister's shadow once. What's changed?'

His words cut, because they were true, and I shrugged off Mira's restraining hand. 'I know we can do this, that's what's changed. Mamă showed me—'

He snorted, incredulous, and I felt fury run through me like a blade. 'It's true, Fen. The *Iele* showed me this route—'

'Which led us straight into danger.'

'They showed me what awaits us,' I snapped. 'And they showed me Kizzy, dancing for him. I can end this, I know it. Perhaps the reason you only saw me in my sister's shadow was because that's where you expected me to be. But where is she now, Fen?' I stretched my arms out to the hushed forest. 'And where am I? Who killed that *strigoi*, who knew it for what it was?'

'It was obvious what it was,' he mumbled, but he sat back down. 'I don't want to fight with you.'

'Then stop saying such stupid things.'

He opened his mouth, closed it again, and laughed softly, shaking his head. 'You sound exactly like Kizzy.' He put his face in his hands, pressing hard. 'I miss her, Lil.' His voice was muffled and sad. 'I want her safe.'

'Me too,' I said, and reached out to him, my anger fading already.

He went on. 'Remember what Old Charani said? That a girl would be putting a promise ring on my finger before the year was out?'

I nodded and swallowed, remembering Cook's reading for Kizzy. *No husband, no children.* I could not tell him; it was too cruel. And besides, Old Charani had seen the ring, seen a marriage for Fen. Whose reading did I trust more, Cook or Old Charani's? I traced the lines on my palm. Would Old Charani have seen the same fate for me, as a *lăutari*?

'We should at least try to sleep,' said Mira.

Fen curled up where he sat, rolling away from us. His shoulders were shaking, and I wished his pride would let him ask for comfort, and that mine would let me give it unasked.

CHAPTER TWENTY-SEVEN

Mira and I lay down facing each other, her head on my arm. After a long while, the fire's warmth sinking into a steady, reddish glow, I heard Fen start to snore.

My eyes adjusted slowly to the darkness. Mira was still awake, still looking at me. Her eyes were glinting wells of silver moonlight. I could feel her breath, warm and alive, ruffling strands of my hair. They tickled my nose, but I didn't dare move. I didn't want to break the spell of her watching me, of her attention binding us like silver thread.

She reached out and brushed the strands away. Her fingertips were calloused with kitchen work. She still smelled faintly of sage and willowherb, and the green, living things of the forest.

Even in the dark, I could tell something in her gaze was different. Fierce and tender at once, mixed up inside one another. She did not take her hand away, but began to trace from my cheek to my ear. My skin tingled beneath her fingers, and I banished thoughts of how I had touched the child's fading face. I wanted to exist only in this moment, with this woman, in this forest, beneath the endless, starlit sky.

I was almost scared to breathe, and she hesitated. I placed my own hand over hers, to show I did not want her to stop. She edged a little closer, and her hand spread over my cheek. I nestled into it.

'Lil?' she said. Her voice was a soft breeze, her breath was the wild mint we chewed each night. I could taste it in my own mouth, was painfully aware of my breath coming a little louder, my heart hammering in my chest. There was warmth spreading through my entire body: I felt I could feel my blood pushing into all the edges of myself. I wanted to fold myself into her, to press along the length of her body, but not how the *Iele* had cleaved to me in the clearing. I wanted to feel her, warm and solid, against me. After our brush with the undead, I felt it was the only way to be sure I was alive.

'Lil,' she said again, and it was almost a sigh. Her hair was soft on my palm. Her smile was brief and sad. I moved closer, and our lips brushed. I paused for only a moment, before pushing my lips fully to hers. They were warm as blood.

The world melted away. I was smoke, or wind, held human only by the places our bodies touched. I had never kissed someone before and couldn't imagine ever wanting to kiss anyone else. She brought her leg between mine and I wanted to disappear entirely, the ache of wanting more was so painful. I pulled her to me, as quietly as I could, and a moan caught in my throat as her lips parted. We kissed as though we were born to fit together like this, as though my body was made for hers—

Fen shifted in his sleep, and we lurched apart. The night air was full of the murmurings of trees, the creaking of insects. I felt it was full of eyes, of judgement. But I couldn't feel ashamed. I could only feel Mira's heart pressed into my chest, hammering, and she threaded her fingers about mine as though we were woven together and could never be parted.

'Mira,' I started, but she closed my mouth with another kiss.

'Sleep, *dragă*,' she said. 'There is time enough.'

There would never be enough time: not for all eternity.

I rolled over and she moved up close to me, nipped my neck playfully. I melted like a kitten carried by the scruff. I wanted to weep, to feel such tenderness after our time in the castle. I thought I would never again know it. It was a gift: she was a blessing. But I had no words to tell her, and as tiredness pulled my lids closed, I prayed to the *Iele* to keep her safe, to keep us together, in this world where there was no place for us.

CHAPTER TWENTY-EIGHT

If Fen noticed the change between Mira and me, he said nothing. I thought it more likely he was simply too caught up in his own thoughts of Kizzy. And though every step brought us closer to danger, and though all our talk was of Kizzy and Kem and the Dragon, I could not help feeling – there was no other word for it – happy.

The guilt of feeling this way whilst Kizzy was in the Dragon's clutches was nauseating, but whenever Mira brushed her hand against mine, or pushed back into me as we rode, I felt a joy spreading through my body that was unlike anything I'd experienced before. It could not be love just yet, but it was something approaching it: a kinship deep and bright and strong.

Her hand in my hand, her lips against my lips, her thigh between my own, her heart beating in time with mine: all of it was a promise I could not keep. But I made it anyway, again and again. She brought me peace, even as we rode towards a sort of war.

But my dreams were far from peaceful. The closer we drew to the Voievod's lands, the worse they became. I saw, often, the castle, thrumming like a diseased heart, my sister and Albu dancing, the Dragon turning to smile at me, the line of red drawn between his and Kizzy's mouth snaking towards my own.

I'd wake screaming, and only Mira's forehead pressed to mine could comfort me. She'd stroke my nose with her rough finger, and though we could not kiss – I would wake Fen too, and besides, in those terrified moments I couldn't stand the thought of anything covering my mouth, even her lips – she'd flutter her wild mint words over my nape, or my wrist, and my heartbeat would slow.

The terrain grew more vertiginous. The forests became sparser, the hills cultivated in square pockets of green and gold, and we passed more people on the road. They watched us with wary, weary eyes, but there was nothing new in that for Fen and me.

Mira found it more unsettling.

'Why do they cross their fingers at us?' she said, as an elderly couple, their donkey bowed beneath kindling, hissed and made the gesture as they passed.

'I'll give you one guess,' said Fen, gesturing at his face. She blinked at him. I think she forgot we were Travellers, a

229

people marked apart from the rest of her countrymen. I loved her all the more for it, but still, it frustrated me how easily she could pass by with her head held high, and how Fen and I must shrink to make ourselves unnoticeable as possible. At night I felt we were growing together, entwining like roots supping the earth, but the looks in the daytime cleaved us again.

A full week and a day since Kizzy had been taken, we came across a village, nestled at the base of a hill. The road took us straight through, and though we had largely skirted any substantial dwellings, we needed supplies as the forest's shelter and provision dropped away.

There was no question of selling my axe, and none of us had left with anything of worth other than Orsha and Dorsi. Both were in good health despite the days of travelling, and we sold the mule easily, to a farmer who would only speak to Mira.

'Are you settling here?' he asked, eyeing us suspiciously. 'You'll need to see Boyar Calazan.'

Mira and I exchanged a look. So this village was under Calazan's dominion, in the realms of the pact.

'No,' said Mira. 'We're continuing north.'

The man made the sign of the cross, an arcane way to ward off evil. 'You know those are the Voievod's lands?'

'We do,' said Fen, but the man ignored him and turned again to Mira.

'You're best to stay here. I could use a house girl.' I didn't like the tone in his voice. His home was small and rundown – I doubted he had more than one place to sleep in there.

'I am not seeking employment,' said Mira stiffly. 'Are you not afraid, living so close to the Voievod?'

'Our master has an arrangement,' said the man. 'Brings him things he wants. Means he leaves the rest of us alone.'

His eyes traced over Mira again, and my hand twitched towards my axe. Kizzy had been a bargaining chip for this man's peace. It did not seem a fair price.

'What "things" does he bring the Dragon?'

The man shrugged. 'Don't know what you're looking for, but you won't find it north.'

'How many days is it to his castle?'

The man crossed himself again: it looked like a twitch. 'This is the last village before his lands. A day's ride.'

I looked at Orsha, standing docile by the house. I was not keen on taking her to the Voievod's lair. But she was a brave horse, and perhaps we would find somewhere safe to hide her.

The mule's sale had given us enough silver to buy a blade from the blacksmith, and the farmer begrudgingly sold us two hard loaves of a quality that confirmed his need for a house girl.

Our bellies stretched by the coarse bread, we rode on, taking turns to walk. As we passed through the scarce copses, Fen searched the trees for more yew.

. . .

In the end, it was not as Old Charani supposed. We did not melt easily into the Dragon's lands as ice into thawing rivers. The boundary was clearly marked by a fence we saw from the brow of the hill. At first I thought the wooden stakes were topped with *demoni*, as Boyar Valcar's castle had been. But as we drew closer, I saw the truth of it.

'*Căcat.*' said Mira. Fen, who was walking beside us, pulled up suddenly, placed his hands on his knees, and threw up. His portion of the coarse loaf splattered onto the ground.

I felt faint, and longed to look away. But my gaze was locked onto the horror of what I was seeing.

The twisted shapes, gaping mouths, monstrous limbs were not stone.

They were flesh, and bone.

They were people. People, impaled upon a fence of wood, stretching as far as I could see.

CHAPTER TWENTY-NINE

Orsha side-stepped, shook her head against the bit. The reins were slack in Mira's hands, and she let them drop. The horse cantered a fair bit back up the hill, Fen stumbling after us, before I could convince her to stop the mare.

I slid off the saddle and held the reins tight.

'Mira,' I said, gripping her ankle. 'Mira, you don't have to do this.'

She stared off into the middle distance, unresponsive. I knew she was thinking of Cristina. In all our night-time trysts she had never spoken of her, but I did wonder if they had been to each other what Mira was now to me.

Fen caught us up, gasping, clutching at a stitch at his side.

'You neither,' I said, turning to him. 'Neither of you need to come. You could take the horse and go.'

They exchanged a look. Fen's face was crumpled and bloodless. He wiped his mouth with his hand. Mira's face was blank, wiped clean by shock and what I recognised as the same numbing fury I felt churning inside myself. I forced myself to look back down the hill. My heart tolled like a death knell.

The castle was beyond that gate, and who knew what horrors awaited me there? All I knew for sure was that I wanted to get there before nightfall. I turned back to Mira and Fen, and he was standing beside the horse, his hands locked together, ready to help me up.

'Are you sure?' I said.

'Quickly,' said Mira, gesturing for me to get on. 'We have to reach the castle before sundown. Before they wake up.'

. . .

All of us kept our heads bowed as we crossed the threshold of the Dragon's boundary. For the first time, I understood his moniker. It was like walking into a dragon's lair. Traveller girls did not enter such places in stories. Knights yes, and other heroes. Never a girl seeking her twin, with naught but her dead mother's axe and some yew to save her.

Mira seemed to have shrunk inside herself since the sight of the impaled bodies. None of us felt much like speaking – there was nothing to say against the horror – but I longed to hear her voice, comforting as a kiss against my cheek. I wondered if Kizzy had seen the same sight, forced my mind away from the horrible possibility of her fate—

No. You saw her. You saw her dancing.

Other voices crowded me.

And Old Charani saw a promise ring for Fen.

And Cook saw none for Kizzy.

And where was Kem in all of this? Not the fence . . . *No.* There was no possibility but to push the thoughts down and go on, until we reached the top of the hill, the fence at its base a macabre necklace of uneven beads.

Before us, atop another hill, almost level, was the Dragon's castle. It was not, as I had seen in my vision, black and pulsing, like a malign organ. It was, with its whitewashed walls and the afternoon sun bearing down on reddish slates, almost beautiful.

The turrets were squatter than the ones on Boyar Valcar's castle, and rather than a dragon coiled atop a mountain, it looked like a stone forest, petrified trunks gleaming. Dread churned in my gut. I had learned my lesson from Malovski: just because something looked harmless, didn't mean it would not crush your throat.

We paused only a moment to stare, before plunging down into the valley. The fence dropped out of sight behind us, but I knew it would stay etched on my mind for all my days.

There was a collection of stone houses at the throat of the hill, but at a glance it was obvious they were abandoned. The roofs had blown away, or were caved in. The sight of the wooden struts, arrowing up through wisps of straw, made me shudder. They looked too like bone showing through tortured flesh.

I gripped Mira's waist tighter. Would I have been so glad of her presence this past week, had I known the terror of what I was leading her towards? Though the Dragon's reputation preceded him, I don't think any of us had approached, in our darkest nightmares, what we had just seen. Even the horror of the *strigoi* child had failed to impress upon me the depth of his depravity. What had turned his heart to stone? Had he been born a monster, or made one?

As we passed through the ghost village, a wind picked up, moaning against our faces and sending doors crashing about on broken hinges.

Orsha reared. Caught off balance, I fell, pulling Mira down with me. Her feet slipped the stirrups and she landed hard on me. I, in turn, landed hard on the handle of my axe, the shaft biting into my ribs.

We rolled up together as Fen tried to snatch at Orsha's reins.

'Woah!' he said, trying to calm her. 'Steady!'

Her hooves smacked down on the packed earth once, twice, quaking the ground. And then she was away, galloping fast up the hill we had just rode down. Fen gave chase for a few paces, but she was too fast, liberated from her load and fuelled by fear.

'Are you all right?' spluttered Mira.

I rolled onto my back and coughed, feeling for broken ribs. But we had had a lucky landing, and an even luckier escape from Orsha's hooves. I took Mira's outstretched hand and winced as she pulled me to my feet. She embraced me, hard, letting go reluctantly as Fen ran back into view.

'Anything broken?' he said. 'I thought she was going to crack your skulls.'

My mouth was full of dust, my eyes watering. I spat. 'I'm all right. I'm sort of glad she's gone. I felt bad bringing her.'

I craned my neck up at the castle. It seemed as abandoned as the village, and less innocent up close. The windows were black slits, emitting no light. It was too quiet, I realised, too still. There were no stakes on the walls, no *demoni*.

'It's so quiet. I can hardly believe he's in there.' said Fen.

'I know,' said Mira. 'But that fence . . .' she shuddered. 'Why protect a castle like that?'

'It's a taunt,' I said. 'No one can stop him.'

'Except you, right?' said Fen, then laughed weakly. But his words hooked into my chest, throbbed alongside the place where I had fallen on my axe.

'Look at the houses,' said Mira. 'They all have crosses on them, see?'

She was right. Above every door was nailed a wooden cross, or a mark where a cross must have been hammered in and then torn down. It was the same Settler superstition as the gesture the farmer had made, so I was surprised at what Fen said next.

'We should take some.' He was already sliding his blade beneath an intact cross, working it back and forth to loosen the nails.

'They obviously didn't work, Fen,' I said, gesturing at the ruins. But Mira joined him, gathering fallen crosses from the ground.

'Then why is the *biserică* the only building still standing?' He gestured behind me and with a jolt I saw the building from my vision: small and square and white. A church. The pointed roof was still thatched, the door pulled closed on unbroken hinges, the windows uncloaked.

'A place of safety,' I breathed. I placed my hand on the door and felt the same surge of energy as I had when I took hold of the yew stake. 'We can shelter here.'

'Now?' said Mira hopefully. No doubt she was already picturing sleeping with a roof over her head, shutting out the horror of our waking reality, if only for a few hours.

'You can,' I said, taking her hand. 'But there are still a couple of hours of light left. I must use them.'

'Surely it would be better to go in the dark,' she frowned, and then realised. 'Ah. But the *strigoi* can't be exposed to daylight.'

'Exactly. That girl only got so far because of her cloak at the cover of the forest,' I said, dropping her hand and rolling my shoulders. They crackled with tiny flames of pain up my back. 'We should get the lay of the land, see how hard it will be to get inside.'

I reached into my pocket and pulled out a handful of *Iele* mushrooms. The red ones had been diminished, but I still had a purple, for bringing on visions. Mira saw me considering it and placed a hand on my wrist.

'Isn't it dangerous? Last time your heart beat so fast I thought it would burst.'

Her hand was causing a similar increase in my pulse, and I moved away so I could think better.

'The *Iele* want to help us, I know it,' I said. 'They've got us this far and may have more yet to tell us.'

'If you take it now, we'll lose the light. You were gone for an hour last time.' Mira's eyes were fearful, and I longed to press a kiss to each eyelid.

I closed my own eyes and breathed deeply. She was right: there would be no time to scout the castle if I took the mushroom now. We had been riding towards this moment for days, and to stop now, to lose the forward momentum felt foolish. But the mushroom was cool in my sweating hand, and I longed to see Mamă again. Longed for her to tell me what to do.

I opened my eyes. Fen and Mira were looking at me, waiting for my decision. I thought of all the times I'd looked at Kizzy like that and knew that I could not rest without knowing I had at least tried to reach her as soon as I could.

Fen must have read my decision in my face, because he squared his shoulders, and turned to the castle.

Chapter Thirty

The road was cobbled, the stones slick though it had not rained in days. It was deserted, and when we reached the castle gates, the wooden doors were wide open. They looked like a leering mouth, waiting for us to walk inside before closing over us.

'Ready?' I asked Mira, who tightened her grip on her stake. She had not wanted a new one when Fen shared them out, and I saw the wood was dark with the man's blood. She nodded. We walked through the gate.

I half expected the doors to slam shut behind us, for *strigoi* to emerge from every corner and descend upon us, or at least for guards to swarm in at all sides.

But it was silent as a grave.

'Where now?' said Fen, examining the outhouses, uncomfortably similar to the boyar's. If we opened the stable door, I wouldn't have been surprised to find Vereski butchered inside. Even being in a courtyard like this brought back vivid, clawing memories, but I forced them aside.

Fen was already crossing to a low barn, Mira close behind. I followed. The windows were shuttered tight, and no sound came from inside. Fen took a deep breath and cautiously opened the door.

At first, I did not understand what I was seeing. I thought the barn was full of sacks, hung from the rafters. But when Mira clasped a hand over her mouth to stifle a scream, backing out as fast as she could, I understood.

They were people. Dozens of people, hanging from their feet. I thought I was seeing another horrific version of the fence, more dead bodies, but one shifted slightly at the sound of Mira's exclamation, and I realised it was almost worse.

These people were sleeping. Upside down, their feet hooked over the rafters like bats, or monstrous vines, strangling the wood. It would have been comical, like a child's game, if every face were not pale as bone, every eyelid red as blood.

'Out,' breathed Fen. 'Quickly.'

We did not need telling twice. The door closed before I could breathe again. We were lucky the last of the sunlight had not touched one of them: it would have set them screaming and brought two dozen *strigoi* down on our heads.

I longed to bar the door, set the whole place alight. With its straw roof, it would go up in minutes, taking every last damned soul with it. But we needed secrecy to find Kizzy, and the sound of shrieking *strigoi* would surely wake any other creature sleeping inside.

'Well Fen,' I whispered. 'Want to check in on any more *strigoi* dens?'

He snorted quietly despite himself, and shook his head, gesturing towards the castle. There was a large door with a set of stone steps leading up to it, well swept and scrubbed, and a smaller one, set low down in the foundations, and it was this one I pushed open.

It was unlocked. I supposed the Voievod didn't need to worry about intruders. The evil of the place settled over me like a shroud. Had he made all those people *strigoi*, like the child we had encountered in the woods?

Behind the door was a heavy woollen curtain, dyed black as night. My heart thudded, shaking my whole body, but I felt Mira's hand, cool against my wrist, and calmed my breath. I gripped my yew stake and pushed the curtain carefully aside.

I barely registered a corridor, broad and dimly lit with torches, before something rose up from the floor. Fen pulled me back, wrenching open the curtain with the other hand. The last of the daylight illuminated a face, eyes gummy with sleep but waking more every moment.

He did not howl, or cower from the light, or dissolve. It was a man. His face was bearded, his eyes blue and wide with surprise. I wondered what we must look like, from our days and nights in the forest, the blood of the *strigoi*'s father still splattering our clothes.

At his breast was stitched a crest: a dragon curled about a heart, the same crest Boyar Calazan had borne. We blinked at each other a moment, before he opened his mouth as though to shout, his hand reaching for his sword.

We acted as though it had been planned. Mira threw her full weight at his arm, sending the sword clattering away into the dim corridor. I pushed the handful of curtain I held into his mouth, stifling his cry. His teeth scraped against my hand as he bit down, leaving my fingers bloody, and Fen grasped hold of his other arm, kicking at his knees until he went down.

We pinned him in place, his breathing loud and ragged through his nose. I sat astride his shoulders and leant down to whisper in his ear.

'I don't want to hurt you, but if you scream I will cut your throat.'

Even saying the words, even hearing his breathing like that, so loud and heavy like Vereski's in the stable, made me nauseous. But there was something else in me, something desperate and dangerous as a cornered dog, that made me certain I could carry through the threat if forced to it. For Kizzy, I could make myself a murderer a hundred times over.

The guard must have realised this, because he stopped struggling almost instantly, going limp beneath us.

243

'Good,' I said, making my voice steady and low, a tone that I learned from Malovski. 'I'm going to move slightly, so you can nod or shake your head. Are there more of you?'

He nodded. Fen looked down the corridor, his jaw clenched.

'Nearby?' I asked. He shook his head. 'But more guards, more men?'

Another nod. Mira sucked in air through her teeth.

I nodded grimly. Calazan's men would guard the castle in the daytime; *strigoi* would swarm the place at night. Rescuing Kizzy seemed like an impossible task. I knew we'd rather chance the men, but it was a close, and unpleasant, call. We needed a plan, and for that, we needed somewhere to be safe.

'The church,' I whispered to Fen and Mira. 'We need to go back to the church.'

'What about him?' Fen looked at the man. He was choking a little on the curtain, his eyes wide and glinting at me. I could not kill him in cold blood.

'He's coming with us. I think he'll be useful.'

Fen looked ready to argue. He took up the man's sword, but I knew he could no more sink it into a defenceless person than I could. Fen slid the sword into his belt. Mira nodded her agreement and the three of us hauled him to his feet.

He was tall, but slight, and gave no argument as I sliced the curtain free with my axe, using the extra length of it to bind his hands, knotting it tight. We pulled the door closed behind us and crossed the courtyard hurriedly. I cast a look at the barn full of *strigoi* and shuddered.

The light was falling fast as we reached the church. Mira loosened her grip on the man and pushed at the door. It would not open.

'It's locked,' she said, leaning against it.

'Can't be,' said Fen, gesturing. 'No lock.'

He was right: the area beneath the handle was smooth, with no place for a key. He ran his hands across it and shook his head. 'Must be jammed. Move out the way.' Mira took his place holding the man as Fen took five big strides backwards.

'What are you—' I began, but, before we could stop him, he ran at the door, shoulder forward, slamming into it with all his weight.

The door didn't budge, and Fen was sent ricocheting backwards, toppling over and falling in a moaning heap at our feet.

'Fen!'

Mira and I crouched beside him, pulling the guard to his knees. Fen's teeth were gritted, and he hissed, 'I think it's locked.'

I bit back a laugh, but Mira snorted, and I was too slow to look away. We caught each other's eye and both began to laugh. It was as if all the horror of the past hours, days, weeks of our lives was forgotten, and I laughed so hard no sound came out and I was gasping for breath.

'It . . . hurts . . .' wheezed Fen through his laughter, still wincing from his shoulder. 'Stop . . .'

But it only made us laugh more. The guard looked between us, nonplussed.

Mira was first to recover herself, sitting up, her stubbled head dusty and cheeks flushed. She looked so beautiful, with the worry lines that had been etched between her eyebrows smoothed, her mouth still wide in a smile.

Something sharp stuck its haft between my ribs and twisted. I longed to reach for her, to pull her back down to the ground, but she dragged the guard to his feet again and I stood with them, offering my hand to Fen.

We brushed ourselves down, and I turned back towards the church. Now I was certain we had to get in, that the doors had been barred for a reason that would be useful to us. Fen's attempt had made no mark on the door, and the windows were too high and small for us to climb through.

'Is there a key?' I asked the guard, and he shrugged. He looked warier than ever since our hysterics, and I wondered if he thought we were lunatics. As I pulled Mamã's axe from my belt, I thought he was not far wrong.

'Stand back.'

CHAPTER THIRTY-ONE

The air was close inside the church. Close, and wrong. It didn't smell of must and burnt-down candles. It smelt of death: not the instant, sharp metal tang of blood, or even of rot – but like a tomb, the air ringing with stillness.

I hesitated on the threshold, peering through the shattered door, cleaved enough to scatter light across the church floor. From the smell, I knew what I would see, and I was right.

Bones, so old they were not even bodies anymore, just piles ranged along the flagstone floor and on the wooden pews. More bones on the altar, and at my feet. Here and there, the earth had broken through the gapped flagstones and breathed green life into the room: moss and mushrooms and small white yarrow. There was nothing to fear here, and much to grieve.

'What is it?' said Fen, and I moved aside to let him see.

'Oh,' he said, and the sound was like a child sighing for their mother.

I reached past him, through the gap Mamă's axe had made, and felt for whatever was blocking the door. My hand found a metal bar laid across the centre, and I was able to push it free.

We stepped inside, bones shifting before us.

'Were they killed?' said Mira angrily, rounding on the guard. Fury blazed strong in her eyes and he flinched, but Fen laid a hand on her shoulder.

'These people have been dead decades. I doubt he had a hand in it.'

'And there's no violence,' I murmured, looking at a small huddle of bones laid next to a larger pile. It was too easy to picture a child, tucking its small shape into the side of its mother. My chest panged for Kem. 'I think these people locked themselves in, to try to be safe. So the *strigoi* didn't get to them.'

'In the daytime,' said Mira, still angry, 'it must have been men who kept them scared.'

It was true. Boyar Calazan's men had left them here to starve.

I swallowed. All my life I saw my inaction as harmless. I was happy to stand by while Kizzy made decisions, while she ran toward danger or threat, answered back to insults. I thought my silence, my stillness, was a fine way to be. But now I realised it made me as bad as those men who took the side of a monster, who watched a locked door as children starved to death inside.

I placed my hand on the small skull. From the moment I had saved myself from Vereski, I thought something of Kizzy's bravery was in me. But perhaps this was me, now. Perhaps I had changed.

I straightened, and carefully moved the bones aside.

'Put him here.'

Fen and Mira manoeuvred the guard inside. He reeled at the sight of the bones, struggling as Mira tried to make him sit. Fen drew his sword and hit the pew, hard. The man stilled, sat.

'Mira, watch him.' I handed her my axe. 'We need to secure this door.'

The light was fading fast, the dusty air of the church blue-grey in the twilight. We pushed any pieces of wood still clinging on back into place and replaced the metal bar. I searched for candle stubs while Fen dragged a heavy wooden table to the door, heedless of the snapping sounds as he heaved it onto its side. This drowned the light completely, and while he checked it was leant securely against the door, I lit the ends of the candles, so we were suffused in a low, flickering light that made the skeletons gleam.

Satisfied we had done all we could to keep the church secure, I turned my attention to the guard. His face was downcast, his eyes closed, and I could smell his fear. We were lucky to have stumbled upon a guard like him, rather than like Vereski. This man had something to live for beside his own twisted desires. A family, perhaps. He could be useful.

Checking the knot tying his hands was holding firm, I pulled the curtain free of his mouth. He collapsed forward and retched, spitting onto the church floor.

'Please,' he said, tears staining his cheeks. 'Please, don't kill me.'

'I'm surprised you don't kill yourself, working for the Dragon,' spat Fen.

The man laughed bitterly. 'You think I have a choice? I am a soldier.'

A servant with a sword. Malovski's words came to me unbidden.

'A soldier for a monster,' snapped Fen.

'I must do what I am told if my family is to eat.'

I had been right, then. I felt a surge of hope. I knelt beside him, holding out my hands to show I was unarmed. 'What is your name?'

A trail of snot glistening beneath his nose as he looked at me, and quickly away.

'I am Lillai.'

'Don't give him your name,' hissed Mira, but I shushed her, not taking my gaze from the man's face.

'Lillai,' he said, as though testing how my name felt in his mouth. 'I'm Tamás.'

'Please, Tamás. We need your help.'

He looked me full in the face for the first time, and his cheeks blanched. The horror I saw in him was absolute, as though he looked into an endless pit.

'You're her,' he moaned. 'You're his.'

'What?'

'Is this a trap?' His eyes were brimming with tears again. 'Are you going to kill me?'

'I don't—'

'He thinks you're Kizzy,' said Fen, in a flat, deadened tone. 'Don't you? You think she's the girl who was brought to the Dragon?'

I watched Tamás's face as he examined me more closely and found my face beneath my sister's features. His whole body slackened, and I had to put a hand out to keep him from falling.

'You're not. But you look . . .'

'I'm here for my sister. Kisaiya.' Even as I said it, my dread grew teeth that gnawed at my belly. 'What did you mean, she is "his"?'

'You're her sister?' He looked dismayed.

'Her twin.'

'I am so sorry,' he said, and his voice held real tenderness.

'What?' said Fen harshly, taking the man by the shoulder and shaking him. 'Sorry for what?'

'Fen!' cried Mira, trying to pull him off. 'Let him speak.'

'Then speak,' said Fen, pacing amid the bones. 'Tell us.'

Tamás hung his head. 'You would be best to ride fast from this place. There is nothing left for you here.'

'Is she dead?' Fen was trying to sound threatening, but his voice had a crack in it, that widened as he went on. 'Did he kill her?'

Tamás shook his head, and when he finally heaved a word into his mouth, his voice was hoarse. 'Worse.'

We all knew what he meant. My sister, my bright, beautiful, blazing sister, was worse than dead. She would never die a natural death, and I would never feel her touch, warm upon my skin, ever again.

My throat was tight, my skin crawling. I felt very hot, as though fire licked upon my back and into my head. I suddenly felt every moment of our journey, from Vereski to the forest, the *strigoi* girl to the impaled bodies.

The church span, and Mira wrapped her arms around me, kissing away tears I did not even know were falling until I felt her lips on them, and then her lips salt on mine. She only brushed them against me for a moment, but it was enough to centre me.

When I pulled my eyes from her face Tamás was staring at us, looking from one to the other, an unpleasant mix of disgust and intrigue on his face. Fen pushed his cheek roughly to the side.

'Don't look at them like that.'

I glanced at my Traveller brother and saw his cheeks were wet with tears too. The look on his face told me he'd known about me and Mira for a while, perhaps since the beginning. There was nothing in his face but love, and sadness.

I wanted to hold him, but there was no time. Kizzy may well be lost to us, but Kem and Albu were not.

'A bear,' I said, so suddenly that Mira startled. 'Did he have a white bear?'

Tamás blinked at me, and I shook him, my patience gone. 'A bear, that she dances with?'

'Yes,' said Tamás. 'Yes.'

'And is there a boy? He's ten, but looks young for his age. He could be much younger to your eyes. He looks like me, with the same curly hair.'

Tamás's brow creased. 'There were many Traveller children passing through. He keeps them sometimes, sometimes he sells them. Sometimes he kills them.' I flinched and wondered if he would talk of his Settled companions' fate with such nonchalance.

'This boy though,' I said. 'He came with the bear.'

Tamás shook his head slowly. 'I'm sorry. I don't know. They all look the same.'

I resisted an urge to strike him, honed from years of ignoring such comments from Settlers. Mira, however, didn't. She hit him hard across the cheek.

'It is only because of this Traveller that you are alive. I would gladly cut you down,' she said. 'In fact, perhaps I shall do so. Lil?'

I knew it was an act, but I appreciated it anyway. 'Leave him,' I said. 'Tell us where the children are kept.'

Tamás shuddered. 'In the dungeons. Just through the corridor where you found me. He let most of them go, though, after – your sister arrived.'

I frowned. 'Why?'

He shrugged. 'No idea. We took them to the forest. We're used to doing that, but usually at night, so the *strigoi* can hunt.' He at least had the decency to look ashamed as he spoke this. 'But this was in the morning, so they had time to get past the boundary. They had a good chance.'

I clenched my jaw, thinking. What had Kizzy's arrival done to warrant their release? And had Kem been among them? Mira tucked a strand of my hair behind my ear.

'What do you want to do, *dragă*?'

CHAPTER THIRTY-TWO

It was a restless night. Only Tamás slept, waking himself up occasionally with his snores. I half-admired him being able to close his eyes, when from outside, all night long, came unnatural swooping sounds, like massive birds taking flight. Shadows chased along the walls, and none of us turned to look at the windows.

My thoughts chased each other through the dark as Fen and Mira whispered ideas and plans. It must have been past midnight when the candles burnt down, and they spoke on in the blackness. But my thoughts kept circling back to the *Iele* mushroom in my pocket. The first vision had guided us this far – it was time. Perhaps it could tell me more of Kizzy's fate, and Kem's whereabouts.

'The mushroom,' I murmured. Though my voice was soft, I heard both Mira and Fen jump. They had grown used to my silence, and I spoke the words again.

255

'Are you sure?' said Fen, and I heard a spark of hope in his voice.

'I don't want you to,' said Mira, groping for my hand and finding it. 'It can't be safe.'

'Mamă left them,' I said. 'All will be well.'

She squeezed my hand in assent, and I felt for the purple mushroom. I put it in my mouth, chewed, swallowed. The same surging filled my body, and I remained only long enough to feel Mira catch me as I fell.

I rose through the church roof. There were bodies knitted into the thatch, scattered to bones even as their fingers grasped for sanctuary. Up I flew, and when Mamă took my hand, she was not the only one beside me.

The air was full of dark shapes, swirling and moving as one, like starlings home after winter. But these were no birds. They were not even human. Their skin glittered like frost, their eyes red as holly berries, glowing like hot coals in the black. I wanted to scream, but I had no voice, and Mamă pulled me higher, above the clouds, so the swooping *strigoi* were obscured from view.

The next moment we were plunging, plunging so fast I swear my heart stopped. Past the *strigoi*, through the church roof, through the floor of bones, to a passage in the earth. My mouth felt full of dirt as we followed it, so fast it was a smudged blur, and when we rose again, this time we were not in a hall, with Kizzy and Albu.

We were bellying through the corridor we had taken Tamás from. More *strigoi* wafted through the stone channels, and I turned my eyes away. We passed through them like mist.

We slid down a set of stairs, unguarded now the *strigoi* roamed, and found a long row of doors. One pulsed with heat. I had time to count *one, two, three* doors along, and then Mamă took me away again, this time to the hall once more, where a girl was dancing—

I leaned forward, willing us faster. Now I would know. Now I would see what was done, and if it could be undone. But just as we drew close enough for me to make out Kizzy's face, I was being pulled back, as though jerked on a hook. Even as Mamă tried to grip me, I felt myself slipping from her.

No, I thought. *It is not over.*

But now there was pain at my scalp, and I snapped back into my body, into a dark church full of bones, and the sound of shouting all about me.

I tried to sit up, but my hair was caught fast beneath something. I could hear Mira crying, 'No!' and Fen swearing, and then my hair was loosened as Tamás's boot crashed down beside my head, stumbling away in the gloom. From the glint in his hand, I could see he had his sword back. He must have wrested it from Fen whilst they watched me as I flew. I felt for my axe, and the stake for good measure.

'Tamás,' I said, my voice steady. 'What are you doing?'

'That's Traveller magick,' he hissed, and the fear in his

voice told me he was beyond reason. 'You're dangerous.'

'Not to you,' I said. 'If you only calm down.'

But there was a scrabbling sound, and then a loud scrape. Fen started forwards, and I heard the slice of the sword through still air.

'Back, Fen. Leave him. Tamás,' I said again. 'If you go out there, they'll kill you.'

'I'm Calazan's man,' said Tamás, his voice shaking with poorly suppressed nerves. 'There's a pact.'

'They won't give a damn about the pact when they scent you,' said Mira. 'We've seen a girl try to murder her own father.'

'We have his word,' he said, seeming to warm to his idea of safety. 'I will not be harmed.'

'You will be murdered!' cried Mira.

But her words were lost to him. He wrenched the barricade clear and pulled open the door. The three of us ran forwards, rushing to replace it. Fen and Mira hurried to right the wooden table, but I paused a moment after I replaced the metal bar, peering through the hewn slices of the door.

Moonlight cast everything in silver. The bare head of Tamás, running for the castle. The soles of his boots, slapping the slick cobbles. Even his cry sounded metallic as he tried to raise the alarm. And then there was the glitter of the *strigoi*'s skin, as they swooped down, and smothered him. Their teeth glinted and flashed, working like blades, until he stopped screaming.

CHAPTER THIRTY-THREE

We found the location of the hidden route from the church to the castle with little trouble, but unearthing it was another matter. It was barricaded better than the door, piles of stones and furniture placed over a great slab of rock.

Daylight began to grow as Fen searched the church for rope, knotting curtain sashes together, and we devised a hoist slung over a low beam to remove the heavier stones. We worked as fast as we could, but the rope kept snapping and had to be reinforced.

After our third try, Fen went out into the sunny village to scavenge for something to help us. Mira and I didn't speak, only sat with our arms around each other, breathing one another in. It was almost lovely, even here.

Fen returned with a long length of rope, a canvas that might have been a sail, and Tamás's sword and tunic. Both were spattered with blood.

'What did you bring those for?' Mira asked, wrinkling her nose. This time we had not sprang apart when he arrived, and it felt good to hold her hand, and have him see it.

'I thought it could be useful,' he said, placing everything down, and pulling on the tunic. Something clinked, and his eyes widened.

'What?'

Wordlessly, he pulled out a set of keys, linked on a small metal ring. He threw them to me, and I caught them.

'All right,' I said, grinning. 'I'll admit they could be useful. But what's with the costume?'

He had hauled on the tunic. It was long on the body, and tight on the arms, but with Fen's dark trousers it was an almost passable uniform.

'You need boots,' said Mira. Fen grimaced, and went out again, returning with the dead man's boots on his bare feet.

We continued to work, fashioning the sail into a sling, and rewrapping the rope so it would hold. Soon we were able to make out that beneath all the debris was a tombstone. It was worn smooth with age, but we could see that it was marked with a single word.

Dracul. Dragon.

This, then, was where he should have lain to rest, and taken his evil with him. But instead, when we heaved the slab off, breaking it in two, we found an empty maw, emanating a demonic chill.

'There really is a passage,' said Fen, and I shot him a sharp glance.

'Of course there is.'

'I wonder who made it,' said Mira, frowning. 'Not the Dragon, surely. *Strigoi* can't enter churches, can they?'

'No,' I said, with more certainty than I felt. But I had no better ideas. I looked at the pit. My skin prickled, and not even Mira's touch could soothe me. But still, I lowered myself down. The tunnel was only waist deep, and I swallowed down a rising nausea.

'We're going to have to crawl.'

Mira jumped down next to me. 'So we crawl.'

There was no hope of light in such dark. Soon the sun-filled church was behind us, and I felt I had been cold and in darkness for ever. I have never had cause to be afraid of small spaces, but this was a primal fear, the earth of the passage loose and crumbling, the whole weight of the castle poised overhead.

I closed my eyes, unable to bear the physical press of the darkness, and felt my way forward. All I could hear was my own breathing, and the breaths of Mira and Fen. Mira occasionally gripped my ankle, just to tell me she was here. *Still with me*, I thought. Even there, that simple fact was a comfort.

After what felt like hours, but could not have been more than minutes, my forehead struck something hard. I felt above me, and to my relief found an iron ring pull, fierce with cold. One hand on my axe, I crouched beneath it.

'Ready?'

'Yes,' said Mira.

I twisted the handle and pushed my shoulder to the door. The trapdoor ground on its hinges but did not swing up. 'It's stuck.'

'Maybe Fen could take a run at it,' said Mira.

'Ha,' said Fen mirthlessly. Mira crawled up beside me, and we pressed our bodies together. I twisted the handle once more, and this time when we placed our shoulders to the rough wood, it grated open.

The noise was awful in the echoing tunnel. I saw that we had emerged into a stone corridor. I looked left and right but there was no one there.

'All clear,' I whispered, and hauled myself out, Mira following behind. Together we pulled Fen up onto the wooden floor and lowered the trapdoor. It was a seamless fit, the lines running smoothly from one join to the next, but the rust from the hinges had left a dark red smear. I kicked some rushes over it, sending staleness into the air.

There were wooden doors set along it, just as Mamă had shown me, and I counted *one, two, three*. 'This one,' I whispered, pulling out the keys. My fingers felt numb with nerves and I fumbled them. Could it really be that Kem was just the other side of this door?

'Calm, *dragă*,' said Mira, and took the keys, trying and swapping them until she found the right one. 'This one fits.'

She moved aside, and I placed my hand on the doorknob. Fen stayed my hand.

'Are you sure?'

I pressed my ear against the wooden door. I could hear a sound, like a dog whimpering.

'What is it?' he whispered.

'A child,' I hissed back, shrugging him off. I opened the door, and the crying stopped.

Before me there were four children, two girls and two boys, huddled together. They were all young, but none were Kem. My heart tumbled. None were pale and blood-eyed either, and I moved hurriedly inside. Fen and Mira hovered on the threshold, watching.

The children shrank back, and I noticed one hadn't moved. A girl, lying prone on the floor. I held out my palms to them in a gesture of peace.

'It's all right,' I said. 'I won't hurt you.' I sheathed my axe, turned my face to the flames so they could see my skin did not glitter and that my eyes were brown, not red.

'I'm Lil,' I said. There was no response. I tried again. 'Lillai. I'm looking for my brother, Kem. He looks like me a bit.'

None of them spoke. The girl's nose was running, and her leg was shaking as she stood, shielding the unconscious child from sight.

'Hello,' I said to her. 'What's your name?'

'You're the dancer,' she said hoarsely, voice thick with tears. 'You're his.'

Her face twisted with fear, and something else, something cold and glinting, that aged her young face. Hatred.

'No,' I said, palms still outstretched. 'I'm not. I have a sister though, Kizzy. Is that who you mean?'

A little boy hissed. 'You are, you're her.'

'We're twins,' I said. 'We look alike. I swear, I'm not her.'

Even as I protested, my heart felt heavy as a stone. What had Kizzy been made to do, to make Tamás and these children fear her?

'It's true,' said Mira, stepping in after me, and at the sight of her pale skin they shuddered. 'We're looking for the dancer though, and her bear.'

'They're his,' repeated the girl, staring at me suspiciously. 'You're really not her?'

'No,' I said. 'I'm her sister. Are you their sister?' I gestured at the two boys, and the figure on the floor.

She nodded. 'They got Olga. She's our big sister. They took her and she won't wake up.'

'Can I see?' said Mira, and the boys moved aside. Olga was lying very still, pale as a *strigoi*. There were two holes by her neck, neat as pinpricks. I would not have seen them had I not known what to look for.

Mira reached out, and the little boy went as though to stop her, but I said, 'It's all right. She's good at healing.'

This seemed to calm him, and the siblings watched as Mira lifted Olga's eyelid. Her eyes were blue, and glassy. Mira lay her fingers to the girl's neck. She looked up at me and shook her head. The girl was dead, then. But she had escaped a worse fate. She was not to be a *strigoi*.

I turned to the girl and boys. 'What's your name?'

The boys looked down at the floor, but the girl answered. 'Alina.'

'Where's your home?'

'A long way,' said Alina. 'Our father sent us. There wasn't enough food, and they would send him some if we came. They said we were heroes.'

'You should get out of here,' I said, swallowing down my anger. What sort of father would send his children to such a place? 'Now, before night comes. We have a way—'

'It's too far,' Alina said. 'Olga says . . .'

'I think Olga would want you to go,' I said. 'She can't wake up just now, but there's a village over the hill. We can show you the way out.'

Tears trailed down Alina's cheeks. 'They told us to wait. We have to do as they say, or they won't let us sleep. They took Olga, so she can sleep now. It's my turn next.'

I sat back on my heels, thinking fast. 'Did they say they would take you?'

She nodded. 'Soon, maybe. He had made a promise, we heard, to your sister and that meant that the other children were let go. But not us. He wanted Olga. She was to be kept a secret from your sister.'

Bile roiled in my throat. Placing what Tamás told me next to this, I was starting to understand what might have happened. 'So you're a secret from her.'

'Only adults now, that's her rule,' said Alina. 'But we were special. A boy too, but he's going to the hall tonight.'

'The hall?'

'That's where Olga went.' She cocked her head. 'He looks like you.'

My heart hammered. 'Like me? Brown skin, brown hair?'

Alina nodded. 'The bear dancer chooses. Since she arrived, she chooses. I don't know why she chose him.' She sounded almost jealous, and I wondered what warped thinking had been bred into this girl, both here and at her village, where they told these children they were heroes.

'And he's going to the hall tonight?'

'Yes,' she looked down at her sister. 'Will Olga wake up soon?'

I reached out a careful hand, and placed it on the girl's shoulder. She didn't move away, only looked up at me with searching eyes.

'Alina,' I said, a terrible weariness coming over me. 'Olga can't wake up.'

Her small face grew fierce, her eyes narrowing. 'Don't say that.'

'I'm sorry–'

She knocked my hand from her shoulder. 'Go away.'

'Alina–'

'Go away or I'll scream!'

I looked helplessly up at Mira and Fen. Fen's face was crumpled, and Mira's eyes shone with tears.

'Take your brothers and leave, Alina. It would be best, safest.' Alina's lower lip wobbled. 'That's a way out.' I pointed at the trapdoor. 'We'll leave it ajar, and the door unlocked. You can go now.'

'We won't,' said Alina, turning back to her sister.

'Then we'll come back,' I said, and stood, leaving in my wake another promise I wasn't sure I could keep.

Chapter Thirty-Four

After letting our eyes readjust to the dark, we moved through the corridor to the steps ahead. We climbed them quickly and found ourselves in the corridor where we had found Tamás. There was no guard replacing him, and the ragged curtain still hung torn from its rail.

I felt sad for him, so strong in his belief that a crest could save him, so unimportant to his master that his absence had likely not even been discovered.

'This way?' whispered Fen, and I knew he felt the same urgency to discover what lay at the end of our journey. I nodded, and we crept along the corridor, towards another thick curtain. Fen pulled it aside.

A guard stood there, his back turned. His head whipped around.

Fen quickly grasped Mira and I by the wrists and threw us down to our knees. In his uniform he looked like any other guard. 'All right?'

The guard ran his eye down Fen's body, from his boots to the crest on his tunic, and finally to his face. He wrinkled his nose. 'Where's the other one? Tall fellow, skinny.'

'Tamás?'

The man shrugged and looking up from the floor I could see he wasn't really concerned, only paying due diligence to this new arrival.

'Sick,' said Fen. 'Sent me in his stead.'

'Right,' said the guard. 'Didn't know there were any free Gyptians round these parts.'

'I'm not a Gyptian,' said Fen, bristling. It was not a lie. We did not acknowledge that word.

I looked up through my hair. The guard looked puzzled. 'No offence meant.'

'None taken,' said Fen.

'What are these?' I ducked my head as the guard looked down at us. 'More of the secret stash?'

It will never not feel like violence, to be talked of like that, I thought.

'Yep,' said Fen, managing to keep his voice steady. 'What's all that about, anyway?'

The guard hoiked some spit up his throat and blew it out of his nose. It glistened on the floor before me and I closed my eyes.

'Seeing as you're new . . . Since that uppity one arrived, he's taken a liking to her. The master. So, she's got demands

– don't they all?' He guffawed and Fen laughed through gritted teeth. 'And one is no more kids. Which I have to say will make my life a lot easier. They hate me down at the village.' He belched, and I thought, *I wonder why.* 'But the pact keeps us safe, and that's what you've got to focus on. It's a tough job, but someone's got to do it.'

'But there are still kids here,' said Fen, in a casual voice. 'How's that?'

'He's keeping them in case she changes her mind.'

I tensed at that, and I could tell Fen had recognised the possibility too. The possibility that we were not too late for Kizzy.

'Changes her mind?' said Fen.

The man shuddered, but I could tell he was enjoying holding court like this. My knees were aching on the stone, and my shoulders twisting with the effort of looking like my hands were bound in rope. I wondered when the guard was going to notice that Mira and I were not actually tied up.

'Look, I don't know much about it. We all clear out around dusk. I've never seen one of the . . . you know. The creatures. But don't ask questions, as I said, and you can make a good living here.'

'Changed her mind how?' Fen repeated, and I knew he had pushed too far. The guard was squinting at him.

'Why are you here again?'

'Bringing them to the hall,' said Fen, forcing his voice to be casual. 'They're part of the feast tonight.'

'Oh,' said the guard, eyebrows raised. 'I thought it was just the one.' He gestured toward a set of wooden double doors, higher than anything I'd seen in the boyar's castle.

'Change of plan,' said Fen, pulling us to our feet and already edging us towards the doors. 'Anyone else in there?'

'Just the boy. Others are all in the den.' The guard narrowed his eyes. 'This is on the Dragon's orders?'

Fen took a step forward. 'Who else's? Perhaps you would like to check with him personally?'

The guard blanched and swallowed. 'Right. Well then,' he said, arm across his face. 'I'll see you tomorrow, er . . . what did you say your name was?'

Fen had reached the door, and had already pushed it open, shoving us through. 'I didn't.'

He closed the door behind us, and collapsed onto the floor, sweating.

'You are a terrible liar,' said Mira.

'We're in, aren't we?' said Fen, who still looked amazed at the fact.

'We are,' I murmured. My head span as I looked around us.

It was the room from my vision, shadowy and massive as a cave. There was the space, cleared at the centre where Kizzy would dance. There was the table, where the Dragon would sit, smiling. And there – there in the centre of the room, was a chair.

And on the chair, was Kem.

His head was bowed, but I would know the dark mass of curls anywhere. He was shrouded in a massive cloak, and as I ran towards him, I saw it was a bear pelt. He shifted, the whites of his eyes showing as his head rolled, and he moaned as I raised his chin, cowering away from me.

'Kem?' I searched his face for signs of sickness, of *strigoi* paleness. But though he was paler, starved of sun, he was warm. He was not a monster. He was a boy, my brother, and I took him into my arms and wept.

'Lillai?' his voice was slurred. Was he drugged? There were so many things I did not understand, not least Alina's claim that it had been Kizzy who chose him – chose him for what? – but I knew I had to get him away as fast as possible.

'Yes, Kem. I'm here.' I held him tightly, whispering his name again and again, to make him solid, make him real.

A tear rolled down his cheek, and I brushed it away though they kept streaming down my own cheeks. Fen was working on the ties binding him to the chair, and as soon as he was free, Kem collapsed forwards, his thin frame hitting mine like a dead weight. He had been drugged, but why? Out of pity for what awaited him?

'Lil,' he slurred. 'Lil, Kizzy . . .'

'Hush,' I said, but Fen pressed close.

'Kizzy what?' he said. I tried to push him away, but Fen would not be moved. 'What about Kizzy, Kem?'

'He . . . he . . .' Kem dissolved into sobs.

'Enough,' I hissed at Fen. My brother, my baby brother was alive and in my arms, and I did not want to let go. But I knew I must. 'Mira, take him.'

'What are you going to do?' she said, holding out her arms.

'I'm going to buy you time.'

'Time for what?' Mira frowned, and I had to look away from her eyes.

Those grey eyes, storm clouds and silver-quick water and moonlight. I had learned them better than my own face, and I knew to look at them now would break what resolve I had left.

'For you to get away.' I hurried on before she could interrupt. 'Take Kem, and Alina and her brothers. Hide in the church. Don't come out until the sun is up, and then get away. You, too,' I said to Fen. 'There's no point us all staying.'

Fen crossed his arms. 'I came for Kizzy. I'll stay.' I could tell he was decided.

'Please, Mira.' I forced myself to look at her. 'Take him. He's a piece of my heart. If anything more happens to him . . .'

'And what about me,' she whispered. 'What about the piece you have of my heart?'

273

I leant my forehead against hers. 'I'll find you. I will.'

'Please,' she said, a gentle sadness in her voice. 'Don't make any more promises.'

She took Kem gently from me, scooping him into her arms even as I spoke.

'He likes fiddleheads,' I said. 'And is scared of the dark. And boars. And most things, actually, and . . .'

'He'll be safe,' said Mira, stopping up my mouth with her finger.

I nodded, hiccupping.

'End this,' she said, and held out her stake to me, dark with the innocent father's blood. 'If you must stay, end it, in whatever way you can.'

Fen held out his lighting flint to her. 'So you can build a fire. Stay off the path.'

She took it, then brought her lips to my ear and whispered something.

And then she was gone, my brother limp in her arms. I realised then that I should have said it back, should have told her I loved her too.

I realised it to be true, because my heart was breaking. Fen laid a hand on my arm, and I knew that he knew.

CHAPTER THIRTY-FIVE

Soon enough it would be nightfall, and too soon we would discover whatever fate my brother had so narrowly avoided.

We formed a plan of sorts. There was some struggle between Fen and me as to who would take Kem's place, but though Fen was taller I could not deny his short dark hair made a more convincing swap. In my vision, I had been at the top of the room, not the centre, and I supposed that as it had gotten us this far, we should stick to what I had seen.

I wrapped the ties around his hands, without binding them, and slid the stake into his hands.

He gripped it tightly, and I bent down and kissed his cheek. Whatever awaited him, I knew he would meet it bravely, but still my stomach churned with guilt that I had not convinced him to go. I was less certain than ever that either of us would survive the night.

I hid behind one of the thick black drapes behind the top table, and waited. Looking up, I could watch the sky darken, but even without seeing the night fall, I knew when the *strigoi* began to stir.

Because as they awoke, they called to one another, in voices that were nearly song, nearly lovely, but they chilled my blood in the same way a wolf's keen does.

Through a gap in the curtains, I watched the hall fill with them. All were dressed in finery, glinting gold and black, glimmering like scales. They were not only men, like in Boyar Valcar's hall, but women too, shining like ghosts. Each set a bone-white goblet before them, but there were no plates, no knives. I felt like I was dreaming and pinched myself to check I was not.

The Dragon came in last.

The whole room stilled, as if suspended in ice. The skin on my arms prickled with tiny knives of cold, as though his mere presence had sucked the life from my flesh. I did not want to look upon him, but I could not look away.

He was tall, taller than Tamás, taller than Calazan. Unnaturally tall, a head higher than any of his guests. The planes of his face were hewn as though from white marble, shining so in the candlelight that his features seemed blurred.

If the other men at the tables were finely attired, it was nothing compared to him. He wore a fur of black that seemed brown beside his true-black hair. He had rings on every finger. A ruby the size of an acorn sat in the centre of one: in another, an opal gleamed milkily, like a rheumy eye. And as he drew close, so close that I could have reached out and brushed his blue-dark hair, I saw he was handsome too. His features were wolfish, vicious, but finer than any man's I'd seen. His eyes gleamed red as the ruby on his finger.

He was repulsive, and magnetic, and elegant. I longed to plunge Mira's stake into his heart. But we were close, so close to finding out Kizzy's fate, and so our own. His final death could wait.

The hushed room fell into deeper stillness. Dracul clapped his hands, and his rings lent the sound an unnatural *click*. The doors at the back of the room opened, and Kizzy and Albu entered, to languid applause.

My broken heart shattered.

Kizzy was still dark, still beautiful, but her skin shone with an unnatural light, as though she were glazed with sweat. Her eyes were red as blood.

I think some small part of me had held hope until then, that Tamás had been mistaken, but now all hope died. I should leap out, kill the Dragon, tell Fen to run. But I felt powerless as I watched my sister and Mamă's bear approaching Fen's chair. He would never fight his way out alive. There must be a hundred *strigoi* in here.

I was caught by indecision. What choice should I make, when the deathless sat at the tables before me? Is this what Mamă had wanted, what she had meant by her sending me a vision? I wanted to weep as Kizzy passed Fen, to drop to my knees and howl. But I only watched as Kizzy took up Albu's paws and began to dance to invisible music.

She was more lovely than ever, lighter than it was possible for a human to be. But she was not human. She was a *strigoi*, and I had failed to save her. As she danced, Fen twitched, and looked up from beneath his thick curls. I saw him see Kizzy, see her shining skin and red eyes, and his shoulders began to shake.

No one noticed, because they were all watching my sister and her bear dance. Not the fine monsters at the tables, not Kizzy, eyes fixed on our white bear. Not even Dracul.

Because when I turned to look at the Dragon, he was looking straight back at me.

CHAPTER THIRTY-SIX

The Dragon smiled, and it was the smile from my vision. The smile I had seen again and again in my nightmares. But there was no Mira here now, to rouse me awake with warm kisses and warmer words.

His sharp teeth glinted in the sliver of moonlight I had carelessly let pass through the curtains, and as my sister danced, he beckoned me forwards.

My legs moved against my will. It was impossible to resist him, though I kept tight hold of Mira's stake. I stepped from the curtain, and the movement made Kizzy falter. Out of the corner of my eye, I saw her stop entirely, loosing Albu's paws. The bear dropped onto all fours, panting.

Every blood-red eye turned towards me, and I felt the temperature in the room drop even further. It was as if every one of them had a hand about my throat and were squeezing.

'Well,' said Dracul, in a voice that was honey and bee-stings, sharp and soft all at once. 'This must be the twin.'

He reached out so quickly I had no time to react. He took hold of my wrist and his skin was so cold it burned. He squeezed and I dropped the stake. It fell to the stone floor with a soft, insubstantial sound that made me wince. How foolish, to think such a matchstick could defeat him.

'We've been waiting for you.'

I hardly dared breathe.

'Look, Kisaiya,' he said, the whole room's eyes upon me. 'Your sister.'

There was something in Kizzy's face, a shadow crossing the pearly beauty, that made me realise she knew me. She was not fully lost to him.

'Kizzy—' I began, but Fen had already acted. He threw off the bearskin cloak, and swiped Kizzy's legs from under her. Albu reared, but I called out Mamă's calming word to him, and something ancient stayed him. He sank back to the ground, growling softly. Fen had Kizzy in a chokehold, the stake pressed to her breast. The room was still, quiet. It was worse than screams.

'Let her go,' said Fen, in a shaking voice. 'Let her go, or I'll kill Kisaiya.'

'Who is this?' said Dracul. 'Where is the boy?'

'Long gone,' said Fen.

'How did you get in?' Dracul's voice was languid, almost amused. Fen didn't answer, but Dracul snapped his fingers and let out a soft *ahhh* of understanding. 'The passage?' He clucked his tongue. 'Of course. The villagers had that dug from my old tomb, in their early efforts to resist my rule. They quickly learned it was a fool's errand. You should have marked that too.'

'We're here though,' said Fen, chin jutted in defiance. 'And you must let Lillai go.'

Dracul chuckled. 'Destroy him, Kisaiya.'

Confusion crossed Fen's face. 'I'll kill her.'

'No,' said Dracul. 'You won't. She could overwhelm you in a moment. She needs no weapon, for she is a weapon. That's what she chose, when she chose to become like me.'

'Like you?' I looked out at the full room. Had all these people made such a choice?

'Oh no. These are my subjects, my *strigoi*,' grinned Dracul wolfishly. He lifted one shimmering, long-fingered hand, and snapped his fingers. The *strigoi* rose, and like wraiths glided from the room until we were alone with Dracul.

'Kisaiya here,' continued Dracul, 'is my swan, my equal. She will be after tonight anyway. She wanted power. And power is what I gave her.'

'She would never choose this,' I said, finding my voice at last. 'She would never choose to become a monster.'

'But you already are a monster to so many,' said Dracul. 'I know how most treat the Travellers. Worse than dogs. Worse than *strigoi*, because their fear of you does not translate into respect. But they will respect her now, as they respect me. I have drunk of her, and now she is *strigoi*. But I offered her even more than that.' He leaned forward. 'She can become like me. All she has to do is drink of me, and then she is free.'

'Drink of you?' My voice was barely a whisper. 'It is no freedom, keeping her here.'

'She chose it.'

'No,' I said. 'Kizzy, it's not true.'

Kizzy raised her head to me, and I knew it was. I passed through fear, and into a great, yawning anger.

'But Kem,' I shouted. 'She would not hurt Kem.'

'She had a choice,' said Dracul. 'She could turn him into one of us or kill him. She decided the latter was kinder. Power is a heavy burden; she knows that now.'

'It hurts, Lillai.' Kizzy's voice was still her own, but layered, mesmeric. 'Losing yourself. I am already . . . I don't feel myself. It's like always almost dying. My heart doesn't beat though it aches. Had I known, I would have made a different choice.'

She leaned back into Fen's arms, and I saw tears running down his cheeks. He kissed her cheek, and she sighed.

'Perhaps,' she said softly, 'I should let someone else do what I could not.'

Dracul sat up straighter, his grip on me tightening. 'If you let him kill you, our deal is off. I'll kill every man, woman and child downstairs. I'll kill every innocent in the land.'

I knew then why Kizzy had made that choice. She had made a deal: her life for countless others. My heart swelled with pride even as it threatened to rip through my chest with rage.

'Then two more lives,' she said, gesturing to me and Fen. 'Two more, and I will never leave your side.'

'You've had enough bargains.'

'Then goodbye,' she said, and wrenched Fen's yew stake from his hands, pressed it so hard to her chest I saw her skin begin to bubble, as the sunlight had done to the child's skin.

'One!' said Dracul. 'One and have done.'

He slid off his gold ring set with the opal. 'This will give one safe passage anywhere on the land. They will not get far without it.' He leaned forward. 'But you may only name one.'

She looked at me, and I knew she was about to say my name. I saw my life branching like the lines on my palms. One path, a life spent living and breathing, loving Mira, watching Kem grow and become a man. I wanted it, I realised then. I wanted it so badly it ached worse than the Dragon's grip on my wrist.

But I shook my head. Kizzy's red eyes flashed momentarily to brown, and I knew she understood.

'Will you let me be the one to do it?' she asked Dracul.

He nodded. 'But first, a show of your loyalty.'

He stood, and I felt dizzy to see how high he seemed, how small I felt. He ignored me completely, eyes fixed upon Kizzy, and as he did so, he drew out a thin knife from his sleeve, so sharp it hurt my eyes just to look at it.

'Kizzy!' I called warningly, but she hissed at me. I saw a glint of sharp teeth, and the sight was so horrible it struck me dumb.

Dracul did not cut her. He drew a line across his arm, and silver blood sprang up, running down his wrist and into one of the ornate cups left by his *strigoi*.

'First you must drink of me.'

'Kizzy, please!' My cry rent the air. Dracul cast a dismissive gaze over me, as though tears were something disgusting. 'Don't!'

But Kizzy lifted the cup to her lips and drained it. She let it drop to the floor and looked up to the ceiling. She convulsed, once, twice silver shimmering on her open lips. Albu growled as the glow radiating from her skin brightened. She seemed to lift from the floor, but then I saw she was growing, becoming taller and taller, like Dracul, until I would come only to her shoulder. Her curly hair grew even darker, taking on Dracul's blue-blackness. Her skin shone like jet.

Finally, the convulsions let go, and she stood straight. It hurt my eyes to look at her, my heart to see her so. More than a *strigoi*, now, but less than human.

284

'Swan,' crooned Dracul. 'Do you feel it?'

'Yes,' she breathed. 'Yes.'

'And your choice?'

Kizzy looked at me and parted her perfect lips.

'Fen.'

Fen shouted, 'No!' but Dracul threw his ring to Kizzy. I watched as she caught it in one hand, the other tight about the stake, and slid it onto Fen's finger.

Then I understood that both Cook and Old Charani were right. There was a promise ring in his future after all, but it was not for marriage. Only for safe passage, away from the woman he loved.

Dracul snapped his fingers again, and the doors opened. The *strigoi* were ranged outside, their shining bodies a seemingly unbreakable mass.

'Well then,' said Dracul. 'Go. I cannot hold them back for ever.'

The *strigoi* began to advance. Albu slunk down, and Kizzy bent and slid her arms about his great, soft neck. She whispered in his ear, and Albu seemed to calm. He swept Fen onto his back as he had with Kem months before, and before Fen could do more than cry out Kizzy's name, he was gone. Gone to Mira, gone to Kem, gone to the life I would never have.

Because now the Dragon was standing, tall as a tree beside me, and leading me to my sister. And she took me in her arms, and they were cold as ice, her skin smooth as glass. I sighed, and leant against her, and she brought her lips to my neck. I could feel nothing: no breath.

Her hair covering me, she whispered into my ear. 'One more chance, Lil. Trust me.'

Her fingers were at my throat, her fingernails sharper than they ever had been in life. Then I felt something slice into my neck, and pain rang like a bell through my body, shuddering me into darkness.

CHAPTER THIRTY-SEVEN

I was cold. Cold as though plunged into an icy river or wrenched from a grave. I sat up, gasping, darkness pressing heavy against my eyes.

'Hush,' said a voice. Kizzy's voice.

'Kisaiya?' I groped in the blackness. It was like being in a tomb. Terror gripped at my throat, and I wondered if the stories really were true, and *strigoi* slept in coffins. I pushed my hands out all around me, feeling for rock, but I felt only soft fabric, beneath me and on the walls. 'I can't see.'

'Sorry,' said Kizzy, and though she sounded like herself, I was afraid. 'I'll light the fire.'

There was a rustle, and I heard her moving, sure and light-footed as a cat. The strike of a flint against – what? Was that her fingernail? I shuddered as I remembered her hands on my throat, the slice . . .

'You cut me,' I said, finally understanding. 'You didn't bite me.'

As the room flared into brightness, I felt for the bandage at my neck. I saw I sat on a fine bed, covered in silks, and more silks were hung on the walls. It was a richly attired room, with a large mirror beside the fireplace. The air was freezing, the window closed by the same thick fabric curtains that hung everywhere in the hall.

My sister was silhouetted by the fire, still crouched with her back to me. She shook her head, perfect ravens-wing curls bouncing.

'He was forcing you. You should be able to choose.'

She turned, and the full horror of her appearance closed over me, as though I really were in a coffin and the lid was bearing down upon my chest. She shone, as though lit from within, but not by fire. By moonlight, that pearly glow caught beneath her dark skin, shimmering and fine. Her red eyes glinted in the firelight.

'Am I so awful, Lil?' She went to the mirror. My blood seemed to freeze in my veins. She had no reflection. 'I can't tell.'

'You're beautiful,' I said, my old loyalty springing up, natural as a bud. 'But yes, you are . . . awful.'

She turned to me and smiled. I could see my terrified face in the mirror, the yawning absence where my sister should be.

'Kisaiya,' I said, tears starting in my eyes. 'Did you really choose this?'

She sighed, closing her eyes, and it was easier to imagine them back to brown, her untransformed and living. 'It did not feel like much of a choice at the time. But then, did I kneel before him, and let him bite me?' She ran her hand over the flawless, shining skin of her neck. 'I did. Memories are already becoming too painful to hold, but that I can remember well.'

'Why?' I shouted. The word burst off the wide walls and bounced back at us. Kizzy flinched as though she were struck by it.

'Because of what Dracul told you.' She spoke his name reverently, without fear. 'The chance to be powerful in my life, to create my own future, and not lean upon fables and fates.' Her voice was becoming layered again, rhythmic, like the terrible music of storms. 'He speaks it well, doesn't he?'

'I want to hear you tell me. Tell me why you chose to become a monster.'

'Much the same reason you did,' she said harshly. Her temper made her seem even taller. 'And if I had done as you asked, you would be *strigoi* by now.'

'But you didn't,' I said. 'So, tell me why you chose it.'

She sat down in a straight-backed chair beside the bed. I could see it, empty in the mirror. I turned determinedly away from the sight.

'Calazan did not bring me directly here,' she said, finally. 'He lied from the moment we left to the moment we arrived. He wanted to take me to his castle, to be his . . . I don't know. His mistress.'

I reached out for her hand and could only grip it a moment before its iciness made it impossible. 'Kizzy. Did he—'

'I gutted him,' she said simply. 'With his own blade.' She looked sharply at me. 'Are you not shocked?'

'I killed Vereski,' I said. 'The night you left, he took me to the stables. I stabbed him.'

I did not expect sadness, but the unrestrained smile that crossed her face was ghoulish. I caught sight of her teeth, very white and very sharp. They did not look like her teeth at all.

'Well done,' she said. 'So we are both monsters after all.'

'Speak for yourself,' I said, and she laughed, the sound water freezing into ice. 'What happened then?'

'His men brought me to Dracul. I think they wanted me to be part of his fence as punishment, but he applauded what I had done. You must know it now, that he is more than a *strigoi*?'

'That is apparent,' I said coolly, and Kizzy laughed again.

'You developed a sense of humour! I like it. Oh Lil, don't look like that. If I don't laugh, I think I shall scream.'

She brought her hands up to her throat, to the scream held there. 'He gave me a choice. He gives all his favourites a choice, but me – he said I was special. That I would not be a *strigoi*, ravenous for a shroud, able to be killed easy as a bug. He drank of me, so I became *strigoi*. But when I drank of him, I became *vampyre*.'

'*Vampyre?*' The word was as enticing and terrible as the Dragon. 'What is that?'

'A whole new order of the undead. A ruling order. And he said I must join it, because we would build a better world.'

'Of course he did,' I said, with a soft laugh.

'No, Lil, listen. He said I was special, and I thought it was because of the blood moon, or the gift, or something like that. But he said no. He said that was all nonsense. Divining days, Seeing, fate, all of it. He said I was special, because I changed my fate. I fought, didn't I? I fought for Mamă, and I fought Malovski, and Vereski, and Calazan – I fought them all. And any possible path I took, I took myself, because of things I had done.'

'That's not true, Kizzy,' I said, frowning. 'We were taken as slaves.'

'But because I fought,' she repeated, a sort of frenzied glaze to her eye. 'We could have run away, when we saw our camp ablaze that day. You wanted to, I felt it. But I went back. Dracul, he says I'm rare.'

'And him,' I said impatiently. 'Did you fight him?'

'At first,' she said. 'But then he told me so many things, Lil. He told me I can have power here. He wants me with him, always.'

'Are you his wife?' I asked, horrified.

She laughed again, and it was crueller. 'He has no need for a wife.'

'Only blood,' I said, disgusted.

'Yes,' she said, looking at me and there was a purr to her voice that made my blood shiver in my veins. 'It is almost unbearable, that thirst. But we are not slave to it as *strigoi* are. Only his control kept those *strigoi* from killing you all in the hall. That is how I can be with you, talk to you, even as I smell the blood in your veins – I am mistress of my desires, Lil.'

'You are monstrous,' I whispered. 'You are scaring me.'

'You need not be afraid of me,' said Kizzy casually. 'But Lil, didn't I tell you, that first night in the kitchens? Didn't I tell you I wanted them to fear me? And they will. Malovski, Boyar Valcar. Dracul says we can avenge ourselves.'

'Kizzy,' I said, my voice almost a whisper. 'This isn't you.'

'It is,' she shouted, rising to her feet, and I reared back, almost falling from the bed. But she only began to pace, back and forth before the fire – which, I realised, was casting no warmth against her fierce chill. 'It finally is. All our lives, Lillai, we've been told what we are. Travellers, *ursar* women, *lăutari*, slaves. And this,' she gestured to herself, pressing at the place her heart used to beat and warm her. 'This I chose. And no man can own me.'

'He owns you,' I shouted back. 'I heard him say so, that if you disobeyed him your deal would be off. What deal is it, Kizzy? What black art have you promised?'

'For the life of innocents, I will bring death on the guilty,' she hissed, and I knew these were not her words. 'He has sworn to stop taking Travellers, to stop taking children.'

'That is not true,' I said. 'I saw children in the foundations. Kept secret. A girl, Alina. Her sister Olga had been killed by the Dragon.'

Kizzy stilled at that, and I realised she had not known.

'And Kem,' I said. 'What sort of bargain is that, that you must kill your own brother?'

'I wouldn't have,' she spat back. 'I would have cut him, as I did you, and freed him.'

'Freed him to the wolves,' I said. 'Freed him to an unsafe world. Perhaps it would have been better that he died.'

'I would have seen him safely away. He is safe, by the way. I followed him and Fen to the border. Some other children too, a girl and two boys.'

'Followed?'

'Flew,' she said, and there was no trace of a lie in her voice.

'What about Mira?' I said sharply, realising she had not mentioned her. Kizzy frowned.

'Mira was here?'

I stilled. I had not meant to give her away. 'Yes. She came with us. We . . .' I trailed off. I could not share what we were to each other, not with this version of Kizzy, glittering and cold.

Kizzy arched an eyebrow. 'She was not with them.'

My heart raced. I thought of her promise to me, then of her promise to Fen. Surely, she had not stayed behind? I looked away from Kizzy, wary of her seeing something in my face.

'But even if he had not gone,' continued Kizzy. 'He would be safe, in this new world Dracul has promised me. He is an innocent.'

'And who decides who is innocent?' I felt exasperation grinding through my jaw. She sounded mad, stupid. But she was also dangerous, even to me. I saw it in the speed with which she rounded on me, how her eyes kept flicking to my throat. She was holding herself back from doing me harm, I could tell. 'You? Him?'

'It is better than the current order,' she said. 'I would not allow Travellers to be slaves.'

'What about the Settled,' I said, thinking of Mira. 'Or do they deserve it?'

'Many of them do,' she said. 'You cannot deny it, after all we were put through.'

'Listen to yourself,' I said. 'You sound as bad as Malovski.'

'I am nothing like her.' She was breathing heavily, but I could not see her breath as I could my own, clouding in the cold air.

'When does it begin?' I said. 'This new regime?'

'When . . . when Kem . . .'

'Was dead?' I said sharply.

'Was free,' she said. 'Those children in the foundations, they would have been freed too, I am sure of it.'

'Do you truly believe you have power over such a man?' I said, shaking my head.

'He is not a man. And yes.' There was the same certainty in her voice with which she'd always spoken of her life as an *ursar*. 'He has searched for a companion such as me all his days. And I have promised myself to him.'

'He still wants you? Even after he saw you with Fen?'

'I will not love Fen much longer,' she said, and there was something close to grief in her face. 'Dracul says that fades, along with all the other human feelings. Weaknesses.'

'And what remains?'

'Purpose,' she said. 'I have purpose now, Lil. Though I can tell you will not join me in it.'

I looked at her then, past the glittering skin and red of her eyes, to Kizzy. Not much remained, and if what she said was true, soon there would be nothing left of the girl I once shared a body with, grew to be two halves of the same soul with. She might not believe in fate, but perhaps the blood-moon had damned her after all.

And as she stared back, her expression almost soft, I knew I could not leave her to face her damnation alone.

295

'You think you know me so well,' I said, and fear and sadness rocked my voice and made it shake. 'But you forget the most important thing.' She jutted out her chin defiantly, and I walked to her and smoothed the set of it away. Her skin was frost.

'I love you, Kisaiya. You might not believe in fate, but I know mine is shared with yours. And no choice I take, earthly or unearthly, can be to step away from you.'

She had no tears to give me, but she held out her hand to mine, fingers splayed. I touched my fingertips to hers, and she gently, gently brought her mouth to my neck. I watched in the mirror as she bent over me. I sat alone, in that reflected world, alone in the shadowy room.

The sharp pain was unmistakable, and I felt a fierce cold spread from the point where her teeth had pierced me, so icy it was almost warm.

'How long?' I whispered.

'A day,' she replied. 'It doesn't hurt. It feels like nothing. And then you can drink of me.'

'Vampyre?'

'Vampyres. Together.'

I sat watching my reflection, wondering when it would fade. And then, the screaming began.

CHAPTER THIRTY-EIGHT

Kizzy ran to the window, pulling aside the curtain. Outside, the moon was a sharp slice taken from the lightening sky, and her skin shimmered in its glow. Daybreak was not far away. Kizzy made a sound like a scalded cat.

I ran to her side, slightly dizzy from her bite, and peered down. The room overlooked the courtyard we had entered, where we had encountered the sleeping *strigoi*. They had returned to the stable after the failed feast, and it was they who screamed.

Because the stable was on fire.

Quick as a bolt of lightning, Kizzy was on the windowsill, and then she stepped off it. I grabbed reflexively at her, but she did not fall. She *flew*.

Skimming the tops of the flames, she darted to and fro from the burning barn, keeping to the shadows cast by the fast-rising sun against the high walls, and I remembered

the wagons ablaze, her determination to save Mamă, her
scalded hands.

But just as it had our home, the fire already had the stable
in its grasp. Shapes fluttered useless and ablaze into the air,
were struck by the sun or else too far caught in the fire's grip.
Kizzy was screaming too, with anger and fear. She came close
to the growing sunlight and I called out.

'Careful!'

And then, she plunged, so suddenly I was sure she had
been struck by the daylight, was dissolving to dust. But as I
watched, my hands clutching at my still-warm cheeks, I saw
her pluck up a figure from the ground. It was so pale, I
thought it was a *strigoi*, but then I saw the shaven head and
realised who it was.

Mira. Mira had burned the barn.

Kizzy flew back up to the window, and I dived aside. Kizzy
tossed her inside. Mira sprawled onto the floor, coughing,
and I ran to her as Kizzy followed after, landing light and
graceful as a swan, throwing the curtain closed again,
shutting out the growing light of sun and flame.

'You little *căcat*,' hissed Kizzy, advancing. 'You murderer.
I'll kill you, I'll—'

'Stop, Kizzy!' I stood between them, the two loves of my
life, shielding Mira from Kizzy's gaze.

'They're *strigoi*, Kizzy,' said Mira from the floor. 'They're
monsters.'

'So are you going to kill me too?'

Now she saw Kizzy, and the wound to my neck, and cried out.

'Saints! *Dragă*, you're not one of them.'

'Perhaps the only one,' spat Kizzy, 'after your antics. The Dragon will not be happy with you. He's spent years building his court.'

'Kizzy,' I said, holding up a hand to calm her. 'Did they choose too? Or did he force them?'

Kizzy hesitated. 'I don't know.'

'You do,' I said. 'He forced them. They're not like you. They're slaves to their needs. We ran into one in the forests, a child. It's a horrible life; you said yourself you would have made another choice had you known. Perhaps this is a mercy.'

The screaming had stopped. The air smelt of sweet smoke, sickeningly strong. Kizzy sighed. 'Perhaps. Though Dracul will not see it that way. He will kill her, you know.'

'Then save her,' I pleaded. 'Get her away from here.'

'It's daylight,' she said. 'She will have to make her own way.'

'I'm not going,' said Mira. 'Not without Lil.'

I looked at her then, and my still-beating heart felt like it would burst. 'I have to stay.'

'Tell her, Kizzy,' said Mira, searching my face. 'Tell her to come.'

'It's too late,' I said, and showed her the holes in my neck.

Mira's silence hit me like a wave. She reached out to me, and her hands were warm and lovely. She spread them across my shoulders, rubbing along my arms, and my longing was so painful I thought it would be better to live without it.

'Lil?' Her eyes searched my face for an answer I did not have. 'Then I'll stay. I'll stay and to hell with it.'

'You will go,' I said voice unsteady with tears. 'Because I cannot have you live like this.'

She wailed like a child, and threw herself towards me, covering my neck in kisses as though that would suck out whatever poison Kizzy had put in my veins.

'No,' she said. 'I came back for you. I came back—'

'And now you have to go,' I said, my eyes hazy with tears. 'Kizzy can take you to Fen and Kem. You will not be alone.'

I wanted to tell her to stay. I wanted to tell her I wished I could give her all my endless days, that I longed to take what she was offering: to take her life and tie it to mine for eternity.

'Kizzy? Will you take her?'

'Fine,' said my sister. 'But it'll have to wait until nightfall. I'll return then, before you are full *strigoi*. It will not be safe for her then.'

She swept from the room, closing the door behind. The warmth seemed to flood back in, the fire blazing brighter.

Mira looked at me, and to my surprise there was a supressed smile on her face. 'Do you want to bite me, Lil? Say you do.'

I laughed too, and an arrow of longing struck hard at my heart.

'Mira—' I began, but Mira pressed herself against me, her lips finding my collarbone, my shoulder, my breasts. I shivered in her arms, my still-warm skin dancing beneath her fingers. I kissed her too, everywhere she wanted, and we moved together as we never could in the forest with Fen close by. It was a bliss I had no words for, could only search for with my hands and my mouth, reaching for every part of her, bringing it as close as I could, until I did not know where her pleasure ended and mine began. And into her ear I whispered her name, and she moaned mine, and it was like she was calling me into true existence for the first, and last, time.

. . .

After, I wrapped my arms around her. I kissed her cheek and returned her whispered words from the hall, a lifetime ago.

'I love you. Forever.'

'It really will be,' said Mira sadly. 'I will stay. I want to stay.'

'I want you to,' I said. 'But it is not right. You know that, don't you?'

The silence was agony, and when she spoke, I wanted to cry with the pain of her answer.

'Yes,' her voice was very small, her breath very warm against my cheek. 'Lil, will you sing for me?'

It was easy as breathing, to share a song with her. I sang it soft, and tender, and sweet as her kisses, and when it was done she rolled over and pressed back against me, her body warm against my length. I looked at her in the mirror, and she looked back with a watchful intensity.

At last, she spoke again. 'Will you forget me?'

I tilted her chin up, and kissed her soft neck, and she shivered. 'Your lips. They're cold.'

We watched each other in the mirror until the fire died. The stars began to burn their places in the sky, and I knew it was done. Some loves are built slowly, brick by brick. But Mira's and mine was forged as a blade: sharp and burning, violence in its beginning, and in its end. She was a wound I felt I would never heal from, a scar I would carry on my heart alongside Mamă.

I watched her face in the mirror as the light faded, and at last, as night fell and Kizzy returned to fly my love away, so did I.

AFTERMATH

I did forget her, of course. I tried to remember, but as the years turned to decades, and the decades turned into centuries, she faded just as I had done in that mirror. I mourned when she died, old by human standards, but without tears grief is not very purging. I decided to let her go.

Dracul kept his word. After I drank Kizzy's blood, he taught me to fly, and we saw a great many things. After a century, another joined our rank of *vampyres*: a Countess who Dracul spared after purging her husband. We liked her well enough.

All our other labels faded, Traveller, slave, until only one remained: *Vampyre*. We were feared, we were powerful. We were allowed to choose our prey, and fed only on those who, by our measure, deserved it. We took Boyar Valcar before his tumour did, his blood sour with sickness, and killed numerous other boyars and slavers. We spared Malovski,

Valcar's puppet, as damaged as the girls she commanded, though I hope our night-time visits gave her nightmares that stalked her to her death.

And she did die, eventually. So did Cook, and Dot, and Szilvie, Albu and Fen and Kem, and my once beloved Mira, though they were free to the end of their days. Soon their deaths were as distant as the horizon.

Men never stopped sinning, and we never stopped feeding. But we kept to the shadows. They didn't exactly forget about Dracul, but truth became rumour, rumour became fable, and so he passed into legend.

We joined him, eventually. They came to call us the three sisters – two dark, one fair – and worse. The beautiful damned, the brides of Dracul, the deathless girls.

And though my loyalty to Kisaiya was my bond, I never knew again what it was to feel my heart quicken in my chest, my blood flood my body at the touch of another. A *vampyre* cannot love, only thirst. And that, above all else, is what truly damns us.

Author's Note

The central joy of re-visioning *Dracula*'s 'dark sisters' is that Dracula himself was a reincarnation, a forging of many different myths into a single enduring creation. Alongside Polidori's *The Vampyre* and Le Fanu's *Carmilla*, *Dracula* became a perfect vehicle for the Victorians to examine their neuroses around sex, gender, and sexuality, at a safe, cloaked distance. Women, of course, bore the brunt of this, and so it was women I looked for when approached to pick a classic to respond to for Bellatrix.

I came late to Stoker's story, but still it has permeated my consciousness for years. In films, TV shows, costumes for Halloween parties, and music; the influence of the ultimate vampire has spread far and wide. This ubiquity means the story is porous and ripe for reimagining, especially in the characters of the so-called 'brides' of Dracula.

Stoker himself doesn't refer to them thus, but of course three sexual, powerful women would not be allowed to exist unattached in the public consciousness. Stoker describes them briefly, as 'two dark, one fair', the 'two dark' having 'high, aquiline noses'. As soon as I read this description, I imagined them as sisters, and knew I'd found the story I wanted to sink my teeth into for the Bellatrix project.

My sisters are Kizzy and Lil, twins and Travellers. This is a much persecuted culture throughout history, and has its origins in Northern India, where my own family are from. Due to their lifestyle and appearance, Travellers were maligned and enslaved throughout Europe for centuries. One of the most notorious slave owners was a fifteenth-century Romanian prince, Vlad Tepes. He was also known as Vlad the Impaler, or Vlad Dracul.

Stoker borrowed this moniker for his own creation, and this is the link upon which my story hinges: a story of persecution, danger, injustice – but most of all, love. Drawing on the darkness of history, and mixing it with the glitter of fantasy, I have found a place for my beloved characters to wrestle with fate, lust, death, and evil. Most of all, I hope I have fulfilled Bellatrix's admirable aims, and gifted these women something of a life beyond *Dracula*'s lines.

Kiran Millwood Hargrave

ACKNOWLEDGMENTS

This book owes most to Helen Thomas, my editor. Thank you for trusting me with this commission, and supporting my story from spark to flame to blaze. Kizzy and Lil would not exist without you, and Bellatrix.

Thank you to my three biggest writing inspirations, and best friends, Sarvat Hasin, Daisy Johnson, and Tom de Freston. I am so grateful to know you, to read your work, to have you read mine. And more than that, I am grateful for your love and friendship.

Thank you to ace writers and friends Katie Webber, Kevin Tsang, Lucy Ayrton, and Laura Theis, for reading early drafts, when I was still feeling my way into writing YA. Thank you to Cat Doyle, Melinda Salisbury, Louise O'Neill, Samantha Shannon, and Francesca Simon. Your encouragement and kindness (and your own writing) drove me to try harder, write better, be more heart-open and soul-deep. Special mention to

Evie Tsang, who cannot read this for a few years, but who I hope knows that her little presence in my life has made it so much richer.

Thank you to my agent, Hellie Ogden, who always knows when I should say yes, and when I should say no. Thank you for being a constant guide and friend.

Thank you to Alison and Olga, for the cover that no doubt was a massive factor in your picking up this book! Thank you to Catinca Untaru, for diligently, patiently, and kindly mending my broken Romanian.

Thank you to my incredible team at Hachette for everything from copy-edits to covers, rights deals and sales pitches, to spare proof copies after cat-related mishaps. I am so excited that *The Deathless Girls* is only the start of our journey together.

Thank you to my family, my favourite humans, and cats, in the whole world.

Thank you to you, the reader, for choosing to spend time with this book. Stories only live as long as they are read, or spoken, or heard. I hope you found something worth sharing in these pages.

Thank you to Tom, for everything, always.

BELLATRIX *[noun: female warrior]*

In literature and in life, women of the past and present
have a million stories that are untold, mis-told or unheard.
In response, we are proud to launch Bellatrix:
a new collection of gripping, powerful and diverse YA
novels by leading female voices. From gothic to thriller
to romance to funny, each book is entirely unique,
but linked by a passion for telling *her whole story*.

HER STORY
THE WHOLE STORY

BELLATRIXBOOKS.CO.UK
#BELLATRIXBOOKS